THE PUPPETMASTER'S APPRENTICE

Lisa DeSelm

PAGE STREET
PUBLISHING CO.

PAGE STREET
PUBLISHING CO.

Copyright © 2020 Lisa DeSelm

First published in 2020 by
Page Street Publishing Co.
27 Congress Street, Suite 105
Salem, MA 01970
www.pagestreetpublishing.com

Distributed by Macmillan, sales in Canada by The Canadian Manda Group.

24   23   22   21   20   1   2   3   4   5

ISBN-13: 978-1-64567-080-3
ISBN-10: 1-64567-080-5
Library of Congress Control Number: 2019957106

Cover and book design by Laura Benton for Page Street Publishing Co.
Cover images: Illustration of hands with puppet © Shutterstock / M3Pics; photograph of sky © Shutterstock / AvDe; photograph of moon © Shutterstock / kdshutterman; vectors of trees © Shutterstock / Binkski, eva_mask and surassawadee
Interior images: Vector of branch © Shutterstock / Binkski; illustration of moon © Shutterstock / Vlada Young
Author photo by Taylor Lutz

Printed and bound in the United States

For my daughters,
I love you, splinters and all. Always.

PROLOGUE

I'VE NEVER HAD A MOTHER, BUT I'VE ALWAYS HAD THE TREES.

I hear them still: the joy of the beech bursting with buds, the oak's relief at shedding fall's heavy fortune, the anticipation of winter's slumber with rugged skins bared to the frost. Their voices rise and fall on every twist of the wind, comforting, yet stern when danger draws near.

Once, a widower walked among them, hunting for fresh wood. The puppetmaster liked to take his time, feeling the bark for smoothness, measuring width for usefulness. Assessing the health of each trunk, he only culled trees who had lived a good life already. He left behind those too young, or too warped by the strange forces of nature.

At night, as he was taking his rest in a small clearing, a woman appeared at the rim of his firelight. She was old, old beyond old—with skin more leather than flesh. Uncertain whether she was human or a force of nature itself, the puppetmaster invited her to share the warmth of his fire. She accepted wordlessly, her legs folding to the ground as spryly as a child's. He offered her his supper, though he hadn't much. At last, sated by the meal, the woman began to speak.

"You are a solitary man, Gephardt."

"Yes, milady."

She knew his name.

"Your heart longs for a companion, a treasure beyond what you can make for yourself."

The old crone's words pierced his heart. The puppetmaster was alone in the world, save for his creations. His parents were gone; his wife had died in childbirth years before, and the babe with her. He so longed for a companion, for a real family. That searing loneliness was his greatest pain.

"Listen well. Soon, the blue moon, the rarest of all moons, will be on the rise," the woman prophesied, her voice skittery as a spider's. "At its waxing, offer up one of your creations, and by the moonlight they will be given breath. Choose wisely who to awaken.

"First, make a cut; finger or hand will do. With a drop of your own blood, mark for the creature a new heart. By the moon's power, the wood will become a living thing again, born of the earth and your blood. But to complete the change, you must say the words."

"Words, milady?" Gephardt stuttered, shocked at these wild suggestions. Such spells were outlawed, forbidden generations ago. Once, men and women sought to raise power from the earth, to bring wooden carvings to life or to entreat a heartbeat from sculpted clay. That age ended when a royal con-jurer's disastrous spell enabled a king to achieve the opposite: he turned the living to wood. Thanks to his blistering temper, more than a few wooden wives, sons, and stewards were lost to the burn pile. His regime finished in ruin, followed by a ruling heralded far and wide against elemental spells.

In an attempt to safeguard the future of the monarchy, all books containing such magic spells were either sentenced to be kept under lock and key or flagrantly destroyed. The latter applied to those still living with magic words tucked within the pages of their memories. Anyone suspected of witchery or sorcery was hunted down and added to the smoking pyres aflame around the royal city. The old, elemental spells were lost, their legacy now mere whispered warnings from mothers' lips. Or so the puppetmaster had thought.

"These are the blue moon's words," the woman rasped. "Take heed now, for there's always a cost, and I'll not repeat myself.

"Bitter moon and solemn blue,
blood of earth and sap and dew,
wake a second life anew."

"Wait, please! What—"

She silenced him by snapping a twig-like finger to her lips. The woman stood and dusted her tattered skirts, which disin-tegrated toward her gnarled feet. Then she left, disappearing into the trunk of a broad oak.

Stunned, Gephardt doused his fire and made his way home. He feared he'd imagined the whole thing. Had his loneliness driven him to madness? If anyone had seen what he'd seen, or heard those words, they were in danger of being pitched straight into a burn pile. And if he were to go so far as to make a living creature using such magic? If discovered, the creature would be burned as an abomination.

Yet in the weeks that followed, he obeyed the old woman, scorned the law and made a girl: the daughter he and his wife had longed for. Selecting pieces of the finest linden, he forsook constructing anything else and worked tirelessly on her. He crafted her legs so that they would be sturdy but elegant, the shoulders even and strong. She emerged from the raw, a girl of about eleven years—the same as his own wee one, had she lived.

When it came to her face, the puppetmaster swore his chisel was guided by another hand, the tools already knowing the way to the features sleeping in the wood. The dark hair, the slope of her nose, the wide eyes; she was always there, he claimed, waiting to be set free.

When the rare blue moon rose, Gephardt remained sequestered at home, waiting for it to peak in power, fearful of returning to the forest to perform the rite in the open. He closed the shop early, bolting the doors and shuttering the windows. He paced wildly, wearing grooves in the planked floors. The marionette had been finished for two days. There was nothing else to do but look at her and *hope*, however outrageous and pitiful that seemed.

He'd asked the old tailor next door to sew him a dress. A new pair of shoes were fashioned by the cobbler. Such requests were not unusual; the puppetmaster often relied on his fellow artisans to complete his work with their finery.

When the moon peaked that fateful night, it was full and lavishly blue, the same shade as the cerulean in the puppetmaster's paint pots. Its light was a living, ghostly thing. He waited until the rays illuminated his far workshop window—the only one he dared crack open.

He held the marionette gently, bathed in moonbeams, as he knelt on the floor. From his pocket he drew a small blade, a long-ago gift from his own father. With a whispered prayer and a deep slice across a scarred fingertip, he painted a heart in the place where a new one might grow.

Then, he uttered the old woman's clandestine words, the marionette's first lullaby. *"Bitter moon and solemn blue . . . "*

In a rush of joy and heartbreak, with a ripping breath that filled the marionette from the inside out, the wooden limbs became warm flesh. The cleverly fashioned joints on the arms and legs germinated from pins and wire to bones and sinew. A human heart hummed in the small chest. Gephardt's blood spilled through newly strung veins, flooding the marionette's cheeks and prodding her eyelids open. In wonderment, the puppetmaster and girl looked one another in the eyes for the first time.

In those first moments, I was, perhaps, still more wood than girl. It's hard to say. Since a tree cannot move about, the only way for it to travel is to stand through time, the pages of its story pressed deeper inside with each passing year. I keep the memories of these first moments tightly pressed within. There are days when I wonder if you were to crack me open, could you still count my rings, each significant moment sealed in a new layer to protect it from the elements?

My father claims I attempted to stand, but my wobbly legs stumbled in a willowy twirl few dancers would have been graceful enough to manage. Like a leaf fluttering to the forest floor. Then came the puppetmaster's hearty laugh and the words that never fail to bring a flood of those early memories rushing back.

"And so it was that I discovered your name: *Pirouette*."

CHAPTER 1

TAVIA'S MARKTPLATZ IS NEARLY FULL BY THE TIME I HITCH Burl to our custom-fitted theater wagon and find an unoccupied corner of the square. Merchant tables and tents unfurl in a patchwork of every kind of ware, both common and exotic, that a Tavian might desire. Burl stands placidly, a bastion of calm among the shrieks and high-pitched chatter of those bargaining their way to fuller stomachs and emptier purses.

"A puppet's pull goes far beyond its strings," Papa often reminds me. "Marionettes aren't just for children. A story—a good one—will grip any audience, young or old."

I desperately hope the audience will be gripped today. I'm already sweating and hungry as I set up our little stage. The ridgepoles snap neatly together, and over them I hang a tailored shade to hide myself and the marionettes, sleeping in their trunk.

I lower the side panel like a drawbridge, revealing rich velvet curtains dangling at the ready. The stage is eye-level for children, though as my father anticipated, adults linger in the back of the crowd to watch, too—a puppet show in the marktplatz is always a welcome diversion. Afterwards, the generous will show their appreciation by placing coins on a narrow ledge bordering the stage. On a good day, I scoop up francs by the handful before returning home. I need today to be one of those days—Papa needs more paint. Again.

Inside the wagon, spools of canvas swing from the ceiling, backgrounds that I can lower and change depending on the story. My fingers stroll through the scenes, each one bearing the evidence of my father's skilled brushstrokes. I select one with a familiar-looking tower in the distance. The crest on the tower's banner is indistinguishable, but the flaming red color means only one thing to me: The Margrave.

Tavia isn't a particularly large territory. There's the sprawling village and surrounding farms, then the inner district where the Maker's Guild and other merchants live and work, all wrapped around the central marktplatz. The Margrave operates as overseer, ruling from his estate at Wolfspire Hall thanks to an ancient appointment of the von Eidle family bloodline. He answers only to King Nicos II, who rules our lands from a city I've only ever heard whispers of—Elinbruk. The king and his rules are so far from here they may as well not exist. Not for us. The Margrave is king here.

With the stage set, I close the curtains ceremoniously, giving a sly wink to the gaggle of children already gathering at the theater's edge. Anticipation builds in me each time I perform, like steam swirling in a teakettle. I settle myself on a three-legged stool and slide open the locks of the trunk with a satisfying *chink*.

The marionettes I perform with are some of our best, each about the length of my arm, painstakingly carved and painted and fitted with costumes that rival any larger stage. Carefully, I lift each performer from the silk-lined depths of their resting place. I hang the ones I'll need later from hooks to keep their strings from becoming tangled.

I select a marionette I carved myself a few years ago, a peasant girl. She's rough compared to the work I can do now, but the unrefined quality of her face suits her. Tassels of dark yarn escape the kerchief around her head and a smattering of freckles dance across her nose. I choose her companion for my opening scene: a gray donkey whose head bobs on its own string.

It's taken years of patient study to become a puppetmaster's apprentice, to learn how to work with wood to produce the pieces I see in my mind's eye. But putting on a show with marionettes, that comes as easy as breathing. I can almost feel myself slipping through the wooden controls, sliding down the strings into the armature. Voices bubble up out of their faces and, just like that, a story is born.

"Masters and mistresses, girls and boys, I offer for your amusement a tale that is sure to charm and delight. A story that will make you laugh and weep. A myth that will stir your very soul—"

"Oh, get on with it, ya laggard!" harps a man's voice from beyond the curtain. "Before we're all as old and gray as Wolf-spire's stones!"

I pause and grin. Without fail, there's a heckler in every crowd.

While my audience cheers, I quickly draw the curtains closed. It's important to never let them see the mess of props I must set to rights before the next show. "Hide the hands behind the strings," as my father would say.

According to the sound of coins filling the wagon ledge, my tale hit its mark. When I reach out to gather them up, I can't ignore small pairs of hungry eyes tracking my penny francs like slices of hot bread. I motion to two hollow-looking faces to join me at the back of the wagon and tuck a few coins into each open palm. Squealing, the children run, slipping away into the crowd. The stand of maple trees at the edge of the marktplatz murmurs approvingly, their gold-tinged leaves rattling like treasure in a tinker's coat.

As I'm resetting the stage and carefully adjusting my puppets, four sharp taps sound at the wagon door.

"Pirouette? It's me."

Bran's voice makes my pulse pick up. I unlatch the door, surprised to see his brown eyes flitting anxiously across the marktplatz. Instead of greeting me, he climbs right inside the wagon and snaps the door shut behind him. Though it's only built for one puppeteer, there's room enough for us both to crouch in the warm, dim interior if we squeeze together closely. I don't mind.

"You had quite an audience going there, Piro."

"Indeed." I smile, shaking the bag of coins.

Bran's handsome face is not smiling. "They're still out there."

"The little beggars?"

"No. The duke and his guards," he says pointedly. "And that big man who's always shadowing the Margrave—the one who does all his dirty work." He leans in, talking low. "I made a delivery and saw you had the whole square enraptured, including the duke. Von Eidle had such a strange look on his face. Like a man seeing the sun for the first time. I don't like it."

"The duke is here?"

That's one downside of puppeteering; I can't see the audience while I perform. I've only ever seen the Margrave's son, Duke Laszlo von Eidle, from afar. I glimpsed him once riding in the carriage procession beside his father, a pale shadow of a boy in a man's body. As a child, the duke was sickly, never going anywhere without a nurse and a rasping cough. Some sort of lung-wasting disease, they said, the same that killed his mother. The Margrave kept his son confined on their castle estate, bringing in tutors and the best doctors while keeping the rest of Tavia at bay. Though that was years ago, he's still widely assumed to be too delicate to rub shoulders with commoners. The duke is rarely seen beyond Wolfspire Hall's gates, let alone watching marionette shows at the marktplatz.

"I wasn't doing anything wrong, Bran! Father is so busy and I must buy more paint—" I whisper. "The wooden soldiers for the Margrave are bleeding us dry."

"I know, Piro."

A tight, stubborn shame spreads across my face, which was so triumphant just moments ago. "It was just a theatrical."

"I know," Bran says sympathetically. "But you need to take care, Piro. Especially if you're going to tell stories like that last one," he adds, eyebrows raised.

It's true that my new story could easily be interpreted as satire; a selfish king's rage turns him into a wolf, and in the end the wolf is struck down by the peasant girl's well-aimed arrow. The crowd loved it.

Bran pets the wolf's shaggy gray head from atop a pile of marionettes. "It's not as if the wolf didn't deserve his end. It was a masterful tale." He smirks. "But you know as well as I, the wrong ears listening…"

"I'll be careful," I promise, pulling the wolf from his grasp.

Shaken, I peer through the small space between the top of the stage and the curtain. If I tilt my head at just the right angle, I have a narrow view of the crowd. I make out a familiar dark shape across the square: Baldrik, the Margrave's steward, hovering around the duke like a crow on a carcass. The duke, a fair-haired man with a red crest on his jacket, surveys the sights from in front of a posse of guards. He strolls the square, looking like a nobleman who knows his place: far above the rest of us. When his gaze turns to my wagon and its audience, though he can't possibly see *me*, his eyes lock onto it with a strange air of possession. My stomach twists at the unwelcome sight.

"The Margrave still keeping you hard at it?" Bran prods me with an elbow.

"Still working on a new order," I mumble, watching the duke's men strut about. "Lately, it's always wooden soldiers. More and more soldiers. Papa wears his fingers to the bone from dawn to dusk. Sometimes I think if I have to crack open another pot of von Eidle red, I'm going to scream."

A line of worry stitches itself above Bran's nose. It only serves to make his face more distracting.

"It's business, Bran. What else can we do?" I sigh. "You and the tailor aren't turning down requests for the marionettes' uniforms, are you? What is it to us if the ruler of Tavia desires a collection of wooden soldiers?"

"It's beyond me to wonder why a grown man would want life-size toys. But I don't like the way he's driving you and Gep into the ground. You already work with your nose to your chisel entirely too much, Pirouette."

I shrug. "We're makers. It's what we do. You don't bite the hand that feeds you."

"Unless it's squeezing your throat."

"Well, I can't complain," I say sharply. "Papa needs me. We'll come out all right. We always do."

Bran brushes his fingers against my arm in solidarity and my cheeks catch flame. That's been happening a lot lately. Then he sneaks out of the wagon, just as skillfully as he came in.

Bran's words sting, but we can't afford to balk at the

Margrave's requests. A year ago, when my father received the first grand commission for an order of life-size marionettes, our little shop was barely scraping by. My father is an artisan of the highest degree, but his beautifully carved dolls, toys, and puppets aren't quite enough to keep us out of patched socks and worn boots. We've always had *just* enough. Papa's always been adamant that we stick to our craft, our calling to produce clever and delightful work regardless of how much money it brings us. So when orders started pouring in from Wolfspire Hall, we weren't in a position to refuse. Gold is gold.

Determined not to let the duke's presence rattle me, I wipe the sweat from my hands and return to work. This time, I choose a common hearth tale about a greedy baker who refuses to sell his own bread. The baker gorges himself until he literally bursts from his gluttony—everyone's favorite part. A tale without the slightest hint of magic or royal mockery, that no one could object to, be they peasant girl or duke.

"I will be careful," I confide to a grandmotherly marionette as I pluck her from the trunk. I find comfort in her softly bent back and wizened, nut-brown face. "But you and I know that careful is not the same as silent, is it, old one?"

"Indeed," she whispers back.

CHAPTER 2

*H*OME. THE PLACE WHERE I AWOKE TO A NEW BEGINNING, startled to find myself in sudden possession of a body and a beating heart and something else altogether foreign—a father. Inside Curio the air is spiced with glue and lacquer, the floor littered with curls of wood shavings that multiply no matter how often I sweep up.

You can't help but admire our shelves, stacked and layered like the best kind of birthday cake, overflowing with toys. Jaunty little wooden men with sticks glued to their backs to make them dance look down upon a menagerie of animals, each more splendid than the next. There are snarling tigers, mysterious elephants, galloping horses, and the great beasts of the sea: the monstrous whale and fearsome squid. Intricate wooden puzzles are tucked into baskets, each piece smoothed to perfection, their mysteries ready to confound minds for many a pleasant evening. Brigades of tiny soldiers line up in rows, waiting for a battle-thirsty master to put them to work. My stomach sinks when I see the soldiers now; I wish the Margrave desired toy soldiers instead of the larger-than-life ones he demands.

And all around, strung from the ceiling or sitting precariously on perches, hangs the pinnacle of his work: the marionettes for which my father is known far and wide. Waiting to spring to action are elegantly coiffed ladies, bashful gentlemen, brash sailors, and sweet little shepherdesses. Some are as small as my hand, others as hefty as the wooden stool behind the counter. Creatures from every old hearth tale and fantastical childhood dream wait, poised for a player's hands to give them voice and motion. I love the marionettes best of all.

My father is a born maker. From the moment he first picked up a piece of wood and a knife as a young boy, Gephardt Leiter has been making the things he loves come to life. That love is evident in every nook and cranny of Curio.

Several of the marionettes are my own creations. My father began training me as his apprentice as soon as he saw I had an inclination toward the work, once I proved myself capable of more than just sweeping up sawdust and sharpening tools. He taught me how to select the best pieces of wood, how to trace shapes onto a rough board of linden or halsa and then, bit by bit, how to transform those rough outlines into curves that speak of movement and expression. My tastes run toward the wild and wondrous: fairy folk and gnomes, lumbering giants and fleet-footed elves, creatures that haunt my daydreams and tiptoe around my nights. After almost seven years, I still find the process utterly thrilling.

If they knew my past, some might think it odd that I am so drawn to carving up the very thing I used to be. But woodworking is my native tongue; I relish the grain against my hands and dust beneath my fingernails, the satisfaction of polishing a piece until it gleams. It connects me with the deepest part of myself, that secret history only Papa is privy to.

Ducking through a curtain, I find him in the workshop, the very heart of Curio. As he sands away at a soldier's rigid torso, his spectacles ride dangerously low on his bulbous nose, and his shaggy gray hair brushes against the rims. I set down the paints I picked up on my way back from the marktplatz.

"Was there enough, Pirouette?"

"Yes, Papa. Just barely. I think we're depleting the chromatist's supply."

"Well, after nearly ninety-some soldiers-worth, I shouldn't wonder," he mutters, tossing a scrap into a jumbled corner behind his workbench.

Back here, every table is overrun with tools and stubs of dark grease pencil. Pots of glue drip slowly and dust motes sail the air, thick as fog. I stop to run my fingers across an emerging face, staring skyward as the iron jaws of a vise lovingly grip its skull.

With his big shoulders hunched to his ears, Papa concentrates on refining the chest of the soldier so that one of Tailor Soren's uniforms will fit snugly as a second skin. The Margrave's orders were very specific: the marionettes are to be as tall as a man, each outfitted with a uniform the tailor would supply. And the faces must be unique, no two alike. I've spent the last year toiling at Papa's side on untold numbers of eyebrows, noses, and lips, until my fingertips were stained and calloused. We've delivered dozens of the soldiers to the Margrave's estate and just received an order for more.

I sit down on an empty stool and poke at an abandoned, half-eaten apple. If I didn't leave him bits of food scattered about, Papa would forget to eat; he's been so focused on meeting the Margrave's absurd deadlines.

"Papa?"

"Yes, Poppet?"

"Why does the Margrave really want the soldiers? Just when I think we're done, a new order arrives."

My father halts the sanding block in his hands, nudging his spectacles up with a dirty shirtsleeve. I see the dazed look of a man getting far too little sleep.

"I don't know, Piro. I've pondered on it much myself. The young duke is still an avid collector of marionettes, so the steward says. He must grow restless, cooped up there as he's always been. Perhaps they are his only source of amusement. I'm sure the Margrave placates the lad any way that he can.

"Of course, it's reckoned by some that the Margrave might prefer to name our Emmitt as heir, though I doubt we'll ever see that come to pass. I can't imagine the young duke would *ever* take kindly to his father's bastard assuming his rightful seat. Though we all know who would make the better Margrave." He muffles the last bit under his breath and resumes sanding.

I am no stranger to the history of the Margrave's two sons. Emmitt Schulze, the clockmaker, is a good friend and long-standing member of the Maker's Guild, and the closest I've come to having a brother. He and his mother, Anke, have spent many an hour at our hearth.

Years before the birth of the young duke in Wolfspire Hall, the Margrave forced a dalliance with Anke, a pretty widow who'd inherited the clock shop from her late husband. Though he never officially declared his first son, the Margrave never concealed Emmitt's existence—much to the ire of his fragile Margravina back at home.

"Whatever the reason for these soldiers, Poppet, it's not our concern. We must be grateful for the work, for it's buying you a new pair of boots and a dress, and me a much-needed saw blade. And then I intend to set some money aside for you. Seems like we never get caught up enough to put anything aside for tomorrow. And," he pauses to blow a fresh pile of dust from the soldier's body, "speaking of tomorrow, we must go gather more wood."

I want to let my father sink back into his work, but I worry what will become of us after the Margrave's commissions. I can't keep it in, can't help but give voice to the fear that's been trickling into my mind for weeks.

"Do you think, Papa, that the Margrave or the duke some-how *knows*? About me?"

Papa jolts, dropping the sanding block on the soldier's stomach. On his face, buried beneath the exhaustion and determination, I see something I have been desperately trying *not* to see these past months: denial laced with fear.

"Surely not, Piro." He lowers his voice to a terse whisper. "No one else in all of Tavia knows about the blue moon's magic except me and you. And you have told no one?"

"Never!"

"Then, it's impossible," he says resolutely, returning to the soldier.

"But . . . haven't you wondered, Papa, about the timing of it all?"

Until recently, I'd assumed the Margrave was hardly aware we existed. He'd kept to himself for years, rarely entering village life to do more than wave a gloved hand in the square at yearly proclamations or parade the duke around in a carriage. There was little contact with the Maker's Guild and the common folk, beyond the odd bit of tailoring and tinkering or the occasional request of a puppet for his son.

"It's been nearly seven years since the last blue moon. Do you think—"

"Impossible." My father growls low, ending any hope of further conversation. "Speak of it no more. You know better, Piro! Now, fetch me that spool of wire, I must attach these arms."

Pressing my lips into a tight line, I hunt for the spool and find it tipped against an empty jar of paint. I hand it over without speaking. Papa can be brusque, but he's never brushed me off like this before. This is new. Along with the tremors in his hands and the drooping bend of his back. Each soldier built seems to sap a little more of his strength.

I decide I will try his method: push down my reservations by working harder. All will be well, if we can just finish these orders on time. I sit on my worn stool with my small back against his mountainous one and dip a brush into some black lacquer. Though I'm weary of soldiers, it's always a thrill to watch wooden eyes open for the first time, the fine fringe of eyelashes growing under my brush.

When I begin to paint the lips, using the Margrave's red, the soldier interrupts my concentration. Like the trees, marionette voices drift from their wooden cores to my ears, speaking in their faint echoes.

"We know who you are," he mutters darkly. "*Sister*. Carved of the same vein and forged in secret. We remember."

A thick drop of red escapes my brush and smudges against the corner of the soldier's mouth, pasting him with a leering grin. Hurriedly, I grab a rag and wipe it away. But the damage is done, the stain too lurid for the rag to erase. I glare at the head, not yet attached to its body. Picking up my own sanding block, I take pleasure in roughly grinding the paint away. In my haste, the lips are gouged, leaving this soldier scarred.

No matter. After all, the Margrave requested that the soldiers appear real. None of us escape becoming real without a few scars.

CHAPTER 3

"PIROUETTE! WAIT UP!" AN EAGER VOICE RISES ABOVE the din of wagon wheels on the cobblestones.

Just near home, Bran catches up to me. I can't help but smile at the sight of him. His face can scarcely be seen, buried beneath a mountainous armload of fabric. He grins at me sideways from behind the rich-hued bolts piled in his arms.

"I see it was another good day for the theatrical arts," he says, referencing the pots of fresh paint swinging in my arms after another market day.

"I don't think you can see anything of the sort, mostly because I don't see how you can see anything at all." I snort, watching as Bran's shins meet an apple seller's crate. He stumbles but catches himself, managing to keep hold of the bundle in his arms. As the tailor's son and chief delivery boy of The Golden Needle, Bran Soren could almost navigate the village sight unseen. Almost.

"You coming to the next Guild meeting?"

I nod as we stop below a sign with Curio etched in winding black script.

"Planning on it."

Bran's grin crinkles the corners of his eyes. "Save you a seat?"

"Same as always."

"Always." He winks conspiratorially and steps backwards into The Golden Needle without looking, the door swinging open to the tinkle of bells and a happy shriek from one of his younger sisters.

"Bran's back, Papa!"

The Golden Needle nestles next to Curio in a long, leaning row of workshops that house their owners in narrow second floor quarters. The tailor, Benito Soren, moved in just two years ago, when I turned sixteen. He and his wife Gita opened The Golden Needle in the sunny space next door and suddenly a whole batch of Sorens, eight in total, overflowed like bunting from every window and door. This included Bran, the oldest, whose tiny attic room shares a wall with mine.

I made the discovery one day when I opened my little cupboard beneath the rafters and saw strange objects mingling with my own. Inside lay a wooden box with a "B" carved upon the lid, a worn measuring tape used for learning the tailor's trade, and oddities like shiny rocks rubbed smooth, a bird's egg, a pocket watch whose face had been rearranged, an assortment of tiny tools and a bag of coins. A note, hastily scrawled on a scrap of receipt, read, *"I see that this is a safe place for secrets. I'll keep mine with yours, if you don't mind. - Bran Soren"*

I did mind—and I told the new boy next door as much when I reached in and poked through what I previously thought was the back of the cupboard. It swung open to the foreign space of his room. He was crouched directly on the other side, as though he'd been waiting for me to open the door.

"I do mind, you know," I insisted, trying to dampen my curiosity at being afforded a window into a stranger's room. It was the very mirror of mine, with a sloping ceiling and a small window resting above wooden slat floors. His bed was draped in a soft gray spread and I could see a pair of smart leather boots tipped over in its shadow.

"Why?" asked the boy from the other side of the cupboard shelves.

"Because this cupboard is mine," I said defensively.

"It seems to me that it is *ours*. It opens for both of us. Seems like we should share it," he said confidently. "It *is* a cupboard with two doors."

I bristled. "I was here first."

"But not really," he replied in a steady voice that made me want to linger in front of the cupboard, though I initially contemplated slamming it shut in his face. "Someone else was here long before us. Haven't you ever wondered who they were?"

"They?"

"The person who built the cupboard. Or persons. Clearly they built it like this for a reason. I wonder if it was an old spinster, shut up in the attic, kept hidden by a vicious master to spin golden threads. Perhaps this cupboard was her only means of sending secret messages to the outside world, through the lonely housewife who took pity on her from next door."

"What?" I said, taken aback.

"Or maybe it was built by a pirate, retired here after a life on the sea, a man now sadly bed-bound, his body ravaged by drink and overwork. He would give away his gold to his many illegitimate children next door, coin by coin, administered daily through the cupboard so that he might never have to touch them and thereby acknowledge all that he had squandered and lost."

I stared at the boy through the cupboard, mesmerized by his words and enthralling dreaminess. I had never imagined that my cupboard had other lives before me. Or that it would open a door to another world: Bran's world.

From that night on, I couldn't close the cupboard door on him. After agreeing upon a secret knock to signal to one another, we began a series of hushed conversations through the cupboard. We would talk about our work, our lessons, or the mundane trifles of our day, sometimes traipsing into the more uncertain territory of the past and our dreams for the future. Despite our closeness, Bran didn't know—*and must never know*—the truth about me. No one could.

Tonight, the cupboard is open while I lie on the floor, my head upon my pillow, bare feet tucked up against the wall where it slopes steeply into the roof. All I can see of Bran through the open shelves are his hands, fluidly stitching the long seam of a soldier's stiff linen shirt, his needle moving like miniature flashes of lightning against a white sky. I love his hands—always so agile and sure. My own often feel at odds with themselves unless they have a chisel or a piece of wood beneath them.

"You really should tell them," I plead for the thousandth time, my voice drifting through the narrow space of the cupboard, where it meets Bran's finely shaped ears and disappears in the light of his room.

A sigh escapes through to my side.

"I will."

"When?"

"Soon."

"You've been saying *soon* for months."

"Soon always comes quicker than we think, Pirouette."

"You have to give your parents time. To prepare."

"I *know*," Bran says a little too roughly. "Emmitt says there's no rush. In the meantime, I've sworn him to secrecy about my plans to apprentice with him. I'll tell them when I'm ready."

It's no secret that Tailor Soren hopes to pass The Golden Needle on to his eldest son. But Bran spends every moment he can spare at Schulze's clock shop, reveling in the stable purr of ticking clocks and marching gears. Though lately, Emmitt spends most of his waking hours aloft in the high gables of the rathaus, charged by the Margrave with repairing the massive, two-storied glockenspiel gracing the town hall. The clockmaker has become Bran's hero. His new choice of vocation will hit his parents hard, but with time, I'm sure they will come to accept it. Bran is not.

Tired of trying to change his mind, I pluck a tiny, wooden dancer from the shelf in the cupboard. She's the first toy the puppetmaster made for me, a little ballerina whose legs dangle with impossibly straight posture, her pointed toes shod in painted slippers lacing to her knees. *Prima Ballerina*, I named her then, delighted with this gift from the warm, gentle man who said I could call him *father*. Dark brown hair, the same shade as my own, dashes across her forehead, topped off by a wooden bead for a bun. I love her still.

"So, what about you?" Bran's voice interrupts my memories.

"What about me?"

"You can't keep ignoring the truth."

I look through the cupboard, blood rushing to my head. The sensation jolts me as it always does. I'm always surprised by how hot and immediately blood flows from one place to another in my body against my will.

What does he mean? I've always been so careful.

"When are you going to say something to Gephardt, get him to see reason? He can't possibly go on like this. Both of you are exhausted. Gep doesn't look good, Piro."

"*He's fine*," I say shakily, trying to convince myself as much. "We're fine."

"Fine is for kettles of fish. You are *not fine*. Neither of you."

I rub my dry and bleary eyes, feeling the delicate clink of Prima's legs against my cheek as I cradle her in my hand. It was past midnight when I left my father sound asleep at his workbench and tiptoed up to my room, too tired to prod him toward his own sleeping quarters. I'm just grateful he's actually getting some sleep.

"You know we have no choice, Bran. The Margrave won't

pay us until we deliver this next dozen. And with the money we've had to spend on paint and supplies . . . his quoted price will earn us a little overage, but still. My father must finish the soldiers. And I must help him."

"If only there were magic words you could utter to render all those pieces finished in a second," Bran groans sleepily. "If only."

"People like us don't have the luxury of magic," I reply softly. "Not anymore. You know that."

"Who believes any of that hogwash anyways?" Bran asks. "Seems like it's mostly superstitions. A bunch of old hearth tales, that's all. There's always a good lesson or a bit of truth in them, like the stories you perform in your wagon. But real spells? Words with power? It's always struck me as funny that the Margraves are so fearful of such things."

My heart constricts at his words. Gephardt always asserted our Margrave is the strictest of them all; Erling considers it a great honor to lock up or burn any supposed conjurer. It was his great-grandfather who started the whole trouble in the first place, that first unruly king of Elinbruk who recklessly destroyed most of his family, nearly wiping out his line.

Closer to home, the story of Old Josipa still rings in my ears. When I was just past what my father marked as my twelfth birthday, a Tavian healer known as Old Josipa was out gathering herbs, bits of bark and roots for her poultices and salves. A child happened to follow her and heard her chanting. The child came running back, telling all who would listen that the old woman was speaking to the earth. In return, plants rose up from the ground, their leaves leaping right into her basket.

Even though the medicines Old Josipa collected were the very things needed to soothe a fever or calm an upset stomach, and she only used her magic for the good of others, it mattered not. When the child's tale made its way to the Margrave's ears, Old Josipa was seized and made an example, her poor body lashed to a pole and tossed on a burn pile like a dried shock of wheat. I'd had nightmares for months after, fearing that Old Josipa's fate would someday be my own.

I must have fallen quiet for too long, for the next thing I know, a hand extends toward me, breaching the empty space between our walls. I sit up and stare at it. Bran wiggles his fingers, and I instinctively drop the little ballerina and place my hand, callused and small, in his own eager and warm one.

Looking at the spaces between our treasures, I can see only parts of Bran, mere slices of the fabric of his face, a strip of eyes shaded by serious brows and then below that, a firm and sympathetic mouth. He squeezes my hand and a flicker of heat trails up my arm. For a moment, he looks like he wants to say something, but isn't sure how to form the words. Bran usually has no trouble finding words when he needs them.

"Pirouette, I . . . "

I watch him search for what comes next, very aware of his hand holding mine. I marvel that, in the two years since we first opened this cupboard, Bran has somehow become my dearest friend. I can't imagine my days without his quick and easy smile, without noticing the way his hair curls up at his collar when his mother gets too busy to give him a haircut, and the way it looks endearingly ragged when one of his sisters does it for him. Bit by bit, like a scrap of sandpaper wearing away a rough edge, Bran has worn down my defenses, all the stiffness, shyness, and quietude of my earlier years. By all accounts, he knows me best, at least, as much as you can know someone without truly knowing their past.

Papa long ago instilled in me the consequences of revealing my origin to anyone else; it would only endanger them as well as me. Of course, Bran's heard the yarn my father told when, out of the blue, a quiet slip of a girl appeared at his side: my mother died in childbirth and I was sent away to be raised by my grandmother until I was old enough to join him in his shop. Gephardt repeated the fable so many times and with such confidence that my newly formed ears absorbed the words like truth, and I repeated it as my own. I've always paid a price for it. Whether it's a misfiring of the magic that made me or a natural effect of my wooden origins, I've learned that anytime I tell a lie, there are consequences. Painful consequences.

"Pirouette." Bran nudges me. "You . . . you know that you can trust me, right? That I care about you, more than I have the words to say."

In spite of his sweetness, all I can think is that if Bran really knew, knew that something about me is both human and *other*, he would be afraid.

Afraid for me.

Afraid *of* me.

I can't bear that.

Bran sighs again, circling the back of my hand with his thumb. My breath catches in my throat.

"Just don't forget that I'm here. Wooden soldiers or not. Margrave or not. Someday, I'll have enough to strike out on my own, and you and Gephardt will never need worry about money. I'll help, I'll—"

"Bran."

"We could be—"

"*Bran*." I cut him off, half-delighted and half-terrified of what he might say next.

More than anything, I want a future with Bran, a chance to be loved the way the milliner loves the milkmaid, with a heart that feels full to the brim of happiness. But it always seems happiness only ever hovers near, a wisp of flame ready to vanish with my next breath. Bran deserves a girl who is fully human, not one whose very existence could condemn him to the Keep.

He looks at me expectantly through the shelves, waiting.

"This is just work," I reassure him. "It's not forever. Surely the Margrave and the duke will run out of room to hold all their toys. Soon our days will return to normal."

"Maybe, Piro," he leans in, gripping my hand, "but normal or not, I want more than this for you."

I dare to read from the hungry look in his eyes that he wants more *from* me, too. My heart swells with something dangerous and thrilling.

"Bran?" I ask, a smile on my lips, offering him the only thing I can right now: the comforting words that have closed every clandestine meeting between our cupboard since we were sixteen. "See you tomorrow. Same as always?"

"Always," he repeats softly, eyes shining in the candlelight.

With regret, he releases my hand and waits for me to be the first to close the cupboard door. I shut it slowly, feeling the same sense of loss I always do when the knob locks into place. Placing my hand over the door, I leave it to rest, foolishly hoping to feel Bran's pulse from the other side.

My heart wants Bran Soren. I can't deny it. But the danger of loving someone is that the closer you get, the more exposed you become. And just like a single lie will work itself out through my skin, I fear the truth will do the same, splintering apart anything good we might have. Far sharper than any lie, I've learned the truth has a way of coming out. Always.

Chapter 4

I BEGIN MY USUAL MORNING DUTIES BY TYING ON MY apron, unlatching the front door and dusting the shelves. Papa hasn't come downstairs yet, he must still be asleep. I'm glad. I don't like the feverish look in his eyes, the sweat I've seen beading his brow.

I linger on the marionettes today with duster in hand, adjusting a crooked arm here, draping a tangled string more loosely there. Each one is so unique, so lovely, it almost pains me to look at them.

"We are not so different, you and I," one of my wise-bearded wizards advises when I tug his handle to make him sit up straight. The tip of his pointed hat knocks the shelf above. "You have strings, too," he mumbles. "Strings you cannot see, but that move you all the same."

Thankfully, the wizard's philosophizing is interrupted by raucous feet bursting through the door to the ring of doorbells. I turn to see the candlemaker's twins: both boys, blond, impish and hardly able to contain themselves. They are regular visitors, but even so, I can only tell them apart on a good day. Their mother dresses them in different colored caps—Dieter in red and Gustav in green—but whether they keep to their correct color depends on their mood.

"Is the puppetmaster here? I've saved all my penny francs, Miss Pirouette," the-boy-who-should-be-Dieter says breathlessly.

"He's saved them all. For weeks and weeks. We need some more wooden men, for our battalion," adds Gustav.

"We're preparing for a great battle," Dieter says seriously, his blond sheaf of hair bobbing in his eyes.

"Are you?" I reply. "That sounds quite dangerous. And who are we fighting this time?"

"Dragons, Miss Pirouette," Gustav—at least I think it's Gustav—pipes up. "There are loads of them here in Tavia. They've escaped from the high mountains in Brylov, didn't you know? And if we aren't careful to watch for them, Father says we'll all be burned to a crisp."

"A crisp!" his brother adds knowingly.

"Indeed. Well, I know the puppetmaster would love nothing more than to help you fight off those pesky dragons, but since he's resting at the moment, will those do?"

I point to the toy soldiers on a low shelf, each with a tiny face and cap and weapon to bear.

"Now, soldiers can be useful in battle, but don't forget, so can a dragon!" I whirl around with a roar, having freed a black dragon marionette from its hooks. I dangle it menacingly over the boys' heads.

They erupt in shrieks and giggles as I make a tiny spray of wooden flames spew forth from the dragon's mouth through a lever my father carved in the beast's neck. While the boys busy themselves on the floor deciding which soldiers their few precious coins will secure, I return the dragon to its hooks and continue dusting. The bells jingle again. It promises to be a busy day.

"One moment!" I call, my back to the door, righting a chess piece from where it had been knocked over.

A male throat clears impatiently behind me. The rudeness sets my cheeks to steaming.

"Yes, I said *just a moment*—"

I whirl around to see the Margrave's steward, the one who lingered near my wagon on market day, a tall, horse-faced man called Baldrik. He has to hunch to fit through our door. He's been to Curio several times now, but always deals with my father. In fact, since the day he arrived in his carriage to bestow his first order of soldiers upon our humble shop, we've seen neither hide nor hair of the Margrave himself.

"What can I do for you, sir?" I ask stiffly, rubbing at my apron with the duster, dispensing dust from the shelves all over myself.

"Here to check accounts," he says briskly. "Margrave von Eidle is eager to complete his latest order, and if our accounts are correct, we are still short eight soldiers." He sniffs, his square jaw and lips grinding like a bull chewing its cud. "Our accounts are always correct."

The man always speaks as if he were the mouthpiece of the Margrave himself, joined to the noble household by some holy union. It's always "we need this" and "we think that." And here he is again, checking up on us, as if we are making mud pies instead of constructing complex pieces of art. I hide my distaste for Baldrik and his master's errand by plastering a smile on my face. The twins eye him suspiciously from the corner.

"Certainly," I say pleasantly, forcing myself to walk calmly to the ledger. Ceremoniously, I heave the curling, leather-bound book on the counter and flip it open to a page marked by a long strip of ribbon so worn it's nearly transparent. I trace my finger down the entries, hunting the one he's asking about. It's the last one on the ledger, one of the only new orders we've listed in weeks.

"Yes, you'll see right here we have eight soldiers left to complete, as you mentioned, in this most recent order of a dozen. But we'll surely have them finished by Margrave von Eidle's deadline, which isn't for another two weeks."

Baldrik shifts around heavily on his feet, which wobble as if they are unaccustomed to supporting such an immense, ungainly apparatus. He looks down at me with scorn.

"We'd like to speak to the puppetmaster himself, girl. Make sure he is aware that this order must take precedence over any other work. The Margrave won't brook any delays."

"He's not down in the workshop at the moment, but I can assure you he has been laboring day and night to complete the Margrave's order."

The twins now stand behind the large man, squabbling

about which one of them should get to hold the prized fistful of soldiers.

Baldrik huffs impatiently, irritated by me and the two small boys. "Call him at once, we prefer to speak with the master himself, not his dusting wench."

Blood rises to my face at his insult, the sensation of roots drawing up water.

"I am the puppetmaster's *apprentice*," I say, unable to hide the edge that slides into my voice. "And if I may repeat myself, he is unavailable. But as his apprentice, let me assure you, we will complete this order, just as we have all the others the Margrave has so generously given us."

Baldrik looks past me, through the open curtain behind the counter to the workshop beyond.

"We don't want your assurances, girl, we want to hear from the puppetmaster himself. Call him out."

"He's not in the workshop," I repeat flatly, not wanting to show any weakness by admitting that my father is still upstairs in bed. It galls me to think of waking him, as though he were a servant at this horrid man's beck and call.

Baldrik places a pair of gloved hands the size of garden rakes onto the counter.

"Where is he?"

"Indisposed. But, I assure you, the Margrave's order—"

"Miss Pirouette? We're all done!" Gustav announces loudly, trying to be heard over the demands of the steward.

"Will be carried out to the letter—every last wooden one of them—and not a day late," Balkdrik barks.

"Yes, sir. We just finished another soldier last night," I reply with forced optimism.

A small fist appears at the edge of the counter and a set of questionably clean hands pushes six soldiers up to the ledger. Baldrik looks at Dieter like he's ready to swat the small boy away like a fly. Then he leans even farther over the counter, scrutinizing my face closely. The man smells of pipe smoke and something sour beneath. "Gephardt Leiter is always in his workshop this time of day. He is a man of regular habits."

"Boys, leave your pennies on the counter. You're all set." I wink at them and they scamper out the door, leaving a pile of warm penny francs behind, new soldiers shoved into bulging pockets. I feel slightly less brave without them here, left to face this particular dragon alone.

"If your master isn't capable of completing this order, other measures must be taken. He knows the consequences. The Margrave has been exceedingly generous with him and this little hovel of a workshop. If he is not able to proceed as planned—well, we hate to think of what will become of him. And," he says, punctuating the threat with a long, tapered finger upon the ledger, "of you . . . "

Baldrik now considers me as one inspects a cow brought to market, his eyes dissecting me for future possibilities. "There's always room in the von Eidle household for one more kitchen drudge or coal scuttler."

"As I said, sir, I am fully trained to—"

"Tell me, girl," he interrupts, "where is Gephardt? Is he gone? Has he fallen ill?"

I teeter on the edge of truth and lie, not knowing which way I will tip.

"No, sir. He's fine! He—"

My words grind to a halt as a splinter punctures the arch of my foot. I bite down hard on my tongue, trying to keep from yelping and giving myself away.

"Has been mixing up some new lacquers for your soldiers' boots," my father's voice booms behind me suddenly. "Dangerous work with those fumes," he says gravely to Baldrik. "Don't trust anyone else to do it but me." He puts a hand on my shoulder. I feel bolstered by its warmth, and blink back my tears. "Not even my finest apprentice. Can't risk her."

Baldrik seems satisfied by my father's sudden arrival, but he also seems to note the white-washed pallor of his cheeks and his fever-bright eyes.

"Well," says the Margrave's man, clearing his throat, "we don't have to repeat to you, Puppetmaster Leiter, the importance of this order to us, nor the ramifications of any failures toward that end. Do we?"

My father shakes his head subserviently. I waver between hating the Margrave's assistant and hating the fear on my father's face. I'm not sure which is worse.

"Good. We'll be by to collect them as soon as they're done. No need to wait until you can deliver them."

With a final flinty look at the both of us, Baldrik stalks from the shop, stooping to avoid a smack across the forehead from our broad doorframe.

A pity.

My father leans against the counter to support what I suspect are a pair of wobbly legs. I put my hand on his trembling arm.

"Don't worry, Papa. We'll finish in time. I was just going to get started when that vile man came in. I'll work all day today, all night. We still have plenty of time if we just keep going."

Papa sighs. "What would I do without you, Poppet?" He tweaks my chin affectionately. "Now, I am much better today . . . much better. Let me go put my apron on and I will join you."

He leaves me, passing through the curtain into the workshop. I wait a moment making sure he's busied himself before reaching down to slip the clog off my aching foot. A patch of red blooms on the arch of my wooden shoe.

You cannot afford to be so reckless, I berate myself.

Easing off my stocking and using my fingers as pliers, I wrench a splinter the size of a needle from my foot, teeth gritted all the while to keep from crying out. I'm grateful this one appeared in a place that's easy enough to conceal. I'm not always so lucky.

For every falsehood that passes my lips, a splinter pierces my skin. They've appeared jutting out of my hand like a claw or piercing my cheek like a thorn trying to escape. I never know where they'll surface. It's a curse that's difficult to hide, especially when all I've ever longed for was to blend in.

When I was newly made, what others mistook for shyness was me drinking in the language and the new faces, the strange customs of humanity. And it was me afraid of being caught in a lie, afraid of losing all I held dear, my short, wonderful life as a girl ending behind bars or in a pile of ashes.

Regretfully, I drop the splinter in my pocket. I keep each and every one, a reminder of the lies I've told, some innocent, some not so. I hide them, wrapped in a bit of cloth beneath my pillow. As a punishment, I force myself to revisit the past and remember whenever a new one is added to their number, mementos of my own cursed frailty.

I must be more careful.

What would become of us if we couldn't fulfill the Margrave's orders? I shudder to think of being indentured in the Margrave's household in order to pay off our debts. Or of watching my father be dragged away to Wolfspire Keep, taken from Curio and his work—all the things he loves most. I cannot allow that to happen. Gephardt Leiter might be the puppetmaster, but I am Pirouette, a girl whose heart is made of stronger stuff than flesh and blood.

CHAPTER 5

S EVERAL DAYS LATER, I WAKE TO THE TEAKETTLE WHISTLING A
sharp welcome from our little kitchen. Papa must be up
already. *He's barely slept again,* I think. *I feel as though I've hardly
passed a wink.* Next door, the familiar hum and shuffle of eight
Sorens moving about their kitchen and shop is unmistakable.

Groaning, I push back my coverlet and go to my small
dormer. I watch the sun break over Tavia, a golden yolk shimmering slowly in a frying pan. This time of day, the brown
peaks of thatched and tiled roofs glisten with dew. The streets
yawn after a brief respite from the trample of hooves, boots,
and rickety wheels.

The kettle whistles on, and I wonder if my father is already
too absorbed in work to hear it. I fling open my ancient
wardrobe and pluck a clean dress off a peg. Bran likes to tease
me because I could have my pick of leftover fabrics from The
Golden Needle, which he or the tailor could cleverly shape

into pretty dresses for me, but I always choose the same color: green. I possess three dresses, two for everyday and one for special occasions. They're all green.

"Make sure to give the girl some pockets, Bran," the tailor noted when I ordered them. "Pockets are like pins and needles, you can never have too many! Especially if you're a maker."

Thanks to him, my green dresses were delivered with some very handy pockets, sewn so artfully the casual observer could hardly see them. But that was last year, back when I had time to think of such frivolities, before the Margrave arrived at our doorstep, arrayed in his carriage with the von Eidle crest emblazoned like a scorch mark upon the side.

I quickly shuck my nightgown and pull a clean dress over my head, in front of the mirror on the door of my wardrobe, an antiquated piece of glass that belonged to the woman who might have been my mother.

I sweep my bangs out of my eyes and hastily run a brush through my hair. I keep it nicked short, at least compared to the way most Tavian women wear theirs. Anytime it grows, which is rare since it grows as slow as moss, I feel compelled to cut it to my chin, leaving my neck and shoulders free to breathe. Having a wad of hair plaited or tied up on my head only makes my scalp ache. I swipe at a smudge of paint on my cheek, leftover from yesterday, and vow to take care of that with fresh water from the kettle that is still sounding its alarm.

"Papa! The kettle!" I yell, hoping he hears me and will take care of the incessant squeal.

I stare at my face in the glass a second longer, marveling

at the fact that it exists. Large, dark eyes look out from under their rim of long eyelashes. A pair of eyebrows arch slightly over high cheekbones. A straight, long nose—a little *too* long for my liking. A small mouth, turned up slightly at the edges. But I can't complain. A tree never considers such things; it's needless, for its entire anatomy is the way that it breathes, eats, and drinks in the world.

I tear myself away from my own reflection and slip my feet into my work clogs, clattering down the stairs past my father's small, empty bedroom and our little sitting room that we rarely find occasion to actually sit in. I burst into the kitchen to rescue the furious kettle from the stovetop. Papa is nowhere to be seen.

My ears strain for the familiar chipping noises of the chisel or the soft scrape of sanding or the creak of a stool, but the workshop is dead quiet.

Perhaps he's finally taking a break.

I run downstairs, quickly darting between the workbenches strewn with the remains of a soldier's legs, the matched pair torn asunder at the hips. The lanterns burn low, like they've been on all night. I dash back up the stairs. The kitchen is deserted. Papa's bed appears unslept in. Returning below, I wander around, looking for clues. He's hardly left Curio in days. Last night, when I came up, he still labored over a new block of wood, just beginning to carve a soldier's head.

That block is still in its vise, but now I see that it boasts an unfamiliar blade sunk deep into the newly carved forehead. I gasp, my heart beating in my ears; it's a short, thick knife, made for utilitarian purposes, like skinning a deer or a gutting a pig. And beneath the blade flutters a note.

We, the Office of the Purser of the Honorable Margrave Erling von Eidle, do render our account with Gephardt Leiter, Puppetmaster, Proprietor of 'Curio,' null and void due to incomplete fulfillment of Order No. 009, for one dozen (qty. 12) full-size, timbered guards. Monetary payment for this order will be withheld until its completion. The proprietor has been summoned to Wolfspire Hall, and will be held in arrears, until such time as his order is completed, or the Honorable Margrave is satisfied at his recompense.

-Baldrik Engleborden, Steward, Office of the Purser

My eyes take in the arrogant scrawling signature. My father has been what—summoned? *Taken?* I didn't even hear anything out of the ordinary this morning while I slept, I was so tired. And we still have several days left, according to the Margrave's original order. We aren't late yet. I am sure of it.

Aren't I?

Nothing else in the workshop seems amiss, except for the foreign blade. Prying it from the head, I slip both blade and note into a deep pocket of my apron and scurry into the storefront.

Hastily, I scroll back through our worn ledger and can see no further notations about this order, no changes made in my father's wiry hand. The order in the ledger still says we have nearly a week left.

Since we first received the Margrave's commission and the

promise of more, Papa's been so obsessed with the idea of getting ahead, of putting money away for tomorrow that I fear he never actually thought what might happen if he couldn't complete the task.

Behind the counter, I flip open a chest shoved in the back where my father keeps old paperwork as well as orders and bills of receipt. Rifling through the papers, my pulse plummets when I come to one from a few weeks ago. It's the full order for the current batch of soldiers: Number 009. It was stuffed far down in the pile, a weak attempt to hide it from me. My heart drops.

Noted at the bottom in smeared ink, as if the writer couldn't wait for it to dry, is an added clause in the steward's hand. It adjusts the date and marks the order due *today* for double the pay.

Why did my father sign off on this? We could barely keep up with the demand as it was! Guilt washes over me. Why hadn't I kept better watch on him? He must have consented to it when I was out to the marktplatz, for I would have pleaded with him to come to a more reasonable agreement had I been there.

In fairness, I'm not sure my father had much choice—those who disagree with Erling von Eidle don't usually fare well. Though we've yet to receive a penny for this most recent order, I'm coming to understand the Margrave sees everything in Tavia as his already. He may consider us already in his debt.

What can I do? I cannot call for the Margrave's guards, for they are most likely the ones responsible for taking him away. With shaking hands, I sling on my cloak and lock up Curio. I dart quickly past The Golden Needle, not wanting to bother the Sorens until I know more.

I run through the main thoroughfare, past the marktplatz, my anger fairly shimmering off me on the path to the lower gates of Wolfspire Hall. I've heard it said that long before this Margrave's time, the first Margrave of Tavia kept wild wolves chained at the gates. Thus the name of the von Eidle's inherited residence, with its towering black spires. These days, the wolves at the gates are long dead. Now I worry the real danger is alive and well within.

When I arrive, the broad gate is locked with a chain and a padlock the size of my head. The two guards standing at attention inside it eye me, clearly bored.

"I must speak to the steward. About Gephardt Leiter, the puppetmaster. It's urgent." I flash them the note.

"You're too late," one of them replies. "He was brought in earlier this mornin' but the steward isn't hearing any more complaints today. You'll have to come back tomorrow."

I argue with the dimwitted guards, but in the end, the exercise is futile. This infernal gate is as close as I will get to Papa today. Banging my fist against it in exasperation, I do the only thing I can think of. I turn and run, as fast as my wooden-feeling legs will take me, back to The Golden Needle.

"But how could they take Gephardt to that awful place?" Gita says, aghast. "The good puppetmaster? He's been looking so worn as it is!"

I drop my head, ashamed I haven't kept a better eye on him, that I haven't forced him take more breaks or seen that he actually ate. He's always been the one taking care of me.

"We didn't see the guards either, Piro, they must have come before first light, surprising Gep at his workbench. And if they won't let you in, his own daughter, there's nothing that can be done until tomorrow," Tailor Soren replies, his lips tight. "I'm so sorry, Piro. It seems you might as well go home and rest. Gita will bring you by something to eat."

"I don't need to rest, I'm fine," I say, and at those well-worn words, I feel the pinprick of a sliver nudge from somewhere inside my palm. *Not a lie, exactly, but not the truth either, Pirouette.*

I must slow down, be careful, mind my speech. I don't want the tailor and Bran finding out anything they shouldn't because I'm too weary to stick to the truth.

"There's no shame in rest, Pirouette. You and Gep are more than entitled to it, after the hours you've been putting in. Rest a little," he says, taking in the shadows under my eyes and the way I'm cracking my knuckles, snapping each joint like nervous twigs.

The tailor himself droops with weariness, more so than I've ever seen. It's a strange sight for a man who normally flits around his shop with the stamina of a hummingbird, seeing to everyone and everything with a large dose of exuberance. I've been so caught up in our work that I forget others are spending late nights laboring over their own workbenches, backs similarly bent under the weight of the Margrave's tasks.

"Thank you, but I must get back to the workshop. There are

still four soldiers left to be finished, and if Papa can't complete them, then I shall."

"Piro," Bran begins to scold, but is silenced by a sharp look from his father.

"Yes, Pirouette. If you feel ready, get a head start on your work for today. That will make Gep feel a little lighter when you see him tomorrow, I am sure."

I nod at him, grateful he understands. I must finish the task set before us.

When I return to Curio I leave the front door to the store open, just like I would on any other day, in case a customer comes in. We can always use the extra francs. Wrapping a heavy work apron over my dress, I tuck my hair behind one ear and a freshly sharpened pencil behind the other and get to work.

Soon I am carving away at a soldier's legs, neatly blotting out the events of the morning, lost in the rhythm of my chisel and hammer striking away at the curve of the calf and the anchor of the knee. The wood we use for these soldiers is different than the typical linden we use for smaller marionettes. The Margrave's men are all made of halsa, a lighter wood that carves with far more ease than a traditional hardwood. Even so, each piece and part of the soldier is time-consuming, especially at their size. When complete, each one stands nearly a head taller than I do.

I don't allow my eyes to linger on the sleeping body of a woodland sprite I started carving months ago, now gathering dust. Even without looking, I know the fairy queen's head rests like a plum on her abdomen, waiting for me to smooth and refine its crude features. My fingers itch to pick her up and keep going.

I find it difficult to summon any joy in shaping this hulking mold of a soldier, who will be delivered to the castle on the hill, pass through its foreboding gates and then become— who knows?

By late afternoon I've finished the lower half of the soldier I started with, and I'm about to begin on the upper when Gita appears at the door with a basket.

"Piro, I've brought some supper. Come and eat."

"Still have more to do," I say, swiping at my forehead with the back of a dusty hand.

"That great oaf's not going anywhere," she says with a nod to the man under my chisel. "He can wait."

Ruling our small kitchen upstairs as if it were her own, Gita ladles me a bowl of roasted potato stew. I feel pitifully grateful, not even realizing how hungry I am until the first mouthful slides down my throat, creamy and hot. By my experience of her, she is a mother to beat all mothers, both stern and sweet. Her entire brood, including the tailor, adores her.

She sits down, calmly watching my face, her eyes probing in the way I've observed some mothers have. I'm unaccustomed to it and it sets my nerves on edge. I avert my eyes and focus on my bowl, trailing my spoon around the edge after every mouthful.

"Do you need anything else, Piro?"

"No, thank you. The stew is delicious."

She smiles. "I wasn't speaking about your supper."

"Oh."

Gita waits patiently.

"We're fine, Gita. Thank you. We'll be all right," I reassure her.

Leaning forward, she places a thin but sturdy hand on my arm. Her eyes refuse to shirk mine.

"Sometimes, Piro, when difficulties come, our first instinct is to manage everything ourselves—the work, the worry. All of it. That's how we survive. We try to lift it all on our own shoulders. And you and Gep, I know you have survived great difficulties before."

I blink, feeling overwhelmed by her quick assessment of my situation and the reminder that she believes my own mother is long dead. *Is this what it's like, having a mother of your own? A pair of eyes that cut straight to the root of a problem before you even know how to form your own thoughts?* I swallow another mouthful of stew.

"What I'm trying to say is, the tailor and I want you to know you're not alone. You and Gep are part of our family, not just our Guild family, but honorary Sorens, if you will." She refills my mug from a pitcher on the table without my asking. "And we will help you and your father all we can. I'm sure he'll be back in the workshop before you know it. And if he won't slow down, I'll give him a few orders of my own," she says with a wink and a squeeze of my arm.

When the warm imprint of her hand disappears and she turns back to the stove, I am struck by how immediately I feel its absence. Bran doesn't know how lucky he is.

After eating two full bowls of stew, I wipe my mouth and make quick work of dropping my dish into a waiting basin of soapy water.

"I'm heading back down. Thank you for the soup."

"'Course. I'm always glad for a few minutes away from my sewing. Though the Margrave may have a thing or two to say if the dozens of seams we have left remain unfinished," Gita says, grimacing as she packs her basket.

"Well, I may have a thing or two to say to the bloody Margrave," I mutter under my breath as we trundle down the steps to the workshop.

"You and me both, girl."

After a full day of work, I journey through the twilight to Wolfspire Hall's locked gate. I want to see my father as soon as possible tomorrow. The guards pay me no mind this time, leaving me to draw my hood and rest against one of the broad stone pillars anchoring the gate. I sink down against the stones, a cloaked puddle of frustration and worry. A large willow within the gates sighs with pity.

"Sleep if you can, while you can," it shushes. "Sleep while you can."

CHAPTER 6

BEFORE THE SUN'S FIRST RAYS APPEAR, THE GRATING SOUND OF the opening gate stirs me from a bad dream. I dreamt the wooden soldiers ran through the streets of Tavia. They ran with jerky, stilted legs across the uneven lanes, their arms pumping rigidly, eyes fixed on the forest beyond. Bewildered, I watched them go, afraid of what their loss meant for Curio yet half-sympathizing with their desire to return to the place from which they came. The poor things didn't know that once you were chopped down and carved up you could never be made whole again. There was no returning to what they were. My father screamed, calling for them to stay, while I silently cheered for them to go, wishing to never see scrap nor splinter of them again.

Blinking, I rub the remains of sleep from my eyes, jittery from the nightmare. The sight of the open gate brings me to my feet. The guards from yesterday have been replaced with new ones. They all afford me the exact same look of disdain. I dispense it right back and step through the gate.

"I must speak with Master Engleborden, the steward," I demand again.

The guard on the left, who has one good eye and one clouded and gray, clears his throat. He spits unceremoniously onto the stones at my feet. "Inside the common entrance, fourth door to the right."

I breeze past them, holding my head high as I walk the long, curving path to the common entrance of Wolfspire Hall. A barrel-bodied washer-woman, whose red face resembles a freshly peeled beet, hurries by with a heaping basket of linens on her head. I pass beneath the curved, stone doorway of the common entrance, which is marked COMMONERS in broad, chiseled engraving across the stone arch.

"Perhaps the grand front entrance has 'entitled imbeciles' or 'uncommonly arrogant' carved upon its keystone?" I mutter. I wouldn't know, for I've never been close enough to see it.

Inside a long, dark hallway, wood-paneled doors are marked with important designations like OFFICE OF THE CHAMBERLAIN or PORTER'S WARD and other offices necessary to the running of a noble household. It's not difficult to find the one titled OFFICE OF THE PURSER and rap my fist upon it.

"Enter!" a muffled voice bellows.

Inside, I'm greeted by the sight of a dour Baldrik Engleborden tucked behind a small table unsuited for his body.

"Yes?" he says, not looking up while he briskly annotates

paperwork, no doubt hard at work writing orders for other innocent Tavians to be brought in for crimes they did not commit or debts they do not owe.

I thrust the notice I found at Curio under his beaked nose.

"Where is my father?"

He blinks, seeing me for the first time, and snatches the note from my hand.

"In a holding cell. Awaiting the Margrave's review, to determine proper compensation for failing to meet a deadline."

"That's not right!" I burst out. "We still had days left— five days now—to complete this last order. We were nearly finished—"

"The Purser's Office is never inaccurate," the giant says smugly. "He agreed to special terms—*a rush order for double the pay*—for this last dozen and did not comply."

I glare at him. Oh, *why wasn't Papa more realistic?*

"When did he agree to such terms?"

"We paid him a special visit several days ago, after the Margrave realized he would need the timbered guards sooner than previously specified."

"But that's impossible—we could barely meet this order such as it is. It's not fair!"

The steward purses his lips. "I assume that Gephardt Leiter, famed puppetmaster, knows his business and is of sound enough mind to enter into business agreements. Especially for double the pay. Is he not?"

"Yes! Well, no, I mean . . . " I flounder, remembering my father's recent state of feverish exhaustion. "He has worn himself to the bone to complete the Margrave's order in such an unreasonable time frame. I'm worried for his health. Please! Let me see him. As his apprentice, I'll find a way to complete the remaining soldiers that are left undone. In fact, I finished another just last night, and it may be picked up if you're ready for it. Now there are only three. I'll see to it myself. *Please*," I beg.

The steward sighs deeply, as though pained day in and day out by such pathetic appeals.

"You may see him briefly this morning, but there is nothing to be done until he appears before the Margrave himself. The Margrave will mete out the appropriate sentence for recompense."

"Fine," I say hurriedly, hoping that if I can just see my father, somehow this will turn out to be a terrible misunderstanding, something I can remedy. "Thank you," I add begrudgingly.

Baldrik draws himself up from his narrow chair and jangles a set of keys at his belt.

"You will only be allowed a few minutes, *apprentice*. Though I doubt you'll want to stay longer." He smirks.

'Til now I've never stepped foot inside the Margrave's estate, let alone the Keep. I know little of the Keep's present reality except what's murmured in the market when another poor sot is dragged from the streets after trying to make a living by stealing what they can. Be they Margrave or Margravina, the noble-in-residence has always used the Keep as a vault, a place to store those branded as thieves and embezzlers, those who shirk their taxes or owe great debts.

Those branded as practitioners of the old spells might also find a home in its depths, if they're lucky enough to escape the burn pile. The Keep is for any who dare to mar the placid tranquility with which the Margrave paints Tavia to the King in Elinbruk.

I follow the towering back of the steward down a warren of narrow passages, some dark, some lit with orange smudges of torchlight. Daylight is not a thing that keeps company down where we are going. I try to mark my way, just as I would in the forest, noting each turn and hall in my mind. It would be easy to get lost down here; I don't entirely trust the steward not to abandon me to the maze.

We stop short at a reinforced door, whose curving metal crossbars remind me of sword blades. Baldrik nods to the guards stationed at the entrance and pushes it open.

"Your father is in 24. All the way down at the end. We'll ring the bell when your time is up," he says, roughly prodding me through the doorway with a leer. The heavy door closes soundly.

My heart races. Here in the depths of the Keep, the inhabitants reside in two stacked rows on either side of a narrow walkway. I can't help but feel like a spectator at a traveling show, walking through a brackish menagerie of caged beasts. Torchlight ekes out every few cells, just enough greasy light to see my hand in front of my face. My feet shuffle on the moldy stones that pass for a floor. I don't know whether it's better to go slowly or hurry toward Papa's cell, but in trying to lick the sudden dryness from my lips I realize I can smell them all before seeing them, the people who languish down here like rotting meat.

The stench of human waste and the acrid burn of urine makes my eyes overflow. I pull my apron up to cover my nose and plunge on, hardly daring to look to my right or to my left, fearing what I will see. Yet, as I stumble my way to number 24, I can't help but see and *hear* them.

As I force myself to put one foot in front of the other, their manic whispers bleed slowly beneath the cries for help. They are the whispers of those talking to themselves, the endless shuffle of raw feet back and forth. Most cells contain barely human shapes, bundles huddled in corners, eyeballs gleaming yellow in the torchlight. I clasp my hands tighter to my apron, feeling disgusted with myself, realizing I am scared of them, these pale specters with matted hair and grasping fingers. Their clawing need is overwhelming.

And what did they do? I wonder, creeping past the rows of hollow eyes and carved-out mouths. *Palm a loaf of bread? Fail to cheer loudly enough from the front row of the Margrave's last feast day promenade? Neglect to contribute to the shares the Margrave insists we pay the King at the end of each harvest after a bad growing season? Find themselves unable to meet some absurd deadline to deliver to him what he already decided was his?* Surely they don't deserve this. No one does.

Trembling, I reach the end of the row and drop to my knees in the damp in front of number 24. My father is curled up on his side, his immense body small in the encompassing dark. A wheezing cough rattles his chest.

"Papa," I call out to him, reaching a hand through the grimy bars.

He doesn't hear me at first, not above the din the other prisoners are making and the thundering of his own cough. I can reach a hand just far enough in to squeeze one of his.

"*Papa.*"

His eyes open and search the gloom for my face. When he finds me, I can tell he doesn't know if I'm truly here. He sits up and comes closer, reaching for me through the narrow spaces between bars.

"Pirouette? I'm so sorry. There wasn't enough time to leave you a note, he wouldn't let me."

"I'm here to see about getting you out. Why did you agree to do the last order, to rush it? Why, Papa?" My voice breaks.

One lens of his glasses is cracked, but still he pushes them up from where they've dropped low on his nose. The sight of that simple, familiar gesture squeezes my heart like a fist.

"I thought if I just worked a little harder, a little faster—I've always been able to meet my orders. And for double the pay! Why, think of what we could do with that money!" Fever coats his eyes and it terrifies me. His cheeks are frighteningly sunken.

"But, Papa, we could never finish that many in such a short time, even with both of us working around the clock. It's impossible. And now what do I do, Papa? How can I get you out of here? This place is . . . "

"Vile," he croaks and then breaks into a deep cough. "I know, Pirouette. But I'm sure it's just temporary. If you can finish the soldiers—"

"I will. I will, Papa!"

"Then perhaps the Margrave will let me go."

"I will do whatever I must, Papa. It won't be long." It couldn't be. Another week in this air and I feared he would no longer be able to draw breath.

"Now, Piro, you'll need to find more halsa, and of course, don't forget to—"

Clang! Clang! Clang!

Above the murmurs and cries, Wolfspire Keep's bell sounds, just as Baldrik promised. A cold hand closes over my collar and I am dragged to my feet.

"I will!" I yell back to my father again, a promise that fades into the dank blackness as I'm hauled away from the dismal sight of number 24.

I will.

I feel that truth deep in my marrow. My pledge to my father is confirmed when no shard of wood comes jarring out of my body in contradiction.

I make a beeline for The Golden Needle, still in shock from what I've seen and heard in the Keep, my cloak reeking of the foul atmosphere in its depths. I interrupt the Sorens at tea.

I made a deal with Baldrik to complete the final three soldiers and have them done within five days, to meet our original deadline. We certainly could have used double the pay—I understand by the empty space inside my father's coffer why he was tempted by such a hollow promise. But if I complete the current order, I will receive only my father in return. Baldrik made it clear no gold francs would pass hands. I will do it for my father. I could live with little and do without many things, but I can't do without *him*.

Bran's face is a patchwork of worry and anger. The tailor's mouth sets itself in a grim seam over the prospect of what I face to set my father free.

"We'll help you, Piro," Bran offers quickly, his flock of sisters gathering around me while Gita presses a steaming mug into my hands. "We all will. Even if we've never picked up a chisel before, surely you can tell us what to do."

"It's not that simple, Bran," I say, my mind frantically ticking off all that must be done to complete the Margrave's order. "We need more halsa, so I'll have to make another trip to the wood. I need more paint—" My voice falters and I find myself blinking back tears to keep them from dripping in my tea. "If you aren't trained, it will take me more time to teach you how to do things properly than it would for me to just buckle down and work on them myself."

I stand up hurriedly, nearly spilling my cup. "I must get started right away,"

"Please, Pirouette, let us help you. I'll bring a bite over later—you mustn't neglect your meals," says Gita firmly.

"I'm coming with you," says Bran, buttoning up his gray vest that had been hanging open over a crisp, white shirt.

The tailor nods. "Of course. I can handle things here."

"I'll help with Bran's work while he's helping Piro, Papa,"

Lottie, the next oldest, says swiftly. Bran's little sisters chime in in agreement, crowding around me.

I look at them all, such hopeful, helpful faces. They have never seen the inside of Wolfspire Keep. For all our sakes, I hope none of us will again.

"No," I say, the word coming out more harshly than I intend. "Thank you, but I need a little time to get things sorted. To figure out what to do first. On my own."

I don't want the distraction of Bran to compromise my planning. There's too much riding on me completing this order.

"At least let me see you home," Bran insists.

Back in Curio, I immediately pick up my chisel and hammer and set to work.

"You know, Piro, if Gep doesn't return for some time—"

"This is temporary." I don't let him finish. "I'll get him back."

"Right. But, if something happens, if he takes a turn for the worse, I—"

"He won't," I say sharply. At this, a splinter prods the skin below my ribs, just under the surface, threatening to poke through.

Blast it all, Piro, I think. *Watch your tongue. It isn't fair, I can't even hope out loud without being reminded of my curse.*

Bran chews on the inside of his cheek. "You can't possibly do it all on your own. Finish an order this size, I mean," he adds hastily, seeing the indignation that colors my face. "Saints and stars, Pirouette! These soldiers are bigger than you are! It's a lot to do in five days, even for one as skilled as the puppetmaster.

Maybe you can alert the Margrave's man again . . . or beg for more time? You can't go on like this or you'll wind up in a cell right along with him."

Bristling at his words, I turn away and resume pounding the handle of my chisel with fresh vigor. *He's never seen the inside of Wolfspire Keep, those emaciated bones reaching through bars, begging for the smallest scraps of human dignity. Well, I have. It's my skin on the line now, my father's life at stake.*

"Easy for you to say! I can't ask for any more than I already have, Bran. The steward thinks he's doing me a favor by even allowing me the honor of finishing this order in Papa's stead. He doesn't trust me as it is, can hardly believe I'm the puppetmaster's disappointing choice of apprentice." I sniff indignantly. "Nice to know you feel the same."

"No, Piro, that's not—I'm just worried for you," he pleads above the noise I'm making to drown him out. "If you'd let us, we could help." He picks up a piece of sandpaper. "The whole lot of us. It's too much for one person. Now's not the time to be a martyr!"

I grit my teeth, needing to feel the chisel bite the wood at every sting of the hammer. *Bran doesn't know the first thing about suffering. How could he? He's known about the village as the Golden Boy, what with his handsome features and sweet nature. Everything comes easily to him; everyone loves him. Bran has no secrets to hide. No past shadowing his future.*

"As you've already said so plainly, I have a lot of work to do." I fume over the noise of my hammering. I refuse to look at him.

A moment later the door bells jangle. He's gone.

They probably all doubt me. But I will complete my father's work. I must.

The size of the pieces don't intimidate me, nor the number. The clock on the wall strikes a new hour, as surely as if I'd used my own hammer to sound the chimes. *Time.* The one thing I can't control, can't wrestle with my hands and pin into place. Yet I wouldn't be Gephardt's daughter if I didn't try.

I need money for paint and supplies, and I thank my fortunate stars Papa's given me a way to make some. Bran's warning from weeks ago, the first time I saw Laszlo out walking the marktplatz, lingers in my mind as I arrange the wagon stage.

"Take care, Pirouette. Take care." For all the good that did! *Father ended up in Wolfspire Keep anyways, didn't he? And Old Josipa still ended her time on the burn pile.*

Instead of taking care, I align the marionettes and settle my shaking grip on the crossbars. I am tired of hiding. If I dare to tell a tale that reeks of the old magic, of a blood sacrifice and cruel fairy folk and magic gifts, the likes of which people here haven't heard in an age, perhaps I'll be able to earn a little more today. The crowd is always thirsty for new stories.

I reach deep in my memory for a fable I once heard from a wandering tinker on a wood-gathering trip, one surely retold countless times under ebony skies filled with stars. It's a grim tale from long before my time, one I guess the elders in the crowd will recognize. I've never forgotten it. Ignoring the worried grousing of the trees at the edges of the marktplatz, I make my voice strong and alluring as a town crier's and plunge headfirst into a story I've never told before.

It's just a story, I tell myself, *to remind them all that the magic still exists. That there is more going on around us than meets the eye. To remind myself of that fact.*

By the end of the tale, I realize I have scarcely breathed the whole time. When the dark fairy reveals that the bread the innocent beauty had eaten was conjured from rocks, hisses emanate from the crowd. With the maiden's belly weighed down by stones, the devastated prince cannot carry her; she is far too heavy to rescue. Instead, the cruel fairy binds the maid to her donkey, cursing them to walk to their deaths, the donkey dragging the poor maid behind him like a millstone round his neck.

The crowd calls out warnings as the fairy carts the prince from the stage, selfishly determined to keep his love to herself. With great flourish, I shutter the curtains to their titilated cries. I am exhausted, but empty of regret.

"Reckless!" a few voices cry above the clapping—though that may be the trees.

My elation is high when many coins, which I know are increasingly difficult to spare, fill my ledge. Performing the tinker's risky story gives me the same morbid satisfaction I feel after a splinter, as if I deserve the torment of my lie. But I know the truth of this tale all too well. Just as quickly as magic may conjure a new gift, it may also weigh the bearer down with a belly full of stones.

That night, I ignore the signaling knock from the other side of the cupboard. I can't bring myself to open it; Bran doubted I could step into my father's shoes and complete the work waiting for me in Curio below. How could someone who belonged from the moment he first squalled in his mother's arms know how it feels to come from some*thing* rather than some*one*? How could he understand this impossible chasm between what I am and how I came to be? The distance between us wraps around me like the cold weight of a dead man's embrace.

CHAPTER 7

THE NEXT EVENING, DESPITE MY EXHAUSTION, I ABANDON MY tools for an hour to join the Maker's Guild at the usual place. It's true The Louse and Flea isn't much to look at, and neither are its regulars, but the smell of the tavern gives me a rush whenever I step in. I don't much care for the foamy beers or dark bottles that keep men planted in front of them until their heads no longer sit upon their shoulders by their own strength, but I love the way the years of soaked barrel staves, rich hops, and laughter coat the very walls in a thick, smoky layer of comradery. Well-worn tables take up most of the pub's dark interior, tables at which many a pair of dirty elbows have ground divots into the wood while eager hands lifted a pint of diversion with friends.

I step inside and nod to Gert, the barmaid, as she expertly wipes mugs with a damp rag and a practiced hand. I wind my way around the narrow common room, having to twist and turn to fit in between the bodies at their stools. Back in a corner, I see them gathering like a brood of hens to cluck and fuss: the Maker's Guild.

Bran's father was responsible for first gathering us together after he came to town, hoping that if we worked as a collective we could share the hardships of our respective crafts and generally look out for one another. If Gephardt Leiter became my father through a bit of magic and love, the Guild has become my family through a stroke of sheer luck. News of my father's stay in the Keep already reached the Guild, thanks to the tailor.

Nan's eyes brighten and she shoves over, making room for me by knocking right into Tiffin and spilling the contents of his mug. Irritation flashes across Tiffin's narrow face, but he moves down and continues silently brooding into his drink. The tall, brown-skinned blacksmith-in-training is built like a marionette, all lanky limbs and loose joints.

As the blacksmith's striker, Tiffin spends his days hefting the heavy hammers that Mort, Tavia's blacksmith, uses to forge metal. You wouldn't think him fit for the job by looking at him, for Tiffin appears to possess the strength and disposition of a string bean left too long on the vine. But his nimble hands work marvelous magic with metal. The young smithy has dreams of one day setting out on his own to be a traveling tinker, free from the confines of our staid village.

Nan fills my glass from a waiting pitcher of water. I shoot her a grateful look and gulp it down. I land my empty water glass on the table a little more forcefully than intended.

"Easy there, Piro, wouldn't want to get too crocked on the

first cup!" chortles Fonso, who by now already has a mug of ale too many down his own gullet. His beefy shoulders shake while he laughs at his own joke, his massive hands thrumming the table. His stocky fingers are crisscrossed with a litany of white and pink scars, remnants of blowing glass over the unearthly temperatures of the furnaces in his workshop.

"I'll try to slow down, Fonso, so you can keep up," I say, filling my water glass a second time. He winks.

"Long day, Piro?" Nan pipes up. The slender potter is wedged into the corner closest to the fireplace. Her dirty boots are slung up on the hearth as she leans back in her stool, exposing an indecent length of clay-spattered red stockings beneath dusty skirts.

"Long *year*, actually. I needed a break."

Nan raises a pair of black eyebrows, more expressive than I could ever manage with a brush. Her dark eyes are probing and don't miss much.

"Well, I'm tired of looking at Tiffin's long face over here," says Fonso. "So thanks to the rest of you showing up." He nods to me and Nan and Emmitt. "At least I'm not having to suffer that burden alone anymore."

Tiffin takes a rebellious swig of Fonso's mug.

"I just got here, too. We're all late, except Tiffin, who has an uncanny ability to be on time even though the forge doesn't keep a clock." Nan eyes Tiffin suspiciously.

"Mort says it would melt in the heat. Not good for the gears," he mumbles.

"True," Emmitt agrees. "Heat is no good for a timepiece."

"Sorry I was late, too." I sigh. "I'm up to my ears in wood chips and soldier parts. I can't stay for long."

Everyone instantly grows sober at the mention of the wooden soldiers.

"How is ol' Gep? Have you had word?" Emmitt asks, deftly rolling a small clock gear back and forth between the knuckles of his right hand. The nimble trick reminds me of our younger days, of the way Emmitt would pluck wee gears from behind my ears as though they'd sprouted there, or conjure extra sweets to tuck into my pocket. Emmitt was always easy to love—tall, dark, and rugged, a visibly healthier specimen than his nearly translucent half-brother up in Wolfspire Hall. Foolishly, I used to wish Emmitt might become my real brother, but over time I understood Papa and Anke's hearts are too tightly tied to their first loves to ever be anything but friends. Thankfully, Emmitt and Anke remain part of my Guild family.

"Papa will be out soon," I say as convincingly as I can. "I'll finish this last dozen. Then I can bring him home to rest." Their eyes fill with hope for the puppetmaster, though the workload still lies heavy on my shoulders. Nan pats my arm and pours me another glass.

"We're a small band tonight, aren't we?" I ask, noting the empty places where my father, the tailor, and Bran would normally be.

"Say, where is the Golden Boy?" Fonso asks, looking to me for an explanation of Bran's whereabouts. "And the tailor?"

"Don't know." I sniff, trying to act as if Bran's location and occupation aren't of great importance to me.

Nan's eyes narrow. I haven't spoken to Bran at all today, ever since I didn't open the cupboard door. It's killing me.

"No puppetmaster, no Bran or the tailor. This is a sad state of affairs," Fonso grouses. "I come to The Louse and Flea to be cheered, distracted from my troubles, not to be thrust right back under a black cloud by you sorry lot."

The glass smith scratches his chin, the bristles of his red beard gleaming like copper wire in the lantern light. Fonso is still attempting to grow in his beard and the fact that he's managed a chin-full thus far is a point of great pride.

"It's a black cloud out there all right," Nan mutters, tossing a glossy braid over her shoulder. "I can hardly afford to enjoy the sun when it shines after the last set of taxes the Margrave levied. A working girl can barely make a decent living in this town!" she complains into her mug.

Nan owns the pottery studio and kiln at the end of our lane. Her small frame, black eyes, and pale skin bestowed by her ancestors in the East often lead people who didn't know her to mistake her for a young apprentice at her own studio instead of the master that she is.

"I've a solution to that problem for you, Nanette Li," Fonso says boldly.

Nan rolls her eyes. "Marriage to you isn't the solution to *my* problems, Alfonso Donati."

Fonso grins. "No? It would be a lot more fun than lower taxes or a sudden windfall of gold. *I guarantee it*," he says, flirting shamelessly.

Emmitt snorts into his cup.

Nan kicks Fonso sharply under the table. "I'll take that windfall of gold any day, thank you very much." She sighs, tucking her small, clay-crusted hands deep into the pockets of her work apron.

I look to Tiffin, who is sullenly tracing patterns in the dew on his mug with a dirty finger instead of drinking from it. He looks particularly troubled, which is a change from his normal state of morose.

"Tiff? What's eating you?" Emmitt beats me to the query, topping off his glass.

"Like the puppetmaster and the tailor, Mort's had a bit of a windfall, too. A big commission from Wolfspire Hall." Tiffin swallows, the sharp knob in his throat rising and falling against his collar.

All ears at our table immediately perk up.

"For what?" says Nan sarcastically. "New ironworks to decorate the Margrave's billiards room? Life-size chess pieces, perhaps?"

The Margrave is an avid player of chess, backgammon, knucklebones, stones—any table game of skill or chance. Since the man isn't blessed with physical prowess, he fancies using what he believes to be a great intellect to soundly beat his opponents.

"No," says Tiffin, shaking his head and setting his tight-knit brown curls bobbing. "Weapons. And not the gaming sort."

The rest of us sit with mouths open like the fishmonger's morning catch of silvertail.

"Broadswords, longswords, rapiers. Knives of various lengths. One hundred of each."

Something in my belly tightens like a screw. We've been commissioned now, after many months, to produce a hundred soldiers in all. Same for the tailor: a hundred uniforms, custom-fitted to my father's creations. *One hundred soldiers and uniforms, with a set of weapons to match.*

"Well, throw me in the kiln and call me baked!" Nan utters.

The blacksmith has never had an order like that before and we all know it. At most, Tiff and Mort are shoeing horses, repairing farmers' tools and working on a custom piece or two at a time. And that's in a good month.

"Well, isn't it about time?" asks Fonso. "The Guild is finally getting some francs from the Margrave. Heaven knows he's as stingy as they come and it's about time we started getting something back for all the taxes we've paid to cushion his overstuffed behind. Don't suppose I could pop in to have a look?" asks Fonso. "I'd like to see what kind of armory is deemed fit to grace the Margrave's walls."

Tiffin chews on a worn nub of fingernail. "I've been pouring and striking for what feels like years, but it's only been a week," he says bleakly. "The only good thing is Mort is paying me overtime, to work at night. Otherwise there's no way we'd be done in time."

I nod. This is the way it is with the Margrave.

"I can't wait to get my hands on one of them broadswords," Fonso says eagerly, thrusting and parrying his mug like a blade.

"I'll be staying far away from any establishment that gives

you free reign on a pile of sharp objects," Nan says.

"Looks are deceiving. I'm exceedingly coordinated, for one so large and strong."

"You won't get the chance," Tiffin says. "The Margrave's man comes and takes them away almost daily, when they're barely even cooled."

"I don't like it," says Nan. "Weapons make me nervous."

"Me too," Emmitt agrees quietly.

"Then how can you stand to be so near these?" says Fonso to Nan, flexing his meaty arms in her face.

"I barely manage," she deadpans.

"But why so clodding *many* all at once?" Tiffin asks the question that rides like a phantom on my shoulder these days.

A burst of light breaks over the dark pub as Bran comes in. Something in my chest tightens. I can't read if he's mad at me, or hurt, or both. Maybe he regrets ever opening that cupboard door. He sits down across from me, claps Emmitt on the back, and immediately orders a drink from Gert. Seconds later she slops a huge mug before him, its contents swaying like the movement of her wide, aproned hips.

"What'd I miss?" he asks the table.

"Like the rest of us, you're late," says Nan. "Fonso thinks the great meat hooks he calls hands are weapons, Tiffin is drowning in a pile of molten metal courtesy of our great and lofty Margrave, and Pirouette looks as if she'd much rather be sitting next to you than me, given the way she's been trailing you like a hawk on a mouse since you walked in."

I blush fiercely and return my gaze to my cup.

"As for Emmitt here, well, who knows?" Nan lowers her voice. "Erundle the chromatist heard from one of the Margrave's washerwomen, who overheard from one of the steward's chambermaids, that the Margrave is definitely considering *someone else* to name as heir—someone more suited to leading," Nan continues, tapping a fine-boned finger on the table. "You know we all have high hopes for you, Emmitt."

The rumor that the Margrave is wavering on naming his heir still hasn't died. Anytime the young duke appears sickly it makes the rounds at market, an undercurrent of promise.

"I can't wait 'til that old goat is put out to pasture," Fonso growls.

"Pure hogwash and speculation." Emmitt shakes his head. "Such things aren't done. Laszlo was reared at Wolfspire Hall, with the best tutors and all the lessons, breeding, and military instruction that comes with it. Much safer that way. What does a clockmaker know of such things? Forget about it. Mother and I have long put those thoughts away. The rest of you'd best do the same."

"Rumors often spring from a kernel of truth, Emmitt! You've always been the first among us to speak up in the market when someone is treated unfairly or give away what you have to help someone else. Why I saw you literally give that wandering minstrel—the one who's perpetually drunk and reeks of rotten fish—the shirt off your back just last week. Surely those things count for more than all the fine tutoring gold can buy!" Nan says passionately.

"Rumors often get the talebearer in a world of trouble,"

snipes Tiffin, irritated at her for speaking of such things in public.

I sympathize with his uneasiness, especially with Papa still in the Keep.

"Fine, you dull-headed chisel of a boy," she snaps back, lowering her voice again. "I understand it's risky. But just think! He is the oldest of the Margrave's sons! To have a maker ruling Tavia? Reporting to the king for us? It could change everything!"

Emmitt raises both hands in protest. "I may be the man's offspring—*unfortunately*—but I'm not privy to his plans." He fiddles with a watch on a gold chain attached to his vest. It belonged to his mother's husband, the late clockmaker. "He speaks of nothing but clocks or the glockenspiel project when he sends for me. Fairly sure that's all I'm good for—another tool he can use to fix something broken. And the duke?" He laughs bitterly. "He's never even spoken to me, though I'm certain he knows who I am."

I try to change the subject. "How is the glockenspiel coming?"

"Ach, I feel as if I will never be finished!" Emmitt sighs, rubbing the back of his head. He's spent the better part of the past year toiling in the old clock tower among the many rows of rusty bells and gears and figurines.

"Personally, I don't care if you ever finish it," I pipe up, taking another drink. "I've never liked it."

"Sacrilege!" cries Nan in mock horror.

The glockenspiel in the marktplatz was installed long

before our time—the village center's sole piece of architectural glory. It was supposed to be a tableau of victory from the time when wolves roamed our land and men struggled to carve out a home among the beasts, but it's always left a bad taste in my mouth. The carousels of snarling wolves chasing farmers, the clash of soldiers at war with the wolves. The tinny, strangled sound of the old bells. Their song always sounded sad, the bells too high and haunting to be happy.

The Margrave put Emmitt to his task when the bells no longer chimed at noonday, like they always had. It's been silent for ages.

"I'm fighting a never-ending battle against rust and damp up there. I'm doing my best to ensure the gears and cogs will last another hundred years or so, but it's tedious work, to be sure."

"If it's your handiwork, Emmitt, no doubt it will last longer than that," Bran says admiringly.

"The thing is, I keep returning to find pieces broken and missing—almost as if someone has been up there at night, messing about. I don't understand it."

"A cog thief?" Nan asks.

"Something like that. The Margrave isn't happy it's taking so long, but there's only so much one man can do in the face of such a monumental piece like the glockenspiel. It's no pocket watch," he adds.

"Probably just some lazy lout's idea of a joke," suggests Tiffin.

"Possibly," says Emmitt, looking worried.

"I'll come help tomorrow, if I can," Bran offers.

"Thanks," Emmitt says, a smile lifting the wide corners of his mouth. "Wish I could lend a hand to you all, but I'm a bit buried at the moment."

As if she timed it just right to bask in his smile, Gert plops a fresh mug down in front of Emmitt, winking saucily.

"This one's on the house, Emmitt Schulze. Don't forget who never lets you go thirsty!"

"I'll not forget you anytime soon, Gert," Emmitt replies, winking back. He downs the entire mug in a single gulp while the rest of us admire his skill. "I'm off! Dawn comes far too soon and I've got more work awaiting me at home."

Emmitt stands and slips the gear he was playing with earlier into his vest pocket. He generously slaps enough francs on the table to pay for his drink as well as everyone else's. "Makers, I regret I must leave you so soon. Piro, send word the moment Gep is home. Until our next gathering." He tips his hat and struts through the crowd, where he is stopped no less than seven times by folks wanting to shake his hand or buy him another mug.

Nan screws up her lips and raises her eyebrows, watching his slow drift to the door.

"Out with it, Nan," Fonso bosses.

"Look at him! The people love him!"

"We're aware," Tiffin says drily.

"I've also heard the Margrave's physician has been spending a lot of time up at Wolfspire Hall. Seems he's been ailing of late." She pauses dramatically.

"So?" I say. "The physician probably has his own quarters

at Wolfspire Hall, what with the duke's recurring illness and now the Margrave living past his prime, as entitled men are wont to do."

Fonso shakes his head. "When you know something real worth broodin' about, I'll join in. Until then, don't be putting more on Emmitt's shoulders, he's got a heavy enough load to carry as it is. Don't go making it worse with your speculatin' about the Margrave dying and him deserving the territory seat. It's a bunch of bosh. And you'd all best watch your tongues about it.

"I heard Peter Baden, the saddler, got hauled off to the Keep for runnin' his big mouth at a game of stones the other night. Rambling on about the rising price of ale and how it's all the Margrave's fault. Which," he says, leaning in with a whisper, "you and I may know is true, but lately it isn't safe to be going on about. The Margrave has ears in every corner, maybe even in The Louse and Flea." He casts a wary glance about. A few uniformed guards sit at a table far on the other side of the room, deep in their cups.

"Well I hope his repulsive ears are burning right this very minute," Nan says imperiously, "knowing that we're talking 'bout him. Fine, if you're not going to let me meddle with Emmitt and what could be, I'll just have to meddle elsewhere. So, what's going on between you two?" Nan says pointedly to Bran and me.

Bran avoids my panicked gaze and looks innocently at Nan. "What do you mean?"

Her eyes narrow. "I wasn't born yesterday, Golden Boy.

The fog between you two is thick enough to cut with a knife."

I choke on my water, my face turning crimson. Bran looks at me quizzically, now assuming I've told her about our argument. I haven't, truly, Nan is just frustratingly observant.

Fonso slaps me helpfully on the back to clear my cough. "Nan," his booming voice warns.

"Well, she's clearly not herself, and I think it has something to do with Bran, just as much as it does with the fact that our ogre of a Margrave has her father penned up in the Keep. Did you say or do something to upset Piro?" She glares at Bran accusingly.

"Well," Bran stutters, looking from Nan to me. "I—"

"No!" I croak, having found my voice again. "He didn't say anything. I'm not upset! Everything's fine with Bran and me. I'm just really tired, Nan, that's all. Not feeling quite myself tonight, just as you said."

A painful hiccup erupts from my throat. Nan watches us both suspiciously. With a groan, I realize I'll pay for my hasty words. Inwardly, I curse my carelessness as a splinter the size of a carpenter's nail protrudes suddenly and painfully from my ear. I try to cover it up with another sharp hiccup and a casual sweep of my hair, but Nan's raven-sharp eyes don't miss it. My stomach plummets as she reaches out a hand toward me.

"Piro! You've got a bit of wood, caught in your hair. And you're bleeding, besides! Great blazes! How on earth did that happen?"

All eyes at our table and the tables next to us are now on me, on my burning face and the ugly splinter that's mysteriously found itself tangled in my hair. Nan's fingers gently pry the splinter free and lay it carefully on the table in front of me. Using a corner of her apron, she dabs at the blood on my ear, studying me, too close for comfort. Tiffin looks confused and Fonso awkwardly clears his throat, unsure of what just happened.

"Here, let me get rid of that," Bran says, reaching to brush the bit of wood away and toss it into the fireplace behind us.

"No!" I bark in a strangled voice, snatching it first. "No, it's just a splinter. A hazard of the job, you know!" I try to laugh it off and distract them as I secretly shove it deep into my pocket. I'm compelled to keep it, to save it along with the other tokens of my wretchedness. Cheeks still aflame, I take another big gulp of water in an effort to wash down the dry lump of fear in my throat.

Feeling too exposed, I stand up so fast I feel dizzy. "Well, I should really be heading back to Curio now. So much to do."

Nan doesn't say anything for once, just continues looking from me to Bran, watching us both cautiously.

"I suppose we should go as well." Fonso leaps to his feet in an effort to help me. "I have an unfinished pair of lanterns I'm trussing up for my cousin, Marco. Remember, the one who works in the kitchens at Wolfspire Hall? Delicate work, you know, lantern glass," he declares. He drains his mug, wiping his hands against his shirt.

"Nanette Li, may I walk you to your studio?"

Nan clears her throat. "I certainly don't require leading about like a horse with a bit." She sniffs. "But yes, you may walk *with* me. I should get back, too," she says, slinging her long braid over her shoulder the way some toss salt for good luck. "Look after that cut, Piro," she says, with a squeeze of my hand on her way out. She pauses to turn around and glare at Bran.

"You'll make sure she gets home in one piece, won't you?" He nods, his lips pressed tightly together.

"I'm done, too," Tiffin says, slapping some penny francs down on the table for Gert. "Cheers," he says dismally, following Nan's lithe back and Fonso's formidable one out the door.

That leaves me and Bran, now unable to avoid one another, no cupboard door to separate us.

"So," he says, a strained look upon his face. "Shall we go?"

Outside, evening light bathes the tops of the tight and twisty lanes, the setting sun casting thick golden strokes across the thatched cottages. Bran is quiet, hands shoved deep in his pockets, eyes down. Still, every housewife sweeping the day's dust from the stoop and every flower girl packing up her cart calls to him as we pass. He barely seems to notice the constant flow of attention coming his way, wave after wave of it, walking through the heart of town. I've lived here longer than he has, and no one calls to me that way.

We walk without speaking, soon finding ourselves at the divide between Curio and The Golden Needle, in that narrow space of a few bricks between our homes. The corners of my mouth can't help but turn up at the sight of several curious little Sorens peering at us through the window.

"I should really get back to work."

"See you later then?" He bites his lip, his eyes hinting at the cupboard.

"Er—" I falter, thinking of all the work that awaits me. "I don't know."

He sits down on Curio's front step. "What's going on, Piro?"

"Nothing" is on my lips, but I can't risk another splinter tonight.

"You mean, besides my father rotting in a cell?" I retort.

Bran exhales sharply and shakes his head. "I know. I mean, yes, besides that. Truly, Pirouette, I never meant to upset you yesterday. I'm worried for you and Gephardt. We all are. I can't stand thinking of him in that terrible place, or of you joining him. And, it's just, with you and me, I can't bear to lose—"

"Bran, I'm sorry I didn't open the cupboard. I'm just worn out. I need this wooden soldier business to be over, so Papa can come home. Then I'll be able to breathe again."

His eyes search mine. "That's all?"

I drop down to sit beside him and squeeze his hand.

"I worry, because I love you," he says simply. "I love you, Pirouette Leiter. Do you think that you love me, too?"

When he leans in, the streets around us shrink like coals in the fire until there is only the ember of me and Bran, here on the stoop, burning in the dim, purple light. And in the one moment when I should have answered truthfully, I find my words stick and my tongue is unable to answer back.

I fall into him instead, my hands tracing the beautiful craftsmanship of his jaw, my lips pressing against his. I am shocked by how soft they feel and how much better a kiss is than a common little word like "yes." This kiss is like nothing

I've ever felt before. A fire and a rushing river compete for space in my veins, sending rivulets of joy down to my toes.

When Bran reluctantly leans back, my lips miss his instantly. He stands, pulling me up with him.

"It's getting dark. We should go in. You know what they say."

"No, what do they say?"

Bran grins. "'Never trust what might happen with a beautiful girl under the moonlight. Might get moonstruck!'"

I nod, brushing a finger across my swollen lips as my heart attempts to recover its regular rhythm. Somehow I must return to work after this. I'm not sure it's possible.

"See you later?" he raises an eyebrow.

I'll be tired, but I can't wait to see him again, even if it's just a glimpse through the cupboard.

"Yes. Same as always."

"Always," he says happily, planting a soft kiss on the back of my hand before slipping through his front door.

Like his mirror image, I follow, dodging into mine. I'm unable to suppress the hope that "always" will be repeated again, and soon.

CHAPTER 8

"THE WOODS MAKE ME UNEASY," BRAN ADMITS AS HE AND I leave Burl behind on the main road with the wood-hauling sleigh. It won't fit among the close-knit trees this deep in the forest.

"There's something about *these woods*, in particular . . . before we came to Tavia, I'd always lived in a town, and we were surrounded by hills and valleys, not a shroud of trees like we are here."

"Mmhmm," I murmur in agreement. There *is* something about these woods. Something Bran can't possibly understand. These woods are my roots. The very fiber of my being.

"Well, you did insist on coming," I reply, trying to swallow the edge that found its way into my voice. It isn't that I don't want Bran's help or his company, but when it comes to the woods, I prefer to be alone or with my father. It's our special place.

Bran follows me, lagging behind as I pick my way through the underbrush with a light step, easily weaving in and out among the great oaks, chestnuts, lindens, and halsa that stand sentry around the land of Tavia. I'm looking for a particular stand of trees from my last trip here with Papa. And, though I don't say so aloud, I'm looking for signs of his presence—a deftly peeled blaze of bark on a tree tagging it for harvest, or a broken branch signifying a directional marker.

Finally, I see what I am seeking: a trio of blazes on a set of three good-sized halsas that will be perfect for completing the Margrave's order. Bran's eyes grow wide.

"You're going to take those down? All three?"

"And you're going to help me haul them back to the wagon," I say with a smile, brandishing the finely sharpened axe I carry on my belt.

"Can I help with the chopping?" he asks, stepping up to survey the leafy canopy above us.

"No, thank you. The halsa's grain is light and delicate, almost like a thick trunk of honeycomb. That's what makes it ideal for carving and toting such large pieces about; if we built the soldiers out of oak, a person would scarcely be able to lift one. I'd better do it, to preserve as much good wood as possible."

He nods and stands behind me to watch.

Before I make the first swing, I lay the palm of my hand over the blaze on the creamy inner skin of the halsa closest me, where it shows through the long scrape of gray bark. My father was the last person to touch this tree. Pressing my palm to the wood, I bow my head and close my eyes, quietly thanking the tree for the life it's about to give, and for the rescue I hope it will provide.

In return, I hear it's humble acquiescence, "You are welcome, sister." The reply tingles up my arm in a buzzing ache, the same strange pain that comes when you strike that tender part below your elbow my father claims is a funny bone. It never feels funny to me.

Bran's eyes are on me, curious. When I'm ready, I position both hands on the axe and let it swing in a graceful arc toward the base of the tree. It takes me longer than my father, but after many sure strokes I have the tree chipped away in a neat angle to its core. Sheathing the axe, I push with both arms against the trunk. The tree falls, landing with a hollow thud onto the forest floor, right where I intended.

Breathing hard, I turn around to face Bran.

"Right. You're up. Move that one out of the way while I begin the next."

With a serious face, Bran nods and goes about his part of the task, helping without asking further questions.

I revel in the sounds of the great wood, the reassuring voices of the trees and the ring of my axe biting into the bark. It's a relief to be away from the watching eyes in town and thoughts of my father suffering alone. Far below my feet I know the close-knit halsa roots grow, their vast tangle spreading out like veins threaded beneath the forest floor. Here in the shadows of the oldest giants, I sense a great breath being taken in and expelled, over and over again—an ancient rhythm as familiar as my own heartbeat. Every moment I spend rooted here in the dirt, something in me loosens until I find that I can finally exhale, too.

Having taken the axe to two of the trees, I break for a moment, leaning up against a nearby linden, savoring its shade. I swipe my bangs away from where they're sticking to my face.

Nearly done. Maybe it's not so bad having Bran with me after all.

I eye the distracting place his neck is flushed pink from the work, where dark curls meet golden skin. He's worked tirelessly, loading everything onto the wagon, following my every command.

"You know, I've heard," he says, dusting his own hands and strolling closer, "that some say the linden is the tree of lovers." He arches his black brows and leans back beside me, the wide trunk large enough to support us both. He crosses his arms nonchalantly, as if he leans up against trees every day, in this very manner.

"Have you? My father told me the linden symbolizes protection and good fortune." I tear the leather work-gloves from my hands and wipe them on my skirt.

"I like that even better," he says, turning toward me.

He pauses a second, eyes locked on mine. "I know things may seem bleak now, Piro, but for you, good fortune will surely follow. I know it. I knew it as soon as we moved in next door and I saw you through that cupboard. There's no one like you."

How right he is, I think, my smile bitter.

"I mean it. There's no one like you, not for me," he says intently, mistaking my scoffing for modesty.

Slowly, he lifts a hand to brush my cheek, settling a wayward strand of hair behind my ear with gentle fingers. Bran cups my chin with both hands, grazing my cheeks with his thumbs. He doesn't speak, just watches me, as though he's marveling at me, seeing something beneath my skin that I never have seen, something rare and precious. It's a heady feeling, watching someone see you in a way that you cannot see yourself.

He leans in and presses his lips to mine in a dizzying kiss that sends any thoughts of gathering wood or waiting deadlines straight to the ether. I can't even hear the voices of the trees, who are surely bustling about what's happening at their feet; I'm diverted from my purpose by stolen kisses. Instead, my ears fill with the sounds of air and light, while warmth surges to the places his hands are touching me.

I kiss him back, my mouth meeting his firm one, reveling in the uncanny way just being held against him makes me feel safe. *Protection and good fortune, indeed.*

The linden tree's bark meets my back as Bran leans even closer into me. His eyelashes flutter against my own and my fingers wind themselves into the rough linen of his shirt.

Kisses from Bran could never be stolen, anyways. I give them willingly.

When I regretfully tear myself from his lips, in part to

breathe—something I've not done much of in the last few moments—Bran smiles but doesn't pull away, just rests his forehead on my own.

"We should get back," I say shakily, knowing this reply sounds more like a question.

"True," he says. "You know, Piro, when your father returns home, you needn't nurse him on your own. My father thinks it's time to call for your grandmother. Do you think she will come if I go fetch her for you?"

I blink, trying to comprehend his words. "Who?"

"Your grandmother."

"My grandmother?"

"Gep's mother? The one who raised you?" he asks, eyebrows raised.

I lick my lips, which have gone dry.

"My parents thought she might come and stay with you. So you needn't be on your own? Surely she'll want to be with him when he comes out of the Keep. If she can make the journey, that is."

I swallow hard. Sometimes I think if I were not cursed by my splintering tell I would be a fantastic liar. It would be so easy, such a relief, just to lie. Instead, at each fork in a conversation, I am faced with dreadful options. Lie and be found out, or tell the truth and possibly be shattered by it.

"My parents, they're worried about you," Bran says. "Worried that you're too young to be on your own, to handle the shop and the care he'll need afterwards, too."

I nod, keeping my mouth shut.

"So, have you written her?" he prods again. "Sent word?"

I shake my head.

How I long to say that she died, or that we lost touch years ago. *Lies.*

I grit my teeth and silently curse my father for making up that part of my story. Then, I am instantly barraged by a wave of guilt. I know my father only intended those lies to protect me. The trouble is, without him here to speak up, they protect me no longer.

"Then, shall I? I'd be happy to help, to go and get her and bring her here to stay with you—"

"*No.*"

"But if you don't have time to reach her on your own, I'll—"

"I'll write to her," I say, the words coming out in a panic. "I'll see if she can come. I've just been so busy with everything, I hadn't even thought of letting her know about Papa. If she's well herself, I'm sure she'll want to come," I stammer, the lie unfurling from my tongue.

Bran looks relieved. I hold my breath, waiting for the familiar pain of a splinter.

It doesn't come.

What magic is this?

When Bran returns his lips to running small kisses down my neck, I feel so free, so happy. I allow myself to relax into his kisses, get lost in them and then it happens too fast and much too late to hide.

A sharp pain suddenly pierces my nose, leaving me gasping.

Bran steps back, eyes wide in alarm. There's no avoiding the huge, barbed fragment of wood rising from my nose. It rears like a sword tip in Bran's awe-struck face.

I shriek in horror, clapping my hands over my nose.

"You know better," scolds the linden tree.

"Piro?" Bran asks, my name suddenly seeming small and shameful, coming from the perfect mouth on his beautiful face. "What's that?"

I promptly whirl and start to run. I'm fast, especially when terrified. Prying the splinter from my nose, I hide it deep in a pocket, hating myself all the while, shamed at having yet more proof of my weakness. Pressing my apron to my face to stop the bleeding, I pray for the ground to open and swallow me whole.

When Bran catches up with me back at the wagon, I am nauseous and dangerously close to losing my breakfast. Blood pours from the wound—just to spite me, I am sure. Masked in my soaking apron, I bury my face in Burl's warm mane.

"Piro, please!" Bran pleads, staying a safe distance back. "Tell me what happened! Are you all right?"

"No, I'm not all right," I growl.

I can't do this. I can't explain. Not yet. Not ever.

My brain burns with humiliated fury, trying desperately to think of a way to escape the moment. If I lie, I will have more splinters to explain. If I tell the truth, I'm not only endangering Bran, I risk losing him as well. Surely, once he knows . . .

"Tell me, Piro. What is it?" He takes a few steps closer.

Burl swishes his tail, nickering softly, prodding Bran to keep going.

Traitor.

"What's hurting you? What was that?"

I bite my lip so hard now I'm bleeding in two places.

"Don't come any closer!" I shriek, pressing my face further into my horse for cover.

"Fine," says Bran, who I see from a quick glance stops at Burl's flank, his hands up in surrender. "I won't. Just tell me, Piro. Did I hurt you? Was it a splinter? Can I help?"

"No," I snarl, knowing that, at least in answer to his last question, is the truth. There is nothing Bran can do to make this better. I must suffer the humiliation of this curse alone.

Retreating into silence, I ignore his pleas for explanation and begin loading the wagon to return home, turning my face away from him at every opportunity. Tears stream freely, seeping with the blood from my nose. I am quite certain I'm the most hideous creature to ever walk the forest floor.

I let Bran take the reins on the drive home, since I can tell he's desperate to do something to help me. I urge Burl along with the crop, eager to put this whole incident behind us. Not intending to be rushed, Burl takes his time, slowly plodding the winding path back to the village. Some days I believe that horse truly loves me, and others that his sole ambition is to make my life more difficult.

My fingers twitch, drumming restlessly on my knees or swiping at my throbbing nose until Bran reaches over to capture one of my hands in his. A rush of heat spreads from his fingers to mine, and for a second, I allow it. Who knows how long I have to savor the simple joy of his touch? I find myself trying to grip tightly to every small delight, afraid such things aren't meant for someone like me—someone who erupts in splinters at the slightest slip of her tongue.

Just as we're about to leave the darkest part of the wood, something among the trees catches my eye. A sharp intake of breath pierces my lungs.

"What is it, Piro?" Bran stops the wagon, looking worried.

Shaking my head to clear my vision, I stare at the spaces between the trees.

"Thought I saw someone," I stammer. "Never mind."

Bran drives on, uncertainty painting his face. I can't help but glance back again. I feel something, *someone*, there still, watching me. I can't explain that I saw *her*—the shape of a little old woman step from the bark of a tree, like a snake shedding its skin. She'd smiled at me, I am sure of it. The hair on the nape of my neck prickles. I force myself to look away.

If there is a little old woman watching me now, a tree-woman who knows the secrets of wood and blue moons, then surely she knows who I am. Who I *really* am, and what I am made of. Against my will, the tight circle drawn around my past widens even more.

CHAPTER 9

"TIFFIN, YOU DOLT, YOU'VE KNOCKED OVER THE GLUE!" NAN shrieks as a fresh wave of glue pours down her skirt. "Again!"

"Sorry!" Tiffin bleats, hurriedly trying to wipe up the mess.

"You might be a wizard with metal, but in here you're a mess," quips Fonso.

It's true. The makers—all who can be spared from their normal occupations and beds—are cluttering up the back workshop of Curio, where they joined me to frantically assemble the final order of soldiers due to the Margrave. I tried to shoo them out hours ago, but my protests were soundly ignored. It's now well past midnight. My deadline looms tomorrow and my father awaits.

A row of three freshly pressed soldier's uniforms also wait on the worktable. Bran and Benito completed them days ago. Two soldiers are constructed and just need their faces to

95

be painted on. The final man is in a near-completed state of assembly. Tiffin was gluing leg joints, with Nan's help, when the latest glue eruption occurred.

"Here, Nan," I say, tossing her a rag and a fresh apron to wear home over the glue. "Tiffin, you'll need to go wash your hands with some solvent unless you want to be permanently attached to Nan's skirts." The smithy's brown eyes widen. Fonso glowers at him.

"In fact, why don't you go home, all of you. Sleep. At least some of us should. I'll finish up here. I'm almost done. I couldn't have made it this far without you."

"I'll stay," Bran says firmly, though the shadows under his eyes mirror those etched beneath my own. "The rest of you go. It won't take us long."

Nan slips the clean apron on over her sticky dress and then presses me close in a tight hug. "Now, I'll have you know we're only going because it seems that the three of us only succeed at making more work for you. But the end is in sight," she says, pulling back to reassure me with her dark eyes. Wisps of hair straggle around her face, but her braid looks as smooth as it did when she first plaited it, many hours ago. "We'll all be waiting to hear the news tomorrow. You'll tell us when Gep is back home?" I nod and squeeze back.

"Say, Piro, what happened to your nose, there?" Tiffin asks the indelicate question I've been trying to avoid all night as he wipes the worst of the glue from his hands. "Slip of the chisel?"

"Your father won't hardly recognize you with that shiner!" Fonso jokes.

"Shut up, you two," Nan says, saving me by wiping her messy hands broadly on Fonso's nice shirt, as punishment for the teasing. "Out! Let's go! Piro doesn't need your bad manners on top of our fine 'help' this evening!"

"Sorry, Piro. Be sure to send word if you need any help getting him home," Tiffin says.

"Thanks, Tiff." I smile.

Fonso steps up next and puts a massive hand on my shoulder. "We'll get him back, Piro. Or the next thing I blow will be a glass knife that will gut the ol' Margrave like a spring pig."

"Let's hope it doesn't come to that."

"A metal blade would be much more effective," Tiffin mumbles under his breath.

"Oh, yeah? Shall we find out?" says Fonso, shoving Tiffin through the door. Nan brings up the rear, rolling her eyes in sympathy to me as they troop out.

I wipe my hands on my own filthy apron and survey the work left.

"I'll dress them, you paint them," Bran offers briskly, holding up a pair of starched uniform pants. They're too big for his lean frame, but fit perfectly against the bulky wood bodies of the soldiers. Since my injury in the wood, Bran has been short with me, a little distant. It's his way of trying not to pry or push me. I know he's also hurt I refused to explain what happened.

"Right," I say, rubbing my aching neck. Days of bending over a worktable have permanently wrenched a sharp crick along my shoulders. My hands are sore, my nails streaked with paint, my fingertips rough and raw from sandpaper.

Bran wrestles the soldiers into their uniforms while I clamp the final soldier's legs into place and begin faces. We work side by side with quiet determination, the kind that only courses through your veins in the final hours of an act of desperation. The next thing I know, the old grandfather clock in the workshop strikes four times, its tinny gong startling me awake from where I'd fallen asleep facedown at my workbench. Bran apparently threw a blanket over my shoulders to ward off the early morning chill. Weak light from a solitary lantern in Burl's stable seeps through the back window.

Standing at attention against my father's big worktable are three wooden soldiers, fully dressed and staring vacantly. Bran snores quietly from his stool on the other side of me, his dark head buried in his arms.

Wearily, I stand and brush dust from a stiff uniform collar. These soldiers are about to join ranks with dozens of others to spend their lives as . . . what? An attraction in the house of a madman? A monument to his absurdity? They hardly even speak to me, these soldiers I've made, not as the other marionettes do. Mostly I sense from them a perplexing emptiness.

"You did it, Pirouette," Bran says softly from behind me.

Straightening the tie on the jacket of the soldier, I let out a deep breath.

"I'm not done yet. Not until I have my father by the hand and can walk him out of that hole and into the daylight."

"Right then," Bran says, squeezing my shoulder. "Let's bring the puppetmaster home."

When the morning sun splays its first rays across Wolfspire Hall's gates, I am there with Bran. The Margrave's final soldiers are piled in the back of the wagon like the spoils of an undertaker. I wait with my hands impatiently tugging on Burl's reins, staring at the crux of the gate, willing it to open, to allow me in, to let my father out.

When finally it does, I knock a guard over in my rush to nudge Burl through.

"Sorry!" I call back, not feeling sorry at all. "Urgent delivery for the Margrave!"

I draw the wagon around the lower side of the courtyard, to the delivery entrance, where the willows lining the drive quiver like old women letting down their hair.

"Hurry, hurry!" they call to me.

Pulling Burl to a halt, I hand Bran the reins and leap down from the wagon seat. I explain my errand to the man at the door and wait breathlessly while he alerts the steward. Eagerly, I unload each soldier with Bran's help and prop them up against the door frame. In the daylight, tipped back against the wall, they look like a trio of nighttime carousers who've found themselves a bit drunk and lost. I am glad to be rid of them.

After a long wait, the guard at the door summons me in with a grunt. Bran starts to follow, only to be stopped by the guard's hand.

"I'll be all right," I find myself saying, reassuringly.

"Shouldn't take long."

I turn from Bran's expectant face and follow the guard down a wide hallway. Brightly lit sconces cast a golden halo on the dull, gray stone permeating Wolfspire Hall. I have the horrible note Baldrik Engleborden left behind in Curio a few days ago still folded in my pocket, and I look forward to ripping it up in his face and marching out the door with my father on my arm. But we walk too far a distance for the steward's office, which is where I expected to end up.

"Where is the steward?" I ask the guard as he hustles me up a long and winding set of stairs. "When will he bring my father?"

"The steward is waiting," he grunts.

"Where? Where are we going?"

"You'll see."

"My debt has been paid, the Margrave has what he needs and I was promised that my father would be returned to me. My wagon is waiting below," I say emphatically, emerging at the top of the stairs.

"Well, the Margrave is waiting up here. I'll let you determine which is of more importance, *Madame Apprentice*," a now-familiar voice intones dryly from above. "A waiting wagon or the waiting Margrave."

I reach the top of the stairs, stunned to find myself in a great hall. Portraits of esteemed men hang in dismal silence, and a richly woven carpet—in the von Eidle family crest's blood-red hue, of course—stretches out beneath my feet. The steward raises unwieldy eyebrows at me.

"The Margrave?" I say, feeling confused. "But I did it! I completed the order. His wooden soldiers are downstairs. Surely our debt is paid—"

"The Margrave wishes to see you," Baldrik says, firmly putting a hand on my shoulder and directing me toward a set of grand doors with guards positioned on either side. I realize with a shudder that their blank faces look eerily similar to the wooden ones I've just spent my days and nights painting.

Before I can protest, the elegantly paneled doors open in tandem. I am ushered into a vast stateroom, where my footsteps are immediately swallowed by thick carpets. The sheer opulence of the room unnerves me. Everything is gold-plated, marble-carved, and polished to a sheen. I can scarcely look around without blinking at the brightness. Elaborate tapestries line the walls, depicting scenes of great battles, brutal hunts, and twisting gardens spreading from one to another. An assemblage of what I assume is the Margrave's household— courtiers, financiers, and advisors—sits behind narrow desks lining the sides of the room. And at the center, in tandem like a sun with its lagging moon, sit the Margrave and his second son.

It's too late for fear. I am already here, standing before the rulers of Tavia, very aware of the poor figure I must present. From the tops of my paint-splattered clogs to my coarse hands and disheveled hair, I know I must look every inch the rough, harried Tavian maker that I am. The gouged skin on my nose is healing, but certainly doesn't add to my appearance.

Because I cannot change the way I look, I use the moment

of silence given to me while the von Eidles look me over to do the same to them. I may never get the chance to inspect them so closely again. The Margrave sits upon a high-backed chair, an ostentatious piece that must rival the king's throne in Elinbruk. Dressed from head to toe in a crisp, black suit broken across the chest by a wide sash of von Eidle red, his feet hardly touch the floor. The sash, emblazoned with numerous tiny medals and baubles, jingles whenever he shifts in his seat. I choke on a giggle at the thought that perhaps his advisors make him wear it, like bells on a cat, to tell when his nobleness approacheth.

He surveys me with a disinterested air, as though my presence is just another trifle in a parade of novelties he's long grown tired of. His anemic face is too narrow for his short, stubby body, though the bushy eyebrows and trimmed white beard lend him an appearance of greatness I already know is untrue. Any man who would throw my father into Wolfspire Keep, force himself on Anke, and keep his love from Emmitt is far from greatness.

My close inspection of Tavia's young duke leaves me rather startled. In complexion, he takes after his mother—the Margravina long dead, whose portrait hangs in memoriam in the hallway. White-golden hair slopes in a perfect wave down to his ears. While Laszlo is quite pale, matching his pallid reputation, his eyes are a piercing blue, his nose straight, and his jaw firm. He reminds me of a statue I glimpsed in the outer gardens of Wolfspire Hall—a man with a face hewn from stone instead of wood.

The corners of the duke's full mouth turn up ever so

slightly as I stare at him, as if we are sharing a secret between us, though we've never met. He's rather beautiful—for a man—and I suspect he fully knows it. His uniform matches his father's, except his red sash is quietly missing accoutrements. How could it have any when at twenty he's barely been allowed off his own estate grounds? Laszlo has never seen a battle, much less commanded a regiment; he's probably never raised a sword with anything but gloved hands.

The Margrave speaks first. "Well, Baldrik," he says, directing his question to the steward who remains behind me, "has the puppetmaster not another assistant? A boy, perhaps, or an apprentice?"

Rage sputters inside me like a flame licking at a candlewick.

"I *am* the puppetmaster's apprentice," I speak up, nearly biting my tongue with the way the words come slicing out. "Pirouette Leiter, My Lord von Eidle," I say with a flourish and a ragged curtsy. "I come in my father's stead."

The Margrave stares at me, visibly concluding I am something sour, a worm in a mealy piece of apple.

"A pity for the puppetmaster," he remarks, leaning forward in his chair, medals tinkling against his chest, "that you were not born a boy." He looks lovingly at Laszlo. "A son is the greatest longing of every man."

Laszlo smiles at him beatifically. I suppress a longing to slap his marble cheeks.

You already had a son before that one came along, one for whom you dangle your affections about like rancid meat above a starving dog.

Instead, I manage to squeak out, "What is it that you require of me, my lord Margrave? Our final order has been delivered to you. Surely my father and I might be on our way, unless there is something else I can do to be of service?"

The old Margrave looks to his son, as if to say, "Go ahead. You need to practice ordering makers about."

Laszlo turns the full light of his alabaster face to me. "We have another order to place with the puppetmaster."

"That would be . . . *splendid*, my lord . . . but as you know, the puppetmaster is currently unwell in the Keep. I must insist that he come home, where he might recover, before we could take on another order of the magnitude of your father's toy— er, wooden soldiers."

"Oh, you are mistaken. Those soldiers are all mine," Laszlo says, glowing. "And I have need of more, don't I, Father?" He beams at the Margrave, whose fleshy bags under his eyes wag in accordance with the nodding of his head. "Indeed, you must take the puppetmaster home and get him well. Though to my way of thinking, as his apprentice," he says, his icy blue eyes raking me up and down curiously, "you should be able to handle this next request."

I look nervously from father to son. Did I hear him right? *My father can come home with me!* My relief is palpable. So is my curiosity at what the duke could possibly wish for that he doesn't already have.

"Thank you, my lord. What is it to be?" I ask, praying it is something small. My father will be too weak to do much besides lift his head from his pillow once I get him home.

"The soldiers the puppetmaster built are brilliant," Laszlo says, blue eyes gleaming. I have a sudden vision of what he must have been like as a little boy, never allowed to go outside and play with other children, knocking about in vast rooms with only his toys for company. *Only his toys.* Perhaps all of these soldiers truly are for Laszlo's amusement.

"They are not enough. We require one more. A *special* kind of soldier." Laszlo watches me carefully.

"One more . . . soldier?" I swallow, feeling a rising dread that I will never be free of the horrid things.

"Yes. Not a foot soldier, though."

"I see," I stutter. *What other kind is there?*

"What I need next, Pirouette Leiter," Laszlo says, drawing my name out, "is a *saboteur*."

I blink, wondering if I've heard him correctly. "A saboteur, My Lord von Eidle?"

"Remind me again, lad, why we need such a thing?" the Margrave whispers none too quietly beside him.

Laszlo ignores his father. "Yes, a custom-built marionette, made in the same manner as the foot soldiers of course, life-size, with the utmost care given to the nimbleness of arm and leg. For this one, I desire it to be everything a saboteur should be: all in black, fully masked, sleek and light as a panther." He sits back and waits for my response.

A saboteur is a night shadow. *A killer.*

It is the strangest request I have heard in all my years at Curio, and I am oddly grateful my father isn't present to hear it. I hate the thought of him groveling at the feet of men like this, being asked to create the wooden form of an assassin. It is far better that it is asked of me.

"Do you agree, apprentice?" Laszlo asks, the tilt of his chin reminiscent of an owl swooping in to devour a field mouse.

I understand that 'no' is not an answer to be spoken in this room without consequences.

"Can you do it?" Laszlo asks, sitting forward on his chair, his eyes wide and expectant, his grin a twist of challenge and allure. Strangely, I get the impression that he believes I can. And though my tongue longs to make excuses, to shout "No! I am not good enough. I am only an apprentice!" I know I only have one choice.

I cannot lie.

"Yes," I say, the grit in my voice surprising us all. "I can."

"Magnificent," says Laszlo, leaning back in his chair with a satisfied smirk, his shoulders relaxing into mirrored slopes of braided gold. "You have ten days, Pirouette Leiter."

"Fifteen," I retort, before my brain knows what my mouth is doing. "I cannot possibly create something so . . . so *unique* in so short a time."

Laszlo bites his lower lip, chewing on my answer.

"Fifteen," he says, nodding slowly. "I will give you fifteen days for fifty francs."

"Yes, My Lord von Eidle," I reply, knowing deep in my heart that this is one "yes" that will return to haunt me. The money will be useful, but in the moment, the price I'm to be paid barely registers; something in me senses the actual cost may be much greater.

"Perhaps we can have all of these trifles of yours finished up by the time the glockenspiel is complete," the Margrave murmurs to Laszlo. "Emmitt assures me he is working on it day and night. Soon the bells in the rathaus will ring again, reminding all within our borders of the greatness of Wolfspire Hall's legacy. Then, I shall be ready to make my fall proclamation and settle the matter of my will—it can't be done properly without the glockenspiel at the ready, to signal the turn of the season! It's tradition!"

"Yes, of course, Father," Laszlo says, patting his father's graying hand with a glint of steel in his syrupy voice. "The clockmaker will surely be finished by then. He's never failed you yet, has he?"

The duke turns his patronizing tone on me. "And neither will you, apprentice. I have grand designs, a whole body of work that is waiting to be done, if you meet this order to my satisfaction."

I choose my words carefully. "Just as the clockmaker served you, I will make what you ask."

The duke's nostrils flare at my praise of Emmitt, but he waves me away with a flick of his hand, clearly done with me. Baldrik's meaty claws clamp down on my shoulders again and I am ushered out in haste.

A guard loads my father's wasting frame into the back of the wagon, tossing him in with no more care than was shown the wooden men we just exchanged for him. I hold Papa's hand and speak to him, trying to make him comfortable, but he just shivers, eyes tightly closed against the starkness of daylight, now used to the gloom of the Keep.

As Bran drives us home, I leave burdened by more than just my father's health. I roll away in possession of a commission I have no choice but to complete, both to feed us and keep the Margrave and his son satisfied. The old tinker's tale weighs on me, crystallizing into one simple truth: sometimes not even magic is required to turn a gift like bread to stones.

CHAPTER 10

"HE KEEPS MOANING ABOUT THE MOON. DO YOU KNOW what troubles him so, dear?" Gita asks, a cool hand laid to my father's forehead, her fingers draped like strips of pale muslin across his sweaty brow.

"Short of a horrible stay in Wolfspire Keep?" says Lottie from the corner.

Fear shoots through me like a well-aimed stone through a window. Since we brought him home, Father has remained in bed, in a terrible state of groaning incoherence. I sit with him every free moment I can spare from the dark soldier I'm building in the workshop below. Gita and two of Bran's sisters, Lottie and Inga, have been taking turns planting themselves like concerned gargoyles at Papa's bedside.

"I'm not sure," I say carefully, because I can only speculate, and of course I have my reasons to keep such speculations to myself.

Father's body was severely weakened by creating the Margrave's soldiers, followed by his internment in that fetid cell. I fear his once clear and swift mind has suffered the same fate. I only catch garbled phrases whose meaning I have yet to parse out, such as, "We are not ready," and "Afraid it's rotting," and "Hardly twice in a blue moon."

I simply haven't the time to solve his riddles. Every spare second I have is devoted to the making of a new marionette that both frightens and fascinates me. The puppetmaster in me delights in the challenge of bringing shape and form to a figurine as grand as the saboteur. Currently, I'm shaping the hands. I asked Bran to create a custom pair of sleek leather gloves the color of coal, to slide over fingers so tapered and slight they'll appear more like claws than squared human bones.

I have five days left to complete Laszlo's request and deliver the marionette to Wolfspire Hall. Baldrik made it painfully clear upon my departure what the consequences will be if I fail to comply with this most recent order. This time, if I don't finish by the Margrave's appointed hour, my father will return to Wolfspire Keep and he won't be alone. I will be joining him, in my own cell.

But I refuse to dwell on the harsh reality of those bars, and am only living and breathing in Curio, in the magic of my craft. My work is the only thing getting me through these long days.

"You're looking peaked yourself, Piro," Gita says thoughtfully, now brushing cool fingers across my forehead. "You are going to wear the flesh from your fingers as well as your poor nose if you aren't careful. Be sure to eat before you go back down."

"I will."

"Mhmmm," she mumbles, looking unconvinced.

After scarfing a hunk of bread and a piece of chicken in the kitchen, I find that I am eager to return to my work. I left the shop front open, hoping that we might gain a little sympathetic business during these difficult weeks as word of the puppetmaster's release trickles about the village. But there are no customers this morning, and so, despite only a few coveted hours of sleep, I set my hands to completing the next phase of the saboteur.

I have enough halsa left from my last trip to the wood, so all my time has been spent shaping what will eventually, I hope, become a saboteur—a saboteur from a hearth tale never seen or heard of before. I pick up a block of wood Papa had wrapped with sanding paper, and using short, practiced strokes, I apply pressure to the jointed fingers. Though it will be as tall as the previous soldiers, this body is being born in an entirely different way than the stiff regiment we previously constructed.

The limbs I've sketched on sheets of onion-skin paper are thick and strong in the haunches and lean in the seams, the torso curved instead of ramrod straight. The muscular chest curls elegantly down to a pair of strong hips, joined by legs that could spring from a window or high ledge at the slightest provocation.

I've made many marionettes; some large, some miniature, some charming and some intended to twist the audience's guts at the very sight of them. This saboteur is one of the latter.

The wood speaks as it takes shape beneath my fingers, a blurred, questioning voice that seeks to know the future. "Where shall I find my place of honor?"

I hope and pray that I will do this piece justice, giving the wood the honor it deserves. In the days that follow, I labor over smoothing every angle, refining every curve and ligature so that its stringed movement will be a thing of beauty. Of feline grace. Of terror.

If it were alive, of course.

I no longer have time to linger at The Louse and Flea, no time to sit and gossip over pitchers with my feet up. The Maker's Guild knows that if we are to gather together, the closest we can get these days is the workshop at Curio. At least those of us that can; Emmitt has nearly completed the glockenspiel, but is sleeping and working by nights in the tower to protect against further thievery.

I'm grateful for my friends' presence, for the eager hands that long to help, for their laughter and their gifts. Each has brought me something special tonight to cheer me: Fonso a new lamp for the workshop, Nan a fresh jar of olive oil, and Tiffin a specially forged rack I requested from him, just for the saboteur.

"Looks like some kind of primitive torture device," Fonso remarks, his hefty shoulders cringing at the metal frame conveying a series of hooks and loops.

"Primitive!" Tiffin grouses. "I'll have you know that rack is as sturdy and strong as it is elegant. Designed it myself," he mumbles. "Didn't even need Mort to help me."

"It is rather . . . *unique*," agrees Nan, gazing at the bars of metal Tiffin fabricated, on a platform bolstered by small wheels. The whole thing does give the impression of a cage for a beast rather than the simple frame on which a marionette will hang.

"It's perfect, Tiff," I say with a tired smile.

The soldiers we could pile in a heap and deliver via wagon, for they were without strings, and had sturdy bodies which could stand at attention like statues with wired armature. But the saboteur requires a full range of movement, and is constructed with strings flying out like spidery threads from every joint, suspended above and behind with sets of crossbars. Though this marionette is made of light halsa wood, because of its size, it will still take someone of considerable strength to stand above and manipulate the body. But the noble son of Tavia requested it be made this way, and my father's life depends on it.

So here it is. The grandest piece I have ever built, though at the moment the entire body is scattered about in pieces. I was joining limbs to torso when the makers invaded my workshop.

Fonso lights his lovely new lamp for me, while Bran rebuilds the fire in the wood-burning stove nestled in the corner. Goodness knows there is always plenty of kindling scattered about. Nan bustles here and there, pouring everyone a cup of tea from a pot Gita sent down, the tea tray laden with scones plopped right down among the glue and mess. Tiffin skulks about, looking out of place and anxious among the marionettes. For a time, the workshop swells with laughter and our inside jokes and jabs, the air fragrant with the scents of freshly hewn wood and scones—two of my favorite things.

"Enough about me." I shove a hot scone into my mouth. "I'm eating, sleeping, and breathing nothing but marionette dust." I lick a drop of raspberry jam clinging to my knuckle. "What's happening out there? How's business?" I ask, looking around, noticing each familiar face appears a little more drawn than usual.

Fonso crosses his colossal arms over his chest and sighs. Nan picks at her nails. Tiffin chews his lip. Bran pretends to study a curl of wood just discovered on the floor. I know them each too well, their eyes, their grim expressions.

"Tell me," I say, swallowing the remaining bite of scone. It slides down my throat in a dry lump.

"You've been so busy," Nan leaps in, "no one wants to worry you."

"Well, now I'm worried."

Silence settles like a stiff sheet as I search their faces.

Fonso clears his throat. "The Margrave isn't just busy conscripting marionettes from you for his son, Piro," says Fonso. "He's raising taxes—again. People will scarcely be able to afford to buy a new lamp or a piece of glassware for their table by next month if it keeps up."

"Just last week people started hoarding food," Tiffin says contemptuously. "The steward is forcing farmers to sell Wolfspire Hall a huge portion of their meat, bread and vegetables from the market at very low prices, next to nothing. That means the rest of us are left to argue over what remains. It's going to be a lean winter."

I blanch. The Sorens have assumed the care and feeding of me and my father these last few weeks, and I had no idea about the growing scarcity, for I've scarcely left the workshop.

"The Margrave's guards are on daily patrols now," Bran says quietly. "Not just positioned at the gates of Wolfspire Hall or at our borders. They sweep through the village daily. People feel they're being watched, more closely than ever before."

I stare at them, experiencing a sensation I recognize faintly from years ago when I woke from a body of wood to find myself inside one of muscle and bone—a feeling of being shocked awake in my own skin.

"What? Why?" I whisper in outrage.

"Dunno," says Fonso, turning up the wick on the oil lamp he'd placed near my workbench. "But it's not good."

"Something is coming," Nan prophesies, her inky eyes glittering. "I don't know how to name it or explain it. But all these strange orders the Maker's Guild has received from the Margrave . . . " She trails off, looking around to the rest of us. "I think those are just the beginning."

"A spoiled brat always wants what they don't have," says Tiffin. "Just think about it. What does the duke not have yet? He has every bloomin' toy a fancy boy like that could want. But what about more territory? There's always Brylov. They are much richer than we are."

Where Tavia has farmland and craftsmen, Brylov, our larger neighbor, has that and more: rich timber and mines. Situated in a sunny valley several days away, our Margrave's older sister, Emmaline, was made Margravina of Brylov many years ago, a move which no doubt pierced Erling to his shallow core. He was left holding the smaller share of the pie.

"What if Laszlo wants an empire here in the south, not just a territory?" Bran poses. "Like his father, his aunt is aging and close to the end of her margraviate. With both the elder von Eidle's nearing the end of their reign, it creates the perfect opportunity for him."

"Even so," I say, confused, "why tax us to death, or hurt the people's livelihood?"

"I think he prefers us weak and desperate." Nan's words slice like cutting wire extracting a pot from her wheel. "So we're easier to control. Hungry people do whatever is necessary to eat—even take up arms."

"Yeah, I think he'd rather us be puppets," says Fonso, absentmindedly fiddling with the saboteur's shoulder joint, flexing it back and forth.

Indignation rises in my chest. I am no one's puppet, no one's toy. Neither are my makers. Even if this saboteur is the last thing my hands ever make, I am determined to do better than merely giving the duke what he thinks he wants. I'll give him what he deserves.

The hour is late. My father is no better than he was fifteen days ago. It's torture to think that bringing him home has no more cured or healed the fever ailing him than weeks in the Keep, so I try not to think about it, and have taken to staying away from the damp, sweating figure twisting the sheets in his bed. He frightens me.

Bran no longer waits to knock at the cupboard, for he knows he'll not likely find me there. Despite the unexplained matter of my battered nose, he visits daily, entering from the door closest to Burl's stable.

Tonight, he surveys the cluttered workshop, appraising the completed dark-clad figure lying in wait on the work table. Usually, displaying my marionettes and seeing others marvel at the visions I've sculpted from wood and paint and wire is one of my greatest joys. *But this time*, I realize, wiping the final layers of dust from the saboteur's body, *it's different*.

For the first time, I feel a pang of regret for making a marionette. Not because I have failed, for the creature on the table is anything but a failure of craftsmanship. I regret it because it's so marvelous. I feel like a desperate mother, forced to abandon my greatest creation to the doorstep of wolves.

"Is it everything they are expecting?" Bran asks carefully.

"Exactly to their specifications," I reply sharply, a defensive vein splitting open in my voice.

"Well," he says, clearing his throat, "the gloves and clothing are a perfect fit."

"I do have an excellent tailor."

Bran grins and then looks thoughtful. "Still needs something," he mutters.

"Like what?"

He pulls a few clock gears from his pocket, their edges filed to crisp planes, and tucks the brass circles into the marionette's vest—a vest of his own making.

"What are those for?"

"An addition to the costume. A gift."

"A gift?" I ask, confused.

"Every soldier should be armed."

"For all we know, this particular saboteur is being assembled to decorate Laszlo von Eidle's bed chamber, like some rusty suit of armor from the old wars. I don't envy any soldier that post. But you won't miss them?"

"No, I have others. And no time to build anything with them."

"Have you talked to your parents yet?"

Bran shakes his head.

"There's no perfect time to bring up a difficult subject," I say sagely, buffing the saboteur's high boots with a soft cloth.

"Yeah," he says with a sigh. "You don't have to tell a clockmaker. Perfect times do not exist." His handsome face looks sad in the lantern glow.

"No," I agree. "There is only now. Only now and what is yet to come."

He hesitates. "Speaking of difficult subjects, Piro." He clears his throat nervously. "I've tried to give you some distance, tried to understand. But I can't work it out—what happened when we were, you know . . . in the woods." His cheeks turn pink.

My whole body freezes. I was hoping to avoid this conversation at all costs, hoping against hope Bran would just forget. But how could he? How could anyone forget seeing a thorn of immense proportions burst through someone's nose?

"In the woods?" I repeat, my voice high and tight.

I can't do this. Not now.

"When I kissed you, the next thing I knew, something had hurt you . . . a splinter dropped out of the sky, or a branch struck you. And you wouldn't even let me see, or let me help. Don't you know I'll help you, anytime I can? I can't bear to see you hurt."

"I know," I say tersely.

"And speaking of my parents again, they've been asking. Is Gep's mother coming? Does she know?"

"Hmm," I murmur, frantically thinking of how to redirect the conversation. I resume boot buffing at a rapid pace.

Bran comes closer, placing a firm hand over mine, to stop the manic polishing.

"Piro, please. I know something is wrong, but I don't know what. It's killing me. Help me understand."

Spruce and ash! The sensation of impending splinters prickles my palms as I search for a lie to hide behind. I know I can't avoid his questions much longer, or his eyes. There's no place to hide. Horrified at the leap I am about to make, I decide to take Bran at his word, to truly trust him.

"Have you ever heard," I stammer, my eyes blurring with sudden tears, "the story of Old Josipa?"

He nods. "It was before my time here, but I've heard it."

I press my hands against my father's worktable, so that the rough surface might hold me up.

"Remember how she used the old magic? Spells long forbidden in our territories?" I mumble.

He nods again, keeping his face steady.

"I am . . . I mean, I was . . . "

"Old Josipa was your grandmother?"

"No, you don't—"

"You're a healer, like the old woman?"

"No!"

"A conjurer?"

"No!"

"A witch?"

"Stars, no, Bran!" I snarl, feeling more like a trapped beast than a girl. "Keep your voice down!"

"What is it, Piro? Where did that splinter come from?" he whispers.

I pause, taking a long, shuddering breath to gird myself for what comes next. The rejection. The fear.

"I wasn't raised by my grandmother. I don't even have a grandmother. Or a mother, or a father, at least, not in the way you do."

He looks confused, but stays silent, watchful. I glance around at the windows to confirm they are shut.

"I come from . . . *there*."

"You come from the countryside?"

"From the wood."

"The wood," he says breathlessly.

"My father, the puppetmaster, *made* me," I say slowly, letting that sink in. "And then there was a spell," I say, with barely a hair's breadth of sound. "A spell spoken under the blue moon."

He stares dumbly, trying to grasp my words. Bran steadies

himself against my father's stool. At least he isn't running—fleeing straight to the steward to tell, like anyone else might. A small tendril of hope uncurls in my chest.

"Your father made you," he repeats slowly. "And the splinters?" he asks, looking up. "Like in The Louse and Flea? I've seen the scars on your hands, your arms."

"Some are from my woodworking." Out of habit, I swipe at my face, and my fingertips graze the wound on my nose. "Some are not. If I speak words that are untrue . . . like I spoke to you about my grandmother, who doesn't exist, then . . . " I shrug.

"If you lie, the magic doesn't let you forget it?" He doesn't force me to complete my thought, he does it for me, though I can tell he's rattled by what he's heard.

"Yes," I whisper, my shame on full display.

"I see," he replies, though I can see he doesn't, not completely.

"I'm sorry I lied to you!" Tears leak from my eyes.

Bran looks utterly bewildered, but bravely hides it. Shaking his head in disbelief, he closes the gap between us and crushes me in a hug.

"There's nothing to be sorry for. I'll admit, it hardly seems possible. Then again, Gep is a great puppetmaster. The greatest. I . . . I don't know how it all happened . . . but I do know that I meant what I said to you that day in the wood. There's no one like you for me. And whether you came from this place or the mountains or the bleedin' moon, it doesn't matter to me," he says staunchly. "I love you, Piro."

Gently, he places a hand on either side of my face, his eyes now a study in curiosity. I can hardly stand to have him look at me so closely while the skin on my nose is still raw. He's seeing me as I really am and it's terrifying.

"No one else can know," I whisper fiercely, digging my fingers into the meat of his arms. "No one, Bran. You understand? Old Josipa . . . " My voice breaks, my mind picturing her old body curling up like a withered leaf among the flames.

"I know. *I know.*" He wipes my tears with a handkerchief he pulls from his vest. "It is enough for me," he says somberly, "to know the truth. And I will protect you in every way I can. I'll tell my parents your grandmother is too ill to come, or better yet, that she died! She's been dead for many years, in fact! I'll make it so that you'll never have to lie about that again."

"Don't lie to protect me," I plead, prompting him to wrap his arms around me even tighter. "Just, please, be careful. We both must be so careful."

In the end, the lies of those who love me only seem to do more harm than good. I know from experience that I can survive the pain of my splinters, but if my secret escapes beyond the small circle of me, Papa, and now Bran, I may not survive the truth.

CHAPTER 11

I WATCH AS THE COLOR OF THE MARGRAVE'S FACE GROWS TO match his coat of arms. Livid and sputtering, he can only manage garbled exclamations of fury.

"Brimstone and sulfur! What in the devil's rotten hoof is that . . . *thing?*"

The younger von Eidle is who I keep my eyes on as I stand again in Wolfspire's great, gilded stateroom. I hold tightly to the arm of the saboteur hanging at my side, suspended on the special rack from Tiffin.

Laszlo leapt to his feet and stared open-mouthed in amazement when I wheeled it in. I feel a thrill of pride at this, followed by a chill that unspools down my spine.

"It's—*not* what he asked for!" growls the Margrave.

"I made it to your exact specifications, Duke von Eidle," I state boldly, though my mouth is dry as wool.

"But it's a . . . that thing is . . . !" The elder fumes.

"She's just as you requested," I interject. "'Larger than life, with the utmost care given to the nimbleness of arm and leg. Everything a saboteur should be: dressed in black, fully masked, sleek and light.'"

"It's atrocious!" the Margrave spits with disgust. "My son wanted a saboteur, a soldier-spy in the form of a marionette, not some feminine, foppish plaything!"

"You never specified that the marionette should be in the likeness of a man, my lord. You only asked for a saboteur," I say flatly, inwardly taking immense delight in his outrage. "And that's what I have created for you."

This saboteur is anything but a plaything. I designed a figure built for stealth and secrets, whose angle of limbs betray the ability to move with clandestine speed and silence. Inconsequently, my saboteur also happens to be a *she*. It's undeniable in the soft curves of her face and lips, the round cheekbones beneath her mask, the unmistakable hint of breasts rising beneath a fitted black uniform that Bran and the tailor labored over for me.

"It's ridiculous! A detestable, unnatural creature! Take it away at once and throw this imposter into—"

"No, Father!" Laszlo exclaims firmly, coming down off the dais to stand before the saboteur. "It's perfect," he says in awe, reaching a hand to cup her cheek. "She—*she* is perfect. A marvel."

His thumb brushes almost tenderly across the pale, lacquered cheekbone and the black mask that wraps around her from the nose up. I painted a few strands of short hair—bright cerulean—escaping in curls from where the mask ties at the back of her neck.

"I could never have imagined it, but she's *just* what I need, Father," the royal son of Tavia purrs with a knowing look in his eyes.

A nauseous surge of panic rises in my throat at the hungry look he casts on the saboteur. I fight the urge to rip his hands away from where he has already laid claim to her, fingers curling possessively around her well-built shoulders. I feel the bite of his grip as surely as if he had just seized my own. This is not what was supposed to happen.

"You must take care . . . very delicate joints." I grasp an iron bar of the saboteur's rack and pull it slowly toward me, hoping to compel him to release her.

But Laszlo just laughs, as if I've made a joke instead of a plea. His hands run down her arms, pausing at her waist before firmly sliding down each leg, inspecting each as if he were scrutinizing horseflesh.

"Very fine craftsmanship indeed. But there's nothing delicate about her, is there, apprentice?" he says with a furtive grin that stabs once more at my gut. "She's a warhorse, I can tell. And custom-made for the work."

My heart sinks. *What dark, blood-stained arena does he envision her in?* Every question I've tried to suppress about the Margrave and his son resurfaces.

Before I can wrest her from his clutches, Laszlo motions to a few guards to follow him. In seconds, they've disappeared behind a door that shuts with a heavy clank, my last glimpse of the saboteur is of her rocking from side to side as the guards wheel her into darkness, with Laszlo leading the way.

I've lost her. Just like that, the saboteur is gone.

I am left to stand before the affronted Margrave, feeling very alone. His anger only serves to make him look unwell, worse than I remember, quite crimson and purple like a blood blister about to burst. I'm on the verge of feeling pity—something about his stooped shoulders reminds me of Papa—when he glowers at me afresh from his ridiculous chair. Remembering I'm naught but stray vermin he'd delight in crushing beneath his gleaming boot heel, my pity disappears.

I don't understand why, in all of Tavia, it's the makers who are looked down upon by the noble class. What has Erling von Eidle ever made with his own two hands? I am sure he couldn't create a sock puppet if he took a stocking from his own stumpy foot right this moment and tried. I cannot abide his silence; it is too full, too billowed with loathing. I must break it.

"My lord?"

"What?" he snaps.

"My payment?"

Disgusted, he waves a limp hand at Baldrik, who has been behind me this whole time, ever the unwanted shadow.

"The steward will see to it."

I turn to leave, knowing I am dismissed. They have taken from me what they need.

"Girl," he says louder, sounding gravelly and hoarse. "How is the puppetmaster faring these days? Is Gephardt Leiter back at his chisel?"

The mention of my father's name from his detestable lips is nearly enough to make me stumble and trip on the long coattails of the steward. The refusal to use my name or proper title sends me spinning back around, irritated. I clench my work-bruised fingers into fists.

"Hopefully soon, my lord."

He offers a small, satisfied smile in return.

"His gift truly is a rare one, the puppetmaster. I've never seen its like, not until one of my own line, Emmitt Schulze, the clockmaker, came of age. You know him, I presume?"

"Of course," I say, taken aback to hear him speak of Emmitt, *to me* of all people. "Everyone knows the clockmaker."

He leans back, looking proud. "Yes, he is very popular among the people, which I do hope—"

A deep guttural sound rises from the Margrave's gullet and sets him hacking, his cheeks burning scarlet as he spits into a golden pot at his feet. I watch to see if anyone will try to help, but his attendants just look on nervously, weighing whether to step in or let him continue in misery. When the horrible sound of his spitting settles and he accepts an offered sip of tea—or something stronger, I really couldn't say—he snorts loudly and continues, pressing a handkerchief to his face.

"I do hope he finishes the glockenspiel in time for my fall proclamation. Much depends on it. You and all those makers will be especially pleased to hear of my succession plan. Thanks to my two fine sons, Tavia's margraviate will continue to thrive long after I'm gone."

Which, from the sound of it, will be soon. I barely dare

to wonder whether he means to name Emmitt as his heir over the younger von Eidle—or somehow in tandem with Laszlo? Could Emmitt's fortunes really be about to change, and all of ours along with it?

Another spitting spell attacks the Margrave, and once again the pressure of the steward's hand on my shoulder spins me around. I am shoved up the long aisle of the stateroom. I have delivered the saboteur and can return to my father with a little money and some news to share.

After my audience with the von Eidles, I carry myself home, my purse filled with the promised francs and my mind with the news that the Margrave may indeed be choosing to let Emmitt lead in his stead. I take some comfort in knowing I have restocked our coffers from my work on the saboteur, if only for a little while.

I return to find my father worsening by the minute.

"Cosima? Cosima? Where are you?" A deep rattle seizes my father's chest at the end of his frantic, wheezing pleas for his wife, the bride who passed away before I ever came to be. A woman small and dark-haired like me, with a great mind for figures, who kept all his books and accounts straight and secure.

I forced myself to send Gita home now that my great work with the saboteur is complete, and have been sitting for hours in a chair at my father's bedside, knees drawn up to my chest. As if I could somehow shield myself from what he has become. From what is happening to us.

I tried to spoon-feed him, but no amount of broth seems to settle him or restore his peace. Teas, herbal remedies, poultices for his fever—we've tried the tried and true, but nothing is proving effective against the heat that burns in his limbs and pours like tears from his temples.

I look at his large, capable hands, whose nimble fingers absentmindedly knead at his sheets, worrying the seams. I can't help but think of what death means. In the wood, death isn't an ending, not really. It's merely a season. If one tree falls, its husk becomes shelter. Its bark becomes food. Its ribs become a ladder for new seeds to climb to reach the sun.

I have faced death before. With the bite of the axe, my first life was cut off from one season and thrust into another. Without ever knowing to hope for it, I was reborn. Will it be so for Gephardt Leiter? Or will he just vanish from the world, a rare breed of creature made extinct at his last breath?

He hasn't seen me, hasn't *known* me, in days. I feel something inside myself start to slip away with him and begin to fade. Who am I, without this man who loved and made me?

The moon is waning tonight, the rounded toe of a pearled slipper peeping beneath dark and clouded skirts. Its light is faint, and yet my father has demanded in these last days that the window shutters be kept open, *always open*, to let the moonlight in.

I know why he hungers after the moon, though the Sorens do not. The moon, in its constant state of waxing or waning, comforts him. He still remembers the magic. He understands its possibilities.

I must have nodded off in my chair, my forehead pressed to my knees, because I am startled awake by his voice. I brush my bangs away from where they stick to my eyes.

"Pirouette," he whispers. "*Poppet.*"

My heart lurches to hear my name on his lips. I look to his eyes, which still burn at the edges but are fixed solidly on my own. He *sees* me. The old maple's branches scratch against the wall, joining me in mourning. "Listen," it says. "*Listen.*"

"Papa?"

He taps his fingers on the coverlet, indicating that I should come closer so he will not strain his voice. I slip to his side, and without thinking, curl up next to him, tucked into his chest with his beard brushing my forehead, my hand over his heart. When I was smaller and a night terror plagued me, I would sneak into his room and settle like this, comforted by the solid rhythm of his dependable heartbeat beneath my cheek.

"Time is fading for me, Piro."

I nod against his chest, which sounds hollow; the heartbeat is still hammering, but faintly.

"There is something you must know, something more to our blue moon story."

He licks his cracked lips and flutters his fingers lightly against my arm. I sense he is trying to comfort me, to stave off the harshness of what will come next.

"The power of the spell, it has . . . a price."

I wait, my breath trapped in my lungs, a gust of air drawn into a blacksmith's bellows.

"You must know . . . you are worth any price, to me."

I cannot breathe. My tears spill freely. He's quiet a moment, garnering strength, and my pulse pounds so loudly in my ears I fear I will not be able to hear what he says next.

"She told me, the tree woman, that when you awoke, I too would be forever changed."

A great wheeze shatters his words to pieces. I wait for the coughing to stop, for him to continue to form the truth I am so afraid to hear.

Suddenly, my father's rasping voice is drowned out not by his cough but by the jarring clang of bells. Loud, discordant peals of bell-song flood through the open window, unleashed like the braying of hunting dogs onto the sleeping city.

I sit up and rush to the window. Hasty lights flicker on in lamps and upper windows all across my narrow view. The deep gongs of bells from the church and the many towers of Wolf-spire Hall roll across the night air for what feels like an eternity, soon joined by confused cries. These aren't melodic bells calling us to services or heralding a feast day. Not in the dead of night.

The frantic drumming of footsteps up the back stair signals the arrival of Bran. He stands in the doorway, out of breath, eyes like golden torches.

"What is it? The bells?"

"The Margrave," Bran says, his lips narrowing to a hard line. "There are criers in the streets. The Margrave is dead."

My mouth drops open.

"They say the duke has announced a period of mourning for the city."

"Of course he has," I mutter, turning back to the window

and the oppressive ardor of the bells, which have not let up.

Nan was right. Change is coming. I just saw the Margrave earlier today; he didn't have a chance to proclaim who would take the seat at Wolfspire Hall after him. What will become of the proclamation about his heir? I haven't yet had the chance to tell Papa what the Margrave said about his two sons.

"Is Gep sleeping?"

"No one could sleep in this bedlam."

"No, Piro, I mean . . . " Bran's voice fades away.

I turn back to my father. His eyes are closed and I know right away because his hands are finally still. His chest has ceased its valiant labor. What no tea or medicine or moonlight could bring him, death has. He is at peace.

I will never get to hear the rest of his story, to know what it was that I cost him, beyond a few drops of blood and some harvested wood. The Margrave has taken even that away from me.

Something in me begins to sink, like a stone cast into a well, and I drop to my knees at his bedside. All I can feel is the drowning, the bottomless depths surrounding a stone hurtling through water. There is no ground here, not anymore.

The bells toll on, and in my heart, I know they are not just signaling the end of the old Margrave of Tavia. They are also singing the end of Gephardt Leiter, the puppetmaster.

CHAPTER 12

BRAN SAT WITH ME AFTER PAPA DIED, LONG AFTER THE BELLS faded, the dawn still ringing with their echoes. He wrapped me in his arms and I cried until I was hollow, my eyes soaking the front of his shirt. When I finally came downstairs, I could only feel grateful not to be alone to do the things one must do to say goodbye.

Benito alerts the church cleric about my father's passing and later that day, a rough wooden coffin is delivered to Curio. I despair at having to release Papa to such a simple box, the same provided for every poor soul when their time comes—unless their family opts for one of Nan's special funerary urns—but I haven't the time nor the wood to make him the casket he deserves. If I had my way, I would bury him in something intricately carved and beautifully constructed. Something befitting a woodworker and puppetmaster such as he.

We wash and dress my father in his best suit of clothes,

arranging him carefully in the plain chest he will rest in from now on. It's strangely like dressing one of the Margrave's wooden men, his body having quickly become a stiff mimic of its former self. It doesn't bother me quite as much as I might have thought to see him this way. It's obvious he isn't really in there anymore, in that brittle, shrinking frame.

The Sorens arrive at noon, bringing food, even though it has been growing ever more precious, especially for their large family. The rest of the Maker's Guild comes too, bearing gifts. One by one, down in the workshop behind the storefront, they tuck items around Papa that he would have cherished.

From Tiffin's forge, a long carpenter's nail, as thick as a man's finger, on whose head is branded a woodland scene of tiny trees.

"Tiff," I gasp, running my fingers along the miniature design. "It's beautiful. How did you manage it?"

He shrugs shyly. "Something new I've been trying. Gep gave me the idea for it."

From Nan comes a small pot of jam; she crafted both the container and the goods. She makes each of us dip a spoon in and taste a bite before she tucks the small vessel into one of his suit pockets. "It was Gep's favorite." She sniffs.

With the sour-sweet tang of currants on our tongues, we watch Fonso place a little doll into my father's other pocket. Her glass-jointed arms and legs betray that she's a puppet,.

"I just thought—" His voice breaks. "I thought the puppetmaster, he might like to have a little reminder of his work with him. I know it's not as good as he would've done, but . . . "

"It's wonderful, Fonso. He would have loved it," I assure him through my tears. And he would have. It's exquisite.

From Anke and Emmitt, a restored pocket watch, polished and refitted with a sturdy brass chain that Anke coils lovingly on my father's chest.

I realize that in the hurry of preparations, along with the chaos of the Margrave's passing, I haven't yet shared the news of what the Margrave had been planning, the possibility of Emmitt being named to the margraviate.

I try to bring it up, but Anke instantly shushes me and tells me not to even think about such things until I've had time to mourn my father. Tears fill my eyes afresh for Emmitt, for he's just lost a father, too. However broken and misguided the Margrave had been, he was his father, nonetheless.

From Bran and the tailor come a handkerchief of fine linen, with embroidered threads outlining the sign that hangs outside of Curio, bearing its name.

After the handkerchief is safely tucked in Papa's hand, I stand at the head of the box, realizing that I have nothing prepared to add. I don't have anything special to give him. Panic and embarrassment well up in the corners of my eyes, until Bran, seeing my distress, speaks up.

"Piro, I wondered if you might send some of his favorite tools with him, that is, if you can spare them?"

Relief floods in, and I nod. *Of course* my father should have some of his favorite tools buried with him. It's only right. The workshop is respectfully silent as I walk around to the various workbenches, looking over every hammer and chisel and saw.

A thousand memories cling to each tool like particles of dust.

I finally select a chisel with a handle worn smooth and glossy, and his favorite carving blade. Reverently, I set one in each hand, feeling a sense of rightness, knowing he will be near to some things he loved even if he cannot be near to us.

Though it is not a common practice in Tavia, and we never discussed it—neither of us ever imagined a future where he didn't exist—I firmly insist that my father be buried out in the woods. He should be laid in a hallowed space at the foot of the old trees, instead of in the small churchyard that lies in the shadow of Wolfspire Hall. I may not be able to give him a beautiful casket, but I can return him to a place where he felt at home.

Late that afternoon, through a haze of villagers already wearing black to make a show of respect for the Margrave, Burl dutifully pulls the old wood-hauling wagon carrying the coffin behind him. It's as if he understands his task; one last trip to the wood with the puppetmaster. Bran rides in the wagon with me, and the rest of our small procession follows behind.

Tears parade down my face at the sight of so many people lining the streets to watch us pass; their heads are bowed, their eyes are wet. Women swipe at their cheeks with work-stained aprons and children run alongside the wagon, tiny legs pumping, gifts for the departing puppetmaster clutched tightly in small fists. I make Bran stop several times, as the candlemaker's twins and others dash up to bestow their treasures on the life-less box where the puppetmaster lies.

One child hands me a beautiful marionette I haven't seen for years, a two-foot-tall lumberjack with a mighty six-inch axe, hanging by his strings from a cross-hatched control. Then comes a jovial clown, whose carved head and hands are attached to a cloth body that pops down into a cone anchored to a long wooden peg. A few toss their offerings into the wagon, as if throwing flower petals. As we proceed through the streets, the air rains with wooden tops and intricate ring-puzzles, small carved animals, wooden blocks and an odd sling-shot or two.

I couldn't have chosen a better monument to my father than things he made that so many children loved. The fall air is cold, but it warms me to think of all the little hands bringing him gifts; hands willing to sacrifice beloved toys to honor the puppetmaster.

We bury my father in a grove of trees where few but he and I have tread. Simple, sincere words are said by the local church cleric, Vincenzo Greco, as is Tavian custom. Vincenzo is widely known to be overly fond of drink, and his broad face is bestowed with a blazing red nose and cheeks. In the moment, I don't mind the cleric's bumbling reputation, for he seems both very kind and sorrowful enough. My father and I didn't often grace the worn pews of the Tavian church in the village. We found our sanctuary in the wood, among the pillars of trees, below the grand cathedral of their branched canopy. The cho-rus of the trees is more beautiful to me than any choir, though their voices drop somber and low now as they sense my pain.

I will hardly remember anyone's words today anyway, for the great trees seem to swallow them up as soon as they are uttered. They disappear like mist into the soft wail of wind and birdsong.

The tailor tearfully says a few words about the beauty and masterwork of creation that I know my father would have loved. Then, beneath the pillars of this sacred place, I drop a handful of sawdust scraped from the floor of the workshop over the mound of freshly churned dirt. The puppetmaster, my father, is gone.

Ashes to ashes, wood to sawdust. We all must return to the soil at some point. *Wooden or not, our roots begin and end here.*

"Not yet, sister," the lindens whisper reassuringly. "It is not your turn to return to the earth yet. You must return to life."

Leaning back against the trunk nearest to me, I let its rough skin and solidness bolster me, drawing from its strength while the rest lay their gifts on my father's grave. With him gone, I am alone now, save for the voices of the trees; my last living connection to what made me. Like the only mother's voice I've known, they hang their heads with me and cry.

Nan stays with me at Curio that night.

"Don't worry, Piro." She interrupts my numb contemplation from where she is curled up on a pallet on the floor of my room. I've been quiet for a long time, buried with the covers up to my chin. "We'll see you through this. Your father is gone, but his work remains. You remain." Even in grief, Nan never skirts around things. The potter always deals solely in raw materials and truths.

"The makers are still here," she continues. "Tavia will stand, though Margraves may come and go. What was it that Gep would say, when he was frustrated at not finding enough good wood in a season, or when a marionette didn't turn out the way he'd envisioned?"

I can barely say the words aloud, but I eke them out anyways, knowing she wants me to humor her. "A maker will always prevail."

"Yes. We will find a way to prevail. But that will be a task best suited to tomorrow. Tonight you must rest."

"'Night, Nanette."

She falls silent again, until uttering her final thoughts. "I will miss the puppetmaster more than I can say. He always knew just what to say to keep me going when I was in a slump. He always knew when I was struggling to make something and not getting it quite right."

He did. He could see it in their eyes, just as he could always see it in mine. "A maker will always prevail," he would entreat them, as if the words made it so. When Gephardt Leiter spoke them, you believed it did.

My mind refuses to be quieted by the fact that it's night. I hear the muffled shuffling of Bran next door, tinkering with his clocks, but I don't dare risk opening the cupboard to see him with Nan here. The cupboard is still a secret, between

Bran and me. Sometimes the secrets we keep, like the lumpy bundle of splinters hidden beneath my pillow, are what holds us together when we feel broken.

Sleep doesn't come tip-toeing in until hours later.

The next day I find myself facing the prospect of running Curio entirely on my own. After Nan departs for her studio, needing to tend her kiln, I tidy my father's room, change his bedding, sweep the floor, and keep the rest of his things just as he left them. Thanks to Gita, our small kitchen is already sparkling. I trudge downstairs to the workshop, and am immediately plunged into reverence at the way the morning light filters through the windows in glittering, dust-mote swirled rays of gold. It's as beautiful as light through a stained-glass visage in a church.

Unfortunately, the daylight also illuminates the fact that I have let things get a bit out of hand down here in the last weeks. With my father in the Keep, and then ill at home, it was all I could do to finish the wooden soldiers and the saboteur. I'd no time for keeping things in order.

So instead of unlocking the shop and pulling back our curtains, as I would normally do in a morning, I keep the front door closed. And I begin to clean. I gather up all the tools I've left scattered about. I sharpen all our blades and chisels, enjoying the repetitive song of metal rasping against whetstone. I catalogue all our paints and lacquers, stacking them neatly in rainbow rows the chromatist herself would surely be proud of.

I spend hours brushing away sawdust and wood chips from the work tables and floor. When I have filled a huge coal-bin's worth of scraps, I slam the lid, satisfied I have enough to burn in the stove to keep me going for a few weeks. Every surface is paint splattered and worn, notched and nicked many times over, but it's cleared of the old dust and ready to be put to use again.

Like any great maker, my father did not have just one piece on his mind at a time. When orders from the Margrave started coming in, he had to suspend the other projects he was working on; it's over these that I linger, remembering. One is an elaborate wooden box, which looks like a traditional jewelry case for valuables on the outside but opens to reveal that the only way to get to the contents is to solve a series of intricate puzzles. As each puzzle is deciphered, a new layer or drawer springs away, revealing the next puzzle and so on, until finally you reach the heart of it: a small nested compartment where a lady might slip a necklace or a gentleman some treasured coins.

I never had Papa's mind for creating puzzles or games, so I dust the box and set it to the side. Perhaps Bran, with his inclination for fitting cogs and gears together, will enjoy taking up the challenge someday.

There are several marionettes still in process, sketches of half-done faces in Papa's broad hand that I carefully lay upon a shelf. Maybe someday I will pick up where he left off, and finish the characters he'd only just begun to flesh out.

By the time I finish putting the workshop back in order,

the sun is low in the sky, and I look around, feeling satisfied at having cared for the place that has given me so much. But my heart can't ignore the sense that something is missing. *Someone.* Papa was as much a part of Curio as the very walls, the beams holding us all up and keeping us together.

Later that night, I curl up in my father's room and contemplate the moon from his window. My gaze falls on the high scaffolding reinforcing the town hall's tower; light flickers from inside the clock tower. Emmitt, the only other person I know who has just lost a father. How awful that my father died the same day as the Margrave, nearly at the same hour. Death comes in threes, the old saying goes. Who else is death lying in wait for, I wonder?

Perhaps Emmitt wouldn't mind some company.

CHAPTER 13

INDING MY WAY TO THE RATHAUS ISN'T DIFFICULT, EVEN IN the dark, for I know Tavia's lanes as well as I know the wood. The old building isn't used much for its original purpose any longer; it used to be a forum to bring disagreements and concerns to light in a public assembly. That's a rare occurrence now. In recent years, the Margrave has taken to making grand proclamations from the front steps, under the glockenspiel, and has set up an office of taxation and tariffs within.

I find the back door leading to the staircase inside the glockenspiel's tower closed but unlocked. Noises drift from above; the tight, chinking sound of ratcheting and the song of a hammer—familiar sounds. I follow the narrow staircase around and around, up its twisted skeleton.

The ancient staircase, barely wide enough to fit my small person, spits me out onto a rickety landing where I can hear but not see Emmitt, another level above, muttering to himself.

The stair disappears and from this floor up to the high eaves there are only ladders rising up to give access to the two tiers of the glockenspiel, whose lower mechanisms and large figurines remain frozen on their carousel. Swallows and doves flutter and snuffle from where they've made nests anchored on the high beams crisscrossing the tower.

Up here, closer than I've ever seen them, the creatures bound to the rotating wheelbase of the glockenspiel look even more garish and gruesome. The wolves' muzzles are blackened with age, the silhouetted bodies of farmers and soldiers wear grim portraits of rage and conquest. The shadows in the corners of the tower feel vacuous; beckoning from them are tall piles of old figurines long replaced, a forgotten tangle of broken limbs and bodies lying where they were tossed. Thick cobwebs drape from the layered apparatus like so many strings on the underside of a tapestry, not yet scissored off by the weaver.

How sorry I am that Emmitt has been laboring away in the clock tower for months, left to his own devices with these hideous pawns for company. My father claims the glockenspiel and its inhabitants are a treasure, precious artifacts of another age—or at least, he used to. But I find them ghastly.

"Emmitt!" I call out, wishing to give him a hint of my presence. "You still here? It's Piro!"

The clatter of a dropped tool echoes on the flimsy wooden scaffolding. A scruffy black head, capped in a halo of burnished light, appears from the second tier above.

"Piro!" Emmitt says wonderingly. "What are you doing out at this hour?"

A single look at my face, and I know he understands. "Oh yes, do come up! It's quite safe. Can you find the ladder?"

I locate the ladder that appears closest to Emmitt's position and begin climbing. *Let's hope a builder of my father's caliber made this thing,* I think. Though I have my doubts. It feels as if it might shatter beneath my weight at any second.

Up on the next platform, the doors that allow the glockenspiel's carousel and carillon to display their show are open to the night. Chilled in the wind, I huddle next to the clockmaker's case of tools and lantern, which cast their own show of shadows against the inner walls of the tower.

"Can't sleep?" Emmitt asks.

I shake my head. "I just feel so . . . so lost without him, and it's barely been a day. I don't see how anything will ever be the same again."

Emmitt solemnly greases a large flywheel with a rag, knowing I won't be offended if he works while he listens.

"Indeed it won't; it can't be. No one can take the puppetmaster's place, nor should they." He raises his eyes, brushing back the shock of hair falling across them. "He was a matchless talent, both as a puppetmaster and a man. I've never known his equal."

My mouth drops.

"That's what the Margrave said," I say, shocked. "Those are the very words he said about *you*, the day he and my father died." I rub my hands up and down my arms to restore some feeling to them. Everything in me feels strangely numb.

Emmitt dismisses my comment.

"But it's true, that is what he said! I know you haven't

wanted to talk about it, but he said he had never known my father's equal as a craftsman, not until you were born. And he took pride in that. And though I know you don't like to think on it, he did say to me he hoped the people would approve of his succession plan. 'Thanks to my two fine sons, the legacy of Tavia's strong margraviate will continue to thrive, long after I'm gone.' That's what he said; I swear it! What else can that mean but that he intended to name you to lead in some way? Have you been contacted by the duke? Perhaps he will make the proclamation himself now that the Margrave is gone. Soon he will have to announce the contents of his father's will and name who shall rule in the old Margrave's stead."

"Ach, if anything, Erling von Eidle probably meant to let me lead as a village councilor or something of that nature. Some people are meant to lead from high seats and grand positions, but not me, Piro. I am meant to wear grease and oil on my fingers; I'm a hidden cog, not the clock face."

"But the face of a clock cannot tell the time without the cogs or the gears. They are essential!"

"Yes, every piece and spring is essential to a clock's function. But some of those do their best work from within, without ever needing to be seen. As I do," he says, grunting as he screws another section on the flywheel. "So, say no more about it. My half-brother will trade the mantle of duke for that of the Margrave easily, and as far I'm concerned, the lad can have it."

"But Emmitt, think of all the good you could do, why you—"

A single, pained look from him silences me.

"Sorry." I didn't come here to hurt him; we are both hurting more than enough.

"Don't be," he says with a sly grin. "I am sorely in need of an apprentice, and since Bran is nowhere to be seen at this hour, would you like to be useful and help me reset the carillon mechanism? I am finally close to being finished! Just another key piece to fit tomorrow and I think I'll have it," he says, standing up on the scaffolding and stepping back to inspect the circular racks of bells that comprise the carillon.

"Will this set the bells off now?" I ask, unprepared to be so close to the hulking chimes when they erupt. It's late, and would wake the whole city. And I've had enough of the bells at Wolfspire Hall ringing endlessly in mourning of the Margrave.

"No," Emmitt replies, rubbing his bleary eyes, "but it will mean that once I get the final piece in place, they shall be ready to ring at noon. The glockenspiel will be fully restored, *finally*. Just a little too late for the Margrave to see it."

"Well," I say, rising to stand with him and survey the inner workings of the tower, "it's an impressive piece. Don't worry about it being too late; your clocks are only ever on time. Tell me what to do."

I slink home late after helping Emmitt and don't feel the least scrap of guilt about it. The hour I go to bed now matters to no one but myself; I bolt the doors and bury myself under my covers, falling into a restless dreaming that barely resembles sleep.

I jolt awake to the screaming and scraping of the tree at my window. "Wake! See to the tower—a shadow is on the move!"

I sit up stiffly, unsure if I've slept at all or if this is just part of the ongoing dream I've felt trapped in since Papa died. *Died.* The finality of that word hasn't released me from its grip.

"See to the tower!" the tree cries again. "Hurry! Before it's too late!"

From the window I spot the distant sputtering halo of Emmitt's lantern in the glockenspiel tower. The sun isn't risen yet; the sky still clutches at the cover of night. But the tree's screams do not let up.

I fell into bed clad in yesterday's dress, so I hastily toss a cloak over my shoulders and shove my feet back into my clogs. After a moment's debate of whether or not to wake Bran, I drop to my knees and scramble to the cupboard. I pry my side open. I shove his door ajar and call through.

"Bran! Bran!"

Within seconds, Bran's weary face appears above bare shoulders in the cupboard. "Hurry! It's Emmitt! The clock tower!"

He doesn't question me.

"I'm coming!" He slams the cupboard door shut.

Meeting in the narrow alley behind our row, we run through the village to the tower.

"He said he was nearly done," I pant. "Only one more piece was required. I helped him reset the carillon just a few hours ago."

Bran runs even faster and I match him step for step. We sprint to the tower's entry door, which is still closed, just as I left it.

"Emmitt!" Bran yells at the top of his lungs, unconcerned about waking anyone in earshot. "Emmitt, you still up here?"

No answer.

"Would never leave his lantern burning . . . " Bran mumbles, thundering up the constricting stairs. The tower seems to be narrowing the higher we climb. "He's always cautious of fire up here! One spark could take down the whole apparatus!"

I was just here. He was just fine.

Did the cog thief return to steal something else? Did he fall? Emmitt was sure-footed, but he was up here alone, working in the darkness. One slip of a shoe on that tottery old scaffolding . . . I instantly fear the worst.

The trees at the edges of the square continue their bellowing, and I can still hear them faintly. "Hurry! The shadow is loose!"

Shadow?

We burst onto the lower-tier platform of the glockenspiel, both of us screaming Emmitt's name like banshees.

"He was up there!" I cry, pointing to the ladder that will deliver us to the second tier.

We ascend, Bran's heels nearly jamming into my head in his haste as he takes the rungs two at a time. A grating sound pours forth above and the scaffolding around the glockenspiel begins to shake. The whole tower feels as if it might take flight. Metal grinds against metal as the large flywheel and gears operating the second tier of the glockenspiel awaken and churn in rotation.

On the second level, still no Emmitt. I look to the eaves, where the doves scatter and beat their wings at the clamor of the glockenspiel coming to life. Higher still, bats swoop and dive from the high cupola. Bran shoves me back against the wall before we are nearly sheared off by the wooden figurines returning to their ancient orbit.

Emmitt did it! He fixed the old glockenspiel.

Up close, the hissing groans of the whole beastly thing are deafening. The wolves and men return to their endless hunt, circling round and round, trying to catch one another's tails.

Creak. Ratchet. Tock, tock. Creak—hiss! Rachet. Tock, tock.

The apparatus picks up pace, making a sad, metallic music of its own. The bells are silent; only the glockenspiel carousel is set in motion. And still there is no trace of the clockmaker.

"Emmitt!" I call again, peering over Bran's shoulder into the dark corners for any sign of him. I only see the same discarded figurines I saw several hours ago. Perhaps he was called away in a hurry. But no, his tools are still scattered at our feet. I know he wouldn't leave them like this willingly, especially not after losing several to recent pilfering.

Bran utters a horrified gasp and pushes me back against the wall once more, covering me until I can hardly see.

"What is it?" I whisper, clutching his arm, straining around him to look.

"No!" he chokes.

"Oh," I cry.

In one shattering moment, death pierces my heart anew. For there, emerging from the dark orbit of the glockenspiel, heralded like a limp banner, speared through the chest on a soldier's pike, is Emmitt's lifeless body.

"No!" Bran yells, shimmying around the platform, hurtling quick as he can toward the control levers to stop the horrific parade. All too slowly, the carousel grinds to a jarring halt.

"Who did this?" I whisper, unable to breathe.

I rush to help Bran tear Emmitt's body from the carousel. It's unthinkable for us both to leave him there another second. No one else should see him like this.

"Who would do such a thing?" I look around, fearful.

There is no place to hide up here except the cluttered corners of the tower tiers, and no way down unless the murderer leapt to their own death from the open glockenspiel doors.

We barely manage to lift Emmitt off the jagged spear and drape him on the small platform while wolves and dead-faced soldiers look on. I can scarcely see through my tears. The birds are nervous above, unable to settle, bleating bereft coos. I pry at Emmitt's torn clothes and attempt to staunch the wounds leaking onto the floor with my cloak, helpless to do anything to save him. Blood bubbles from the corners of his lips, painting his beard red. The three of us are soaked in his blood now, red as the Margrave's peculiar carmine.

I was too late. Whatever shadow visited the clockmaker came just before we arrived.

"Piro." Bran shudders, sounding mortally wounded himself. "Look."

He gently tilts Emmitt's head from where it rests on his lap, pointing to a brass clock gear the size of a walnut embedded firmly between the clockmaker's eyes.

CHAPTER 14

BRANCHES SNAP ACROSS MY FACE, TWIGS BITE AT MY CHEEKS and tear at my hair, but I barely feel their claws. I run as fast as I can into the woods, hurtling through the narrow spaces between trunks and the jutting roots that sink knobby knuckles into the forest floor. I register the aching tread of my boots against the ground, the harsh strokes of my pulse carving channels inside my skin.

To avoid the inevitable visits from the makers checking on me, I rose very early, packed a small bag of supplies and left without Burl while there was only a thin, watery spoonful of moon in the sky. I don't know how long I'll be gone, but I brought a few woodcutting tools so that if I'm stopped I can get away with the guise that I am scouting for new trees or taking a few samples.

Or, I realize with a jolt, *I could say I'm visiting my father's grave. Haven't done that yet.*

I press ever farther into the trees, like a child running into her mother's skirts. They welcome me with open arms. Pain prompts me to reach for my nose. The wound from weeks ago is nearly healed, but my heart is still raw. I'm used to the pain of my splinters, but yesterday's terror—that's something I'll never get used to. Seeing Emmitt trussed up in the glockenspiel is an injury that will stay with me long after my physical scars fade.

The isolation of the forest is a salve to my wounds. For two days, I am unable to do anything but lie coiled in the hollowed base of an old beech, not far from the grove where my father now rests. Ingesting the chatter of birds. Watching life skulk along the forest floor. I stare at the light straining through the canopy above, the way it changes from white to gold as the day moves until it is finally swallowed whole by the shadows of night. I make a fire when I grow cold and I eat when I feel hungry. But mostly I just huddle inside the cradle of the beech and cry, letting myself sink into its deeply rooted life, listening to its sonorous voice reassure me over and over, "All will be well."

It surely does not seem like it.

Having to leave Emmitt's body and run to tell Anke and rouse the rest of the makers—that is a journey that will haunt me as long as I live. Bran was shattered, wouldn't leave the clockmaker's side until he'd been carried from the tower in Fonso's arms. Anke wept, rocking herself back and forth, a pendulum of disbelief. Bran's tears finally fell as we left her alone with her son's body, to grieve.

Before I ran for the others, we removed the clock gear from Emmitt's forehead—no easy task—so that his mother wouldn't have to see it. I sense the weight of it now, still in my pocket where I stashed it to keep it from sight. Still crusted with Emmitt's blood.

I can't bring myself to touch it. Is there some meaning to the killer striking that first blow against Emmitt using a piece of the glockenspiel? Or did the murderer just pick up something convenient and close? The clockmaker had many such pieces in his tool trunk.

All I know is that my father and Emmitt are dead.

"Yet, the old magic still lives," the beech tree hums, her voice in my chest evidence of that very fact. "Men may make laws and proclamations, but what are those to powers that spring from the earth unbidden?"

Death has come to us in threes, just like I feared. What else will come marching that I am ill prepared for?

Three tiny ants, bustling with purpose, march across my bare arms, undeterred by the sudden presence of a girl-creature in their path. Beetles scuffle in the rich, dark soil at the foot of the great tree, oblivious to my staring. A pair of chipmunks avoid me until they decide I pose no threat, then begin darting past me to enter their underground tunnels at the mouth of the beech's hollow. Birds sing their endless pronouncements: *Day is here. Night is coming. Where are you? Here I am. Here I am.*

On my third night, the cold draws me out of the tree and I sit facing a small fire, trying to forget the events of the past days and absorb warmth into my stiff limbs. I provoke the fire with a sharp stick, feeling justified when a high spray of sparks shoots up into the blackness and rains down on my arms.

I don't move to brush any off. I let the tiny embers pulse and die on my skin.

At least I am alive. I am still here. Why me and not my father? Why Emmitt?

The trees try to answer my questions, but even they don't know everything. They resume their singing, ancient songs about the coming of winter and the folly of men who have passed under their boughs. I scratch in the dirt at my feet, scraping the pointed end of my fire poker back and forth as if I can etch my sadness out. This branch, this piece that used to be part of something larger, is now cut off. Alone. *Like me.*

A blur of shadow from a large tree across the fire catches my eye, and I grip the stick tighter. A gasp tries to climb its way out of my throat.

Like a specter who walks through walls, an old woman steps out from the massive column of trees across from my fire.

It's her.

Hair the color of dead leaves hangs long and loose around her shoulders. Her robe is rough, giving her the appearance of being wrapped in sheets of bark. Her skin is nut-brown and deeply creased, and the wrinkles at her eyes and mouth fold in on themselves when she smiles. Which she does, promptly proceeding to sit down, cross-legged and easy as a child, with the fire between us. Just like in my father's blue moon tale.

Her hands and feet are bare and knotted, the swollen joints and thin bones reminding me of twigs shooting off new buds in spring. Her eyes read me with the same masterful air my father possessed when appraising a tree. Something about their black, bright knowingness makes me think she is both very old and not done growing yet.

"Welcome, elder," the trees around me croon. I sense their excitement at the arrival of this guest at my fire. "The elder one is here!"

I shift awkwardly to my knees, not knowing what to do or say.

"I am hungry," she says plainly.

Startled by her simple need, I flounder around in my bag and find the end of a loaf of rye and one of my apples. Her knotted fingers close tightly around the food as I sit back on my heels to watch. She eats everything with gusto, including the core and stem of the apple, savoring the seeds and licking her fingers at the end. It feels impolite to gawk, yet I'm not capable of doing anything else while an ancient tree sprite eats so close to me. I've decided that's what she must be. Some kind of wood elf; a living dryad untethered to her fortress.

When she's eaten, her fingers collapse again in her lap, forming an empty hollow like a bird's nest. It's all I can do to stare at her dumbly. I have questions for her, questions I know I should ask, but I forget them all. I don't feel afraid of her, not for one second, but I don't feel at ease, either. Her hair and skin crackle with an energy reminiscent of shivering aspen leaves, a palpable static keeping her in motion though she's sitting still.

"You are alone, young one?"

The simple question comes out like a statement. She calls me what the trees call me.

"Yes."

"Your maker is gone?"

Her voice is high and light, the sound of wind racing through treetops. I have nothing to hide from her; the tree woman sees me as I am.

"Yes," I croak.

She nods, looking mournful for a brief flash. "I saw his resting place."

I think of the mound of dirt not far from where we sit, exposed to the night air and the stars. I haven't been able to bring myself to walk to it yet.

"You know me?" I ask stupidly.

She blinks. "I remember when you were naught but a sapling, all eager shoots and limbs. I watched over you. I watch over them all," she says, waving her fingers to the trees standing sentinel around us. "When a puppetmaster takes a tree from the woods, who do you think plants a new one?"

Something small inside me bursts open, like a seed splitting its husk. It feels good to be known. To be seen.

"Why have you returned to the wood?" she asks.

My answer comes tumbling out in a heap of grievances. "Because I cannot abide the sadness at home. With my father gone, it hurts too much. I'm all alone now. And even hearing the trees' warning, I didn't get there in time to save my friend; he was killed! I fear this curse will be the end of me as well, if I'm not careful."

Her brows furrow.

"Curse?"

"When I lie . . . something happens," I stammer. "I think

it's a mistake—or a punishment, perhaps. Splinters burst out of me. Maybe I deserve it, even. For the lies. But it ruins everything," I add angrily, touching the still-tender tip of my nose.

Indignant, I pull the small bundle filled with my tell-tale splinters from my bag. As I hastily gathered my things to run away, it suddenly felt foolish and risky to leave such a strange thing behind for someone else to find. *Why have I kept them all these years?*

"It's not fair! I didn't ask for this!" I say, opening the bundle, holding a fistful out as evidence. "Or for these scars!" I pull up a sleeve and point to my arms.

She raises an eyebrow. "I see."

Resuming her intense scrutiny, she then commands, "Give that big stick here, girl."

Cautiously, I reach across the fire, passing her the stick I had grabbed in defense, a branch nearly as tall as I am. She snaps it in half as neatly as if it were a piece of kindling, a mere twig.

"A tree cannot lie, girl. It's impossible," she says, pointing to the jagged interior of the stick, where I see the white core exposed. "You cut a tree and you can see its history, its age, its injuries. By its very nature, it's telling the truth about who it is and where it comes from. That is why the splinters find you. You are no different."

Anger rises like bile in my throat. "But I am! And that's just the problem. I *am* different from everyone in Tavia. And trying to explain to anyone what I really am, well, it's impossible! Not to mention *forbidden*," I hiss, lowering my voice as best as I can, suddenly remembering that anyone could be out among the trees watching or listening. "Whatever magic made me was banished from Tavia long ago, don't you realize that? Surely you've heard? If I let anyone see me as I am, I put us all in danger, just as *you* endangered my father by giving him the blue moon's spell years ago. Why, if anyone saw me here, right now, with you . . . it's unthinkable! We'd both be tossed into this fire as kindling!"

I take a deep breath. "Tell me why you did it? Why did you come to him, just as you've come to me now, on a night like tonight? It would have been far better if you'd left him alone. He would have been better off without me!"

"Your father chose his path. Just as you will choose yours."

"But what if my splinters give me away? I didn't choose them. I don't want to spend the rest of my days shunned or locked in a cell, and I certainly don't want to be burned alive!"

Tears pool at the edges of my vision as I remember the dark corridors filled with filth and desperation spanning the length of Wolfspire Keep.

"You are human in every way that matters, girl."

"Then why do *slivers of wood* pierce me from the inside out every time I lie? Others don't have this difficulty," I say bitterly.

"But they do; some carry a family birthmark, or inherit a crooked nose from a grandfather, or a mother's hasty temper. Part of who we are is who we come *from*. There's no escaping that, not for any living creature."

I ponder that for a moment, knowing she's right but hating the stupidity of it all.

"Isn't there any way to change it?" I plead. "For me to be free of this curse? Is there a spell you can give me, something you can do to make me wholly human and not part of the wood any longer? How do I rid myself of these splinters?"

The trees begin to murmur, disappointed by my longing to be different from them.

"Shun falsehoods."

"I don't *want* to lie," I say, exasperated. "Please understand, it's not that I want to be able to lie, it's just that now that my father is gone, I have no one else to hide behind. The splinters will give me away. I'll be cast aside as something less than human, something to be hated and feared."

"What if I were to tell you your wooden nature makes you *more* than human, not less?" she asks, one wispy eyebrow cocking up like the spread of a bird's wing.

"My curse is not helpful in any way!" I grumble. "And I still don't know what it means, my splinters, for . . . for *love*," I say, a wash of heat burning my cheeks. "Can I marry one day without harming my husband or my children? Without making them swear to keep the truth hidden, endangering those I love most?"

"There is one that you love?"

I nod, my thoughts filling with Bran.

Her eyes bore into mine like two black beetles tunneling into a burrow. "Understand, the moon's spell may have bought you breath, but the power of your father's love gave you *life*, girl. The heart of the maker will determine the course of the marionette.

"You will become as you wish when you give life to another under the blue moon's magic, just as your father did for you. You know the words already, I daresay," she says, stirring the fire with the broken end of my stick.

Of course I know the words. The words of the blue moon spell are as branded into my skin as the lingering tracks of my lies. *Is there really a way for my splinters to be gone?*

The tree woman stands abruptly, ready to depart my fire just as quickly as she arrived. She gazes upwards to the canopy, the bespeckled shell of night sky hollowed out between the treetops. I don't want her to go, don't want to be left here alone.

"It will rise again you know," she warns, still holding tightly to the two halves of my broken branch, which she plunges into the ground on either side of her. "Soon. There's no such thing as once in a blue moon. The sacred blue moon will rise again while you walk 'neath the night. Trust it and you'll have your chance. Remember to count the cost."

Afraid she might disappear again, I blurt out a final question for this strange half-woman, half-wild thing. "Please, what was the cost of my father making me? He warned the magic always has a cost. What cost?"

"His strength," she rasps bluntly. "The blue moon is a patient mercenary, girl. She may bide her time, sometimes for years, but she always collects."

My heart squeezes in misery. *My father lost his strength because of me? It wasn't just the burden of the Margrave's demands or his stay in the Keep?*

He had grown weaker, aging so rapidly these past months. Tears burn my eyes and they drop on the tops of my knees, which I clutch like they are all I have left in the world.

I am the real reason for my father's death.

In gaining me, he ultimately lost a vital part of himself. I cannot swallow; grief clogs my throat.

"Better to hold the seed of the great oak in your hand and sense its towering potential, than to never let it pass through your fingers at all," she answers, reading the thoughts crowding my mind.

"I beg to differ," I mutter bitterly. Especially if that seed steals your precious life while it grows.

She turns her back on me and stalks through the shadows to another massive beech. Placing a hand fondly on its broad trunk, she aims a final piercing glare over her bony shoulder.

"Take heed, young one: a figment created for good will collect less from the maker, but one born of dark purposes always takes more. Sometimes *much* more."

"But what—"

The old creature vanishes into the bark like a fleeing vapor, leaving me full of questions and emptier than ever.

CHAPTER 15

I WAKE AT DAWN TO A PILE OF COLD ASHES IN THE FIRE, A DAY drizzly with mist and fog. As I sit up and look around, I rub my eyes to make sure I'm not hallucinating. Overnight, the two halves of the dead branch the old woman stuck into the earth grew covered in buds, fat and ready to burst. Winter is just around the corner, but here they are, growing right from where she'd grafted them to the forest floor as if it's the first day of spring. Her message is not lost on me; a reminder that impossible things *can* happen, that even dead and broken things find a way to grow.

The two new trees growing from the broken halves look as if they've been here all along, and weren't remnants of a dying season just hours before. I can't stop examining the waxy buds that hold within their grasp flags of green ready to unfurl as soon as the sun reaches them. The tree woman is a strange magic all her own.

I reluctantly clean up my little camp near the beech tree, using an evergreen branch to scatter the remains of my fire and sweep away my footprints. I wish it to be like I was never here at all, as if a girl named Pirouette never came to seek solace among the trees, never met a dryad with a blue moon premonition on her lips. Also, I've run out of food.

I am resolved to return to Curio, back to the makers who will be trying to piece together the remnants of our little family, now without the puppetmaster or the clockmaker. Though I'm sure I will have to keep my mouth shut more than I'd like to survive, I will keep the shop going, if only for my father's sake. I owe it to him to try. He lost his strength because of me, so at the very least I can keep him from losing his legacy in Tavia, keep his name from fading like a memory.

Before leaving the shelter of the wood, my feet carry me a few moments' walk away in the gloom. Early fog swirls through the forest like a cat wrapping itself around cold ankles. At Papa's grave, the lumberjack marionette's legs dance in the breeze, swinging from the wooden cross marking his head.

I stoop down, sinking my fingers into the soil, just knuckle-deep. Closing my eyes, I pause a moment, just to breathe. And to . . . talk? Think? Pray? I don't know how to describe the torrent of feelings surging against the walls of my heart. The trees are silent around me, for once.

With tears rolling down my cheeks, I find myself taking out my bundle of splinters and unwrapping them for the last time. Near where my father lies I dig a few shallow scoops of damp earth and drop the remains of my lies into a grave of their own. I don't need to keep or carry them any longer. According to the old tree woman, someday I might be free of them completely.

Before I leave him, I settle for simply saying, "I love you, Papa. A maker will always prevail."

He would understand this is the best I can do right now. I will come again, when I can.

I leave feeling a little lighter, though the air this deep in the wood gathers thicker than Gita's pea soup. I can scarcely see the next tree in front me. From time to time, the split of a twig or the crackle of leaves shifting sends a jolt down my neck. My fingers tighten around the handle of the axe hanging at my belt. I turn to look behind me, staring blindly into the fog.

I am being followed. I am sure of it. But my eyes see nothing. Nothing but trees and haze.

I hear whispers, the old trees fretting and shushing, "Shadows are on the move."

The same warning they gave the night Emmitt died.

I half expect to see the tree woman emerge from the mist, but when I look again, still nothing. I plunge on, unable to ignore the feeling that someone is near. Fear coats my palms with an inescapable itch.

I stop to rest, leaning back against a halsa to draw some strength from its deceptively solid trunk. I close my eyes a moment to rid myself of the dryness plaguing them after days spent crying. Even then, the sensation of being watched raises the hair on my arms to gooseflesh. I open my eyes, straining into the fog. *Still nothing.*

Suddenly, from behind, soft as a breath, I feel a tap on my shoulder. Stifling a scream, I force my eyes downward. A trio of fingers rests on the exposed skin at my collar. *Spruce and ash!* It is a hand I know well. I created it.

The masked face of the saboteur stares unblinkingly at me from behind the tree. Out of habit, my fingers clutch at my axe, trying to squeeze some comfort from its blunt edges. I squint and blink again, sure the fog is playing tricks on me. With little rest and even less breakfast, no doubt I am prone to seeing things in my state of grief. Especially things that cannot be.

But when I look again, the creature is moving from behind the halsa, wide eyes searching, watching my every move. With sickening fascination, I can't help but stare back. She's still all wired joints and carved limbs, same as when she was taken away in the cold stateroom at Wolfspire Hall. But the strings connecting her to the crossbar controls have been cut. Walking freely, the saboteur comes closer, splayed hands swinging loose at her sides, knees bent so she might bolt at any moment, like a deer. Instinctively, I take a few steps back. *She's alive.*

Yet . . . she is not like me. The blue moon hasn't risen yet. She's not human. She can't be. What is she?

"How?" I breathe aloud.

The saboteur glances around quickly, as if afraid of what my voice might summon.

She hears me. Can she speak?

Quickly putting a claw-like, gloved finger to her lips, she motions for me to be quiet. *Oh, saints and stars.* Anyone with eyes can see her sharp finger drips with blood. Dread fills my lungs instead of air. My legs are locked in place, unable to move.

The saboteur's painted eyes examine me, trying to understand my response. She seems as curious about me as I am of her, if that's even possible.

"What—" I croak again, but the saboteur cuts me off with a shake of her head, beckoning me forward with long, slender fingers.

Unsatisfied with my stupefied inability to comply with her orders, she tugs at my arm, dragging me through the fog, into a dense stand of pines. Her bloody fingers curl solidly around me, her grasp like iron. She points, indicating I should tuck myself into a small space between two tall overhanging branches. Shaking and wobbly, I don't fight her. She wedges herself in front of me, standing silent sentry between me and the thinly veiled opening in the pines.

Touching her shoulder, I pick up the sound of her voice, a silky remoteness repeating over and over words I don't understand.

"Leben consurgé! Danger among us. Consurgé! Danger among us!"

It's dark between the trees; the pine boughs gouge at my neck and face. I fidget worriedly, unsheathing my axe to have it at the ready, wondering what on earth is happening and how I will explain to all of Tavia that a marionette of mine walks the woods before dawn.

The saboteur's body tenses, a string down her spine tightening. Then I hear the reason: through the trees comes the distinct sound of marching, of men moving in metered unison. I wait, holding my breath, peeking over the saboteur's black-clad shoulder, the leather tunic Bran hand cut providing the frame to my view. At first, we can only hear them; a small army on the move. Surely this is the duke's doing, sending men in the direction of Brylov under the cover of near darkness and fog. And then, to my dismay, I see them.

They are not men at all.

My father's wooden soldiers, fully animated, destroy the forest floor beneath dirtied boots as they sweep across in lines five deep. It's like my nightmare from the gate of Wolfspire Hall come to pass. They stomp onwards, their gait brittle, their advance unyielding. The soldiers pass us by, never noticing us sequestered among the pines. I recognize each blocky face, a set of eyebrows here, a bulbous nose there.

Like the saboteur, they do not blink; their eyes stare ahead undaunted, summoned by an invisible beacon. Their boots gather muck from the forest floor, but even in the graying light, their uniforms are as crisp as they were when my father and I delivered them. I take this as a sign that this is their first time out of Wolfspire Hall.

The saboteur doesn't allow me to move a muscle until they are long gone from sight, their footfalls a distant echo. Only then does she break from the pines, indicating I should follow. I realize she's been protecting me, keeping me from the path of the soldiers who would have been on me in minutes had she not found me first.

Has she been sent on the same mission as the soldiers or was she sent ahead to spy or stir up trouble? Whose blood is on her hands?

The possibilities set my stomach churning.

I have so many questions, yet I know from her eyes and stiff-jointed mouth she can't give me real answers. If I were seen with her now, what would people say? Old Josipa's wrinkled face rises up to haunt my mind. The saboteur lives by some form of the same old magic, that banned and dangerous kind.

Unconcerned about the soldiers now, she crouches down beside me, intently scooping up a little of the black soil. She sifts it through her gloved fingers, and dirt clings to the bloody, sticky patches. Perhaps she hears the forest speaking through the earth, for she plunges five fingers down farther and dips her head, listening.

Part of me wonders if I should turn and follow the soldiers, to see where they might be going, but I'm so mesmerized by the saboteur it's impossible to leave her. I squat down beside her, sitting back on my haunches, just as she does.

Logically, I know she is without a beating heart and a brain and all the other encumbrances that make a creature human and whole. But here she is. Functioning on magic I can't begin to understand.

"What did he do to you?" I ask softly, so as not to startle her. My voice sounds fragile, like it might shatter when it touches the air. "What did he make you do?" I assess the blood-stained gloves.

Her head inclines toward me, curious. Her expression remains unchanged: intense, sharp, and self-assured. At the time I was carving it, the wood gave me no other choice. Hers is not a beautiful face, but it is one you cannot look away from.

Lost in my own spell of wonderment, I lift my hand in greeting, splaying my five fingers wide. She regards this gesture and lifts the hand that has been communing with the dirt to mirror my own. I make a fist and open it again. Fluently, she matches me move for move. Taking the game even further, I press my sweaty palm to her wooden one. A shiver races down my neck to feel the pressure returned. Her gloved hand is cool and hard and pushes back with a strength that far outweighs my own. Unprepared, I tumble back into the dirt.

Taking a handkerchief from my pocket, I reach out cautiously to wipe the blood and dirt from her open hand. She observes my fingers, the way I utilize the scrap of fabric and pat her gently when done, the way a mother would, cleaning a child's scrape. Once I've finished, I find her reaching to take the handkerchief for herself. My cheeks burn as she turns it toward me, gently dabbing the still-visible wound on my nose.

"A splinter," I explain. "Apparently, where we come from," I point to the trees, "splinters are somewhat inescapable."

She nods, seeming to think me daft for not knowing that before.

"Come," I reach for her hand, sensing the mounting danger of being out in the woods, in the open, with her. "Come with me."

"Danger among us!" her voice reverberates in my skin. "The shadows are loosed."

"You will be safe. You needn't go where Laszlo has bade you. You don't have to do what he says. He is not your master," I insist. "I made you."

Bearing an undeniable guardianship for the saboteur, I long to protect her from him. My mind cannot conceive what the young duke intends for this dark creature, but I understand now her true purpose is a hostile rather than decorative one. That he would take something so beautiful and use it for violent ends!

The power of her animated form almost makes me feel ashamed of the naive exuberance with which I built her, of those exhausting days at Curio when her construction consumed me, of the joy carving her gave to me. Building her was a relief, especially after the rigid limitations of a year spent laboring over wooden soldiers, a distraction from the pain of watching Papa grow weaker. I poured the full extent of my skill and imagination into the saboteur, not holding anything back, ultimately delivering to Wolfspire Hall a marionette the duke wished to wield like a freshly forged blade.

This is all my fault—our fault. We presented the weapons right into his waiting hands. The soldiers. The uniforms and broadswords. The saboteur.

I wonder how to smuggle her back to Curio. Perhaps I could persuade her to go limp, and drag her down the back alleys to the rear workshop door? I could hide her in my attic room, keep her locked away if necessary, somewhere she could do no more damage. Where I wouldn't have to watch my best workmanship ruined by Laszlo's abuses. Or perhaps I should take her away from here, high into the mountains. If we ran far enough from his reach, maybe the magical ties binding her would be broken.

"I made you," I repeat, hoping to appeal to whatever loyalty she might possess. "You belong with me. Let's go now, it isn't safe here." I pull at her hand, but her fingers slip through my own like water. Her head darts, watching the surrounding fog.

She hears something again, something I cannot. Connected to the forest in a deep and primal way, she motions for me to retreat back to the safety of the pines.

Soldiers again?

I obey as she deftly reaches for something in her vest pocket. Then, the saboteur leaves me behind in the trees, her dark head drifting away like a departing ship on a sea of fog. I wait and watch for a few tense moments. Then, in the distance, a sharp zing meets my ears, the sound of an arrowhead striking true.

Then I hear a cry. A very human cry. The trees fall silent.

I stay a moment more, hoping she'll reappear. But the saboteur never comes back. With my throat burning and fear supplying the last of my strength, I decide to leave, with or without her. I must return to Curio, to make sure the only family I have left will be kept safe from the havoc of wooden soldiers set loose on the territory. A havoc I helped unleash. I must warn the Maker's Guild.

Shivering, I creep slowly from the evergreen hollow. Wading warily from tree to tree, more fearful than ever of what lurks behind them, I nearly trip over the startled body of a Wolfspire Hall guard. My foot tentatively prods his side, but the man doesn't stir. This soldier is fully human, dressed in the Margrave's livery, just like his wooden counterparts. Bending down to examine him, I see his skin is still warm to the touch, the look on his face one of frozen shock. With fresh dread, I spot the cause of his demise: a finely notched brass clock gear planted between the eyes, embedded deep in his skull.

Unable to suspend my terror, I retch beside him into a wide spray of leatherleaf ferns, my empty gullet heaving without respite. Stumbling blindly around the body, I tear into a run through the trees, straining for the edges in the distance where thicket meets the meadow.

As I gallop away like a wounded animal, the weight of the matching clock gear in my pocket nearly buckles my knees. I cannot catch my breath. Where I fled to the wood days ago seeking a place to hide and lick my wounds, now I crave air and light. The trees feel too close, too towering. I am too small in their accusing shadows, their branches casting pointed blame directly on my head.

The saboteur is lost to me now, untethered and out of my control. My hopes for returning home to start anew after Papa and Emmitt's deaths are soundly crushed. How can I pick up my chisel and hammer again, knowing a creature made by my own hand has stolen life—*more than once*? As though a pack of wolves bite at my heels, I run for home, dragging my own millstone around my neck.

CHAPTER 16

I RUN LIKE FURY, SPRINGING THROUGH THE CROOKED LANES toward Curio. My eyes scarcely see anything but the soldier with the clock gear struck between blood-filled eyes and Emmitt's body draped on the glockenspiel. I'm so distracted, it isn't until I'm several streets past the marktplatz that I realize everything around me feels . . . wrong.

It's morning, a Tuesday, though it feels like an eternity has passed since I first ventured to the wood, running away from my problems. Instead of the normal bustle and slosh of hawkers and busy housewives, there's entirely too much stillness.

Many shops and homes look dark inside, despite cold sunshine grazing the rooftops as the fog flees. Windows aren't flung open; they remain shut. The usual rag-tag assortment of laundry flutters stiffly from lines strung across the upper windows of each home, like so many flags of surrender. I spy the milkmaid carrying full pails into the cheesemonger's, but she scurries past with her eyes downcast.

Through my tears, I see Erundle the chromatist tossing a bucket of water across her back steps, leaving a puddle of murky rainbows on the cobbles. No doubt the remainder of the morning's grindings of powders and herbs.

"Erundle!" I call, waving and gulping great breaths of air, relieved to see a familiar face.

She hesitates, looking pained to see me. She nods roughly and turns around to go back into her home, quickly slamming the door shut behind her. *Strange.* We've always been on excellent terms.

No lights emanate from Curio's windows. I enter through the back, flinging open the door to Burl's stable. The horse nickers in surprise. I left him plenty of fresh hay and water, but it's evident his stall needs immediate attention.

"I know, Burly," I apologize, scratching his nose. "Papa left us. Then I left you, too. I'm so sorry. Everything is slipping away from me and I can't stop it or slow it down."

As I fumble around in my room after bathing and changing clothes, there is no way to escape the persistent knocking coming from the cupboard door.

"Piro?" Bran calls from the other side.

There is so much to tell him—to tell them all. I just don't know if I have the strength to do it. To tell them what I've just seen. Or if I even should.

"Piro, please? If you don't want to see me, just listen through the door. Just knock back—do something, anything—so I know that you're safe. You've been gone for days," his muffled voice pleads worriedly. "I know you're there, I can hear you. At least, I hear *someone* over there, and if you're not Pirouette, I'm going to beat this cupboard down and—"

Reluctantly, I knock against my side of the door in our secret pattern.

I hear his breath catch, relief flooding his voice. "Thank you. Are you all right?"

I tap again for "yes."

"I've missed you."

The longing in his voice is a balm to my wounded pride and sore heart. I yank open the door of the cupboard. His door flies open, the space immediately filling with his face.

"Hi."

"Hello."

This moment suddenly feels reminiscent of the experience I had years ago, of opening the cupboard to see his face for the first time, realizing there was an actual person on the other side.

"Bran—" I begin to explain myself and where I've been. As I search for the words, Bran intently clears away the shelves, sweeping everything onto his side of the cupboard with the arc of his arm. Our odds and ends instantly tumble down onto his rug.

"Wait. What are you doing?"

"Something I should've done long ago," he mutters, biting

his lip as he wrenches each wooden shelf from its moorings. Quicker than I thought possible, there is nothing between us, no more doors or treasures to separate my room from his.

There's just us.

"Piro?"

"Yes, Bran?"

"Would you like to come in?"

I nod, startled; I would.

I've only ever seen Bran's room, the mirror image of my own, in bits and pieces, but for once nothing stands between me and the warmth of it. I crawl through the cupboard on my hands and knees, and find myself in a place I've only been able to see slices of, never the whole.

His bed and wardrobe look the same, but on the side where I have nothing but empty wall he has a full worktable, with clock parts and pieces filling the shelves mounted behind. A finished mantlepiece clock ticks soundly with a crisp, regular rhythm. Shelves of books occupy another corner and below the window sits a wooden bench, the perfect place for watching life go by on Tavia's streets.

And then, there's him. After I catch myself staring open-mouthed at his room, the lamp by the bedside bathing everything in golden light, I find I can't look away from his eyes. He perches on his heels, back against the wall, as if he's been here forever, waiting an age for me to come through the cupboard. I crouch awkwardly on my knees.

"Bran, I couldn't—"

Again I attempt to explain where I've been, but I am cut off by his hands on my cheeks, by his mouth kissing my battered nose gently on the tip. His lips move from my nose to my forehead and then make their way down in a cascade across cheeks and chin, until one kiss, the most tender and insistent of all, lands squarely on my lips.

He is knee to knee with me, and I reach for his shoulders to steady myself. The heat of his breath against my skin sends a flutter down to my core, warming me through in a way the golden light in his room never could. Bran himself is made of light and warmth. The tightly wound knot of fear and shame I've been holding begins to loosen in my chest. His kisses send me reeling and I want nothing more than to just exist here beyond the cupboard door, with Bran, forever.

Until I remember all the sorrows that have befallen us both—and that I am the cause for most of them.

I pull away from his lips, but am unable to fully escape him; he pulls me into the welcoming space beneath his arm. Sitting this way, we fit against each other as neatly as two layers in my father's puzzle boxes.

"You missed Emmitt's wake yesterday," he says softly, disappointment thick in his voice. "Same day the Margrave was interred."

"Oh!" Regret twists deeper in my chest.

I should have been there to say goodbye. To help Anke bury her son, just as she had helped bury my father. To help Bran mourn the loss of our friend. The Maker's Guild needed me and I fled.

"I'm sorry. How is Anke?"

"Not good."

I know the feeling.

"Where'd you go, Pirouette?"

"To see Papa."

He sighs, the strain about his eyes making him seem older. Suddenly, I clam up, unable to speak about how I ran to get away from my own sadness, only to meet the truth face to face in the woods. I cannot burden Bran with the old tree woman or the saboteur. Certainly not with how I fled from the dead soldier with the clock gear buried in his skull, just like Emmitt. I can't fully grasp it all, myself.

"But Bran, the soldiers." I steel myself to explain at least this much. "We have to warn everyone. The wooden soldiers are . . . well, they are marching around. Like real men, but . . . "

"I know, I heard. Word has already spread. The innkeeper's boy was out getting water, and the poor lad came back screaming his gullet out with an empty bucket in his hands, saying there's a full lot of 'em on the move. Said they were heading into the wood before the sun was even up."

"Oh." My pulse thunders like it might burst from my ears.

"The boy said there was something not right about the soldiers . . . that they were more like figurines than men." Bran gives me a long, worried look. "I don't know how to explain it. Could someone be resurrecting those old spells, Piro? But how? Everyone's keeping inside until we have to venture out for the proclamation."

Others had seen the soldiers marching, too. And the chromatist and almost every other maker in Tavia knew my father and I made them.

How had the duke wrought that magic out? And what of the saboteur—what if she were seen, with fresh blood on her hands?

It's horrible to think of what she might do, or what might be done to her if she were seized and attacked.

"When's the proclamation?" I gulp.

"Announced yesterday. Every man, woman, and child, be they from the farms or the village, is *requested* to present themself to the rathaus on the morrow at noon," he says, his voice laced with sarcasm. "Until then, we're all to be doing nothing but mourning Erling von Eidle. Even the market was canceled today in honor of the late Margrave."

"Canceled? Well, we have to warn the others, Bran. The duke is certainly planning something. Though I'm afraid I don't know what."

"I went to see him, about Emmitt, you know," he says, anger creeping into his voice.

"What? What do you mean?"

"It isn't right! Our friend was murdered, practically right in front of us! And beyond whispering fearfully, no one was doing anything. My father wouldn't go, Fonso and Tiffin were too spooked and Anke was too grieved. And you weren't here, so *I* went. I went to see the steward. I asked to see the duke himself, but they wouldn't let me. Someone had to!

"I know the duke had something to do with his death. I just know it! I'm convinced Laszlo used a paid mercenary to kill Emmitt before the Margrave's will could be read. Perhaps even just to silence the rest of us. His father might have made allowances for a maker to rule in Tavia, but the duke—the real bastard, in my opinion—could never stand the thought of playing second fiddle."

"What did the steward say?"

He laughs bitterly. "He pretended to listen to my complaint and then said, 'We're already looking into the matter of the clockmaker's unfortunate death. The duke is *most concerned*, especially since the glockenspiel wasn't completed before the fall proclamation, per his father's orders.' So, in other words, they're doing nothing and couldn't care less about what really happened to Emmitt. They're upset about the blasted glockenspiel not being complete! And soon, we all have to go hear the duke's proclamation, which, no doubt, puts that conniving usurper exactly where he wants to be."

"It's his right, he's the Margrave's only legitimate heir," I say sadly.

"Yes, and he took that right, like a greedy child stealing a biscuit from his father's plate. Emmitt didn't even want to be Margrave! He didn't want anything to do with it and look at the price he paid. Some of us are meant to be makers," he says, the pressure of his fingers squeezing my hand, "and some are takers. I'm under no illusions about which sort the duke is."

"Yes," I agree. My own illusions of safety and happiness are long gone.

"I am so sorry about Gep," Bran says sincerely. "We've not even had any time to talk about it, just you and I. Everything has happened so quickly."

Even hearing my father's name aloud still hurts, a hammer

striking a fresh bruise. As an offering, Bran presses something round and warm into my fingers. It's a pocket watch, trimmed in brass.

"Pretty." I admire the elegant hands, marking time without any concern for the past, only inching us forward. A bit of blue velvet ribbon is strung through the loop at the top. "One of yours?"

"Yes, finally finished it. This is the first I've built completely on my own."

I turn it over in my hands, noting the scrolling pattern of leaves and flowers engraved on the back, embellishing an ornate "P." I look up at him.

"Your name does not begin with a 'P.'"

"I am pleased you remember, since it's been so long since we've seen each other," he says with mock gravity.

"Is it for me?"

"Well," he replies with a long exhale, "I was rather hoping that Prudence Shoemacher, the cobbler's daughter, would want it, but alas, she has her eye set on the fetchingly large frame of the milliner's apprentice. There's no chance for me, a lowly tailor's son and fledgling watchmaker with very slender shoulders to catch her eye. So, I suppose you could have it. Seeing as your first initial is also 'P'. It makes sense."

I snort. "Prudence Shoemacher has been sweet on you since you moved into The Golden Needle and you know it." Her and every other Tavian girl with a pair of eyes in their skulls.

"Well, then Prudence Shoemacher will have to be disappointed," he says with a look that causes my heartbeat to overflow into my cheeks, "because I made that watch for you, Pirouette Leiter."

I look down at the watch again—it *is* a beauty.

"As much as I hate to disappoint Prudence Shoemacher," I say, with a grin, "I will keep it. Thank you." I nestle it into a pocket and reach again for one of his hands, eager to absorb some of his heat.

"You remember, Piro, what we talked about the night you finished the saboteur?" he asks, brushing my nose gently with his thumb.

As if it hasn't been on my mind nearly every waking moment since, despite all the chaos.

"I'm so glad you told me. So many things about you make sense to me now."

"Was I that confusing?"

He tips my chin up, so that my eyes are forced to meet his.

"Not confusing. Complex. I've never known anyone touched by magic before. But the way you work with wood and the way the puppets seem to come alive under your hands . . . that look you get in your eye sometimes when you're carving, as if you're hearing voices; it all makes sense now.

"What," he prods gently, "was it like? Do you remember?"

"Before the spell, or after?"

"Both."

"Ah." I start haltingly, unused to speaking of such personal memories out loud. "I remember my father and how big he seemed, how kind. And my body, how strange it felt, to move and to walk—to go wherever I wished! People are always gallivanting about, chasing after things and looking after things. It all took a good deal of time to get used to."

"And before?" His voice drops low, his breath on my ear sends a flutter down my neck.

"Before . . . " I remember back to what seems like eons ago, when I stood with roots and not feet, with branches bared beneath every storm and phase of the moon. A time when the passing seasons were the only clock I knew. A time that felt sacred. "Before, it was different. It seems that in some ways, I knew *more*, then. I understood things I've now forgotten—the language of the birds, the way of the flowers, the signals of the sky. So many things I've lost."

He presses his lips to the top of my head. "When I was younger, I used to imagine that all of my lost things—a favorite rock, or a bit of paper, or my best sewing kit—had lives of their own that had just gone on without me. They weren't lost at all. Perhaps that's how it will be for us someday, Piro. We'll realize the things and people we've lost aren't really lost at all, they've just gone on journeying without us," he says hopefully.

"Perhaps." I squeeze his hand and nestle my head into his shoulder.

But Bran's fanciful idea brings me little comfort. I've lost a father, a friend, and a masterpiece in the space of mere days. And now one of those has begun a journey into darkness beyond the limits of my imagination. Would that I could turn the clock back, to the time before we all were lost.

CHAPTER 17

THAT EVENING, BEFORE THE DUKE'S PROCLAMATION, I FORCE myself to go out to meet the makers, to warn them about the soldiers. To make my apologies for missing Emmitt's burial. I watch the street corners warily, my eyes hunting for signs of approaching soldiers or a glimpse of the saboteur. But the streets are quiet tonight.

I am the last to arrive at The Louse and Flea, which is nearly empty. Without a word, I settle myself beside Bran and inspect each maker's face. Fonso pours a mugful from his pitcher, Nan at his side. He appears calm, while she looks like a kettle ready to blow, eyes bright and furious, busily biting her nails. Tiffin looks glum, staring at the surface of the old trestle table as though trying to divine some mystery from its grain.

"Perhaps it won't be so bad," Nan finally says in a stilted voice.

"What?" Tiff asks.

"The proclamation. At least we'll get to hear it for ourselves.

The duke can be assured of his position, and then maybe we can all go back to normal. Sorry, Pirouette," she says, reaching across to squeeze my hand. "As normal as we can, now, with fewer of us at the table. On the other hand, I've half a mind to come tomorrow with my pockets full of stones to take that gormless maggot down a few notches."

"That's my girl." Fonso looks at her admiringly.

"Stoning isn't painful enough for the likes of him," Tiffin replies flatly. "Besides, your aim is too good, Nan. It would be over far too quickly."

"True." She sighs.

"You may want to save your rocks or whatever weapons you can lay your hands on for another foe. Rumors are flying thick as flocking geese about the duke's soldiers," Bran says. "Real or wooden, it's all anyone can talk about, everyone that comes in the Needle. Troops have been seen gathering in the woods, setting up boundaries. Patrolling the edges of the territory. People can't tell if they're real men or not." He looks at me from the corner of his eye.

Nan nods. "They're afraid—afraid there's magic at play, but everyone's too scared to speak out or question it."

"I've seen them," I confess, dropping my voice low. "Our wooden soldiers. In the woods. Just a glimpse of them, but still. Somehow, they're moving about. Wearing *our* uniforms and brandishing *our* weapons." I look at each of them pointedly. "We could all be blamed for what's to come."

"Keep your voice down!" Tiffin whispers. "I say it sounds like you been seein' things in the fog, Pirouette. A trick of the mist. You'd best keep those observations to yourself. It's not safe to speculate otherwise."

"What if he is planning to invade Brylov, to try and secure his place there, too, like we thought? We could all be conscripted to fight," Fonso says bleakly. "I don't want to leave Tavia."

"Perhaps because we're part of the Maker's Guild he'll excuse us from whatever he's planning," Bran adds, hope in his voice. "Without Tiffin and Mort in the smithy and Fonso in the glassworks, or my father and me in the tailor's shop, what would people here do?"

Nan sucks her teeth. "You're greener than grass if you think anyone is going to be 'excused' from what is to come. If the duke declares his intentions toward Brylov and needs an army, I guarantee that if you can lift a sword or tote a hatchet he'll be putting your arms to his own uses. Meanwhile, Piro, Gita, and I will be left here to try and keep food in our mouths and the village from being overrun by outlander thieves and wandering vagabonds."

Fonso reaches a hand out to steal one of Nan's from being bitten to stubs. She stills and lets him hold it. Bran takes one of mine under the table, twining his fingers firmly through my own.

"Well, if anyone can scare away thieves and vagabonds, it's you, Nanette Li," Fonso says with a serious air.

Nan looks at him for a moment, unsure whether to take his words as a compliment or an insult, but in the end she bursts out laughing. Her laugh is contagious and the pressures of the last days burst in all of us, laughter spilling like a welcome flood across our parched table. We garner stares from the few other grim-eyed patrons of The Louse and Flea, but none of us care. Nan laughs until tears streak the corners of her eyes, and even Tiffin, who rarely even smiles, is left clutching his stomach.

I marvel at the gift of small moments like these, despite all I've lost. They are all the family I have left now, these makers.

The next day finds me locking Curio's door and heading to the marktplatz, to stand with the others in the shadow of the clock tower at the rathaus. I've never seen the village in such a state. People mill about anxiously in a din of angry whispers and worried glances. Guards—real men, thank the heavens— patrol about, keeping their eyes searching for any who might cause trouble.

I push my way through the crowd, searching for the makers, and quickly land on a familiar set of bulky shoulders sporting a shaggy red head. Fonso. Tiffin, Nan, and the Sorens are here, too. Nan stands at the far edge of the cluster, arms fiercely crossed, her face a storm cloud. Gita appears deep in an argument with her husband with the baby fussing at her hip and Bran's sisters clinging to her skirts. Bran's eyes light on me. He steps out of range of his parents' squabble to pull me in close.

A few minutes before noon, the duke's black carriage arrives. People part like waving wheat to allow his retinue through. With great pomp, Laszlo von Eidle ascends the steps of the rathaus, one crisp boot-fall at a time. Before speaking, he gazes up to the clock tower and the glockenspiel, which is still frozen in the position it stopped in when Bran pulled the lever to shut it down. The duke smiles. Then he begins his proclamation, his voice surprisingly strong and resonant.

"Good people of Tavia, it is with great honor that I announce the end of our period of mourning for my father, Erling von Eidle, your late and favored Margrave. His tenure is now complete, and it is my privilege to announce that I shall ascend to his position as sovereign head of the margraviate of Tavia, as set forth in his final will and testament. This was my father's greatest wish, being that I am his *only* heir."

Anger vibrates from Bran, who squeezes my hand so fiercely I cannot feel my fingers. I glance at Anke, whose lips press so hard together they've disappeared in her distraught face.

"Henceforth, I endeavor to return Tavia to its former glory. The glory of an age before my father's time, a time when we produced the kingdom's finest goods, grew the finest crops, and lived with our enemies kept firmly in hand. Surely you know there are many who say our borders should be expanded; that the margraviates of Brylov and Tavia should be joined, to form a strong and solid southern seat in the kingdom. There are those who say only one such as I can unite them."

"And by 'those' he means himself," Nan spits under her breath.

"Time will tell," he continues, "though my aspirations are great. I make no secret of that. If it becomes necessary to unite us through force, I trust every man and boy here will be prepared not only to defend Tavia on our own soil, but to take up arms in support of our unification."

Distressed whispers scatter through the people like crumbs shaken from a tablecloth.

"You should also know I aim to keep the laws set forth from Elinbruk, and will tolerate no thieves or traitors among us. Nor will I allow any of the old superstitions, the old fabricated spells and magic to spring up under my reign, just as my father before me. Such things were banned by my elders for good reason. Those laws still stand. Elemental spells are pure wicked foolishness, and a danger to any man or woman who would let them pass their lips.

"In keeping with history, and as a demonstration of my commitment to a peaceful and law-abiding territory, let this be a warning to those of you who might endeavor to seek out the old ways."

The trees begin to fret from their position at the edges of the marketplatz. Blood boils in my veins.

"We have among us one accused of such practices. Let it be known that I will not tolerate such flagrant disregard for the law."

Baldrik, the steward, glares at me calculatingly from the duke's side.

What is happening?

I grip Bran's fingers harder, having lost sensation in my own hand.

"Bring me the puppetmaster's apprentice," Laszlo's voice booms across the wide square.

CHAPTER 18

HORRIFIED GASPS ERUPT AROUND ME. BEFORE I CAN TAKE A breath, guards swarm me, their red jackets bleeding across the crowd like gashes. Rough hands pry me away from where I stand, still clutching Bran's hand as if it were a string that could hold me fast.

No, no. This can't be happening.

"Piro!" Bran's little sisters cry. Nan claws at the guards, trying to grab me. Tiffin and Fonso hold her back. Bran pushes his way through the jostling crowd, following as I am dragged to the front, calling my name all the while.

My deepest fears are stripped and laid bare; years of suppressing nightmares of Old Josipa and the burn pile now rise to the surface. I failed my father in keeping our secret; now I'm cursed to be shamed in front of everyone. The trees wail in protest of my ill treatment.

The guards drop me at Laszlo's feet, where he and the

steward can better glower at me from on high. I see a blur of fear and fascination in the faces of the crowd. What I feared most, I have become: no longer one of them.

But how? Was I seen with the old tree woman? Did my father give our secret away during his time in the Keep? How has it come to this?

"If you've seen wooden marionettes afoot, waking and walking as men do," the new Margrave pontificates, pointing a gloved fingertip at my nose, "she is to blame. The puppetmaster's apprentice resurrected the old spells and bewitched the soldiers she made and delivered to me, hoping to harm me and cause dissention. They are enlivened by her charms, and have been set upon the village. It's clear she hopes to exact revenge on any she can for her father's death!"

"No!" I cry. The crowd answers in a wail of boos and hisses, some in fury, some in suspicion.

Bran's face is a picture of devastation; it takes three guards to keep him from flinging himself at me.

"She's just an apprentice!" a voice cries.

"Where's your proof?" the tailor's voice calls out.

"Proof? You want proof? The wooden men ambling about the village, that she and her swindling father made, aren't proof enough for you?"

"We don't believe it!" my makers call.

"I see," says Laszlo, pacing back and forth in front of the podium, hands clasped behind his back. "It does seem unbelievable doesn't it? Figurines of wood, coming to life? Well, in that case, I submit to you further evidence of her sorcery—

a deadly creature made by her own hand!"

With that, he flings an arm up to the clock tower. As if by command, the clock strikes noon and the glockenspiel carousel springs to life, the creak of gears and wheels adding to the cacophony in the square. The bells, though, are silent. *Emmitt never had the chance to fit that final piece.*

The saboteur emerges from the tower, astride a wolf on one of the carousels. Springing from the wolf's back, she descends the tower's stones, nimble as a black spider, gloved claws sliding effortlessly over the stone.

How dare he use her to condemn me! He is the one using magic, not me!

I scream my innocence, but my voice is lost in the terrified cries of the crowd. No one has seen anything like her, awakened and moving. The saboteur slithers down the tower, dropping elegantly on the steps near the Margrave. She crouches with her hands on the stones, a waiting gargoyle. The crowds push back, giving her a wide berth.

She is still under his spell.

I waver, wishing I knew how to rip her from his control and fearing what her sudden appearance means for me. Laszlo holds up his hands to calm the crowd. He whispers a few commands out of the side of his mouth that fall on the wind.

Can they not see? It's all him! Practicing the very thing he's accusing me of.

"Fellow Tavians, do not fear. I have this situation well in hand. I will keep the soldiers, both man and wooden, under my control. For your protection, the puppetmaster's apprentice will be taken away to the Keep. No more will she be allowed to threaten my sovereignty or ensnare our children with her witchery! For I am certain that she spews out evil magic and ancient curses with her paltry puppet stage, all while her listeners remain unaware! Have your children been seen acting strangely after hearing one of her little plays? Taken a fit the next day? I've seen it myself! That is all her doing. She is a public danger!"

"No!" call the voices of my friends against the recoiling crowds.

"Let her go!" Bran yells. "She hasn't done anything!"

Laszlo turns to address him directly.

"Hasn't she though? Did she not make these wooden creatures with her father's help? Did she not deliver them directly to Wolfspire Hall, planting them in our midst, to ensure they would rise up to hurt me and my late father the moment she let loose her vile incantations? I have only narrowly escaped harm myself, thanks to a remedy I found in an old book in the annals of Wolfspire Hall. Alas, such countermeasures were not discovered soon enough to be of benefit to my father, who I suspect died at the hand of one of her unlawful brutes." Laszlo motions to the saboteur and glares at me accusingly.

He aims to lay blame for his father's death on my back?

"No! She's done nothing!" Bran yells again.

"If you are so certain of her innocence, perhaps we should let the apprentice speak in her own defense. Hear from her own lips what menace she's brought upon us all."

The guards force me to stand, where I gaze miserably at the

crushing throng of Tavians. This is how it must have been for Old Josipa. I just know it.

"Tell us, apprentice, how you came to live in Tavia! What is the lineage of your mother? Let us hear about your fraudulent father, a shirker who failed to complete his work and pay his debts. Tell us how the two of you schemed to use these dangerous figures to your advantage, to strike at the margraviate!"

He folds his arms across his chest, looking as if he has all the time in the world, delighting in my agony. The masses fall quiet. All I can do is blink at my feet and grind my jaw. Every fiber of my being wants to tell the tale of my fabricated family origins and declare my innocence. But I cannot speak the truth without betraying Papa. I cannot defend myself. Not like this.

"Surely it's not that difficult to talk of your past? I have it on good authority you learnt your sorcery from your father, a man beloved and trusted by many here. A man who, behind closed doors in his workshop, practiced those old spells which long ago wreaked havoc upon our law-abiding society. Spells that go against the very laws of nature!

"You have a choice here: speak now and tell us the truth, or go to the Keep. Did your father use magic to bring his creations to life? Were you not only his apprentice, but his accomplice?"

I refuse to answer. Laszlo grips my jaw tightly, mashing my cheeks in with his fingers, willing me to speak.

"I am not uncharitable. I'm willing to make concessions for the truth, if you are capable of telling it. I'll have the guards release you now if you'll only answer me honestly. So what shall it be? Your freedom? Or your dark secrets?"

I look around at the blur of faces through my tears, the saboteur still poised and waiting behind me. I wish I knew the words to send her barreling into the duke, to rip the smug conceit from his face.

I will not give the new Margrave nor the gawkers the satisfaction of seeing my splinters. It's better that I resort to my old standby: silence. I will go silently to the burn pile if I must, in honor of my father. I won't betray him by bellowing the truth. He gave up his strength and life to make me; this last stand of silence is all I can do to protect his good name.

The crowd hushes, waiting, while the makers look on, urging to me to speak up. But I cannot. I tear my face from the duke's pincer grasp.

Laszlo sighs, looking pained on my behalf. "I am afraid you must accept the consequences of your father's actions, and your own folly. It's necessary to protect the people. Take her away."

"No!" Bran screams, this time having broken free from the guards, running up to Lazlo, kneeling below us on the steps. "No! Her father *did* practice the old magic, I saw him. Why, I overheard it myself, one day in his workshop."

I look at him, horrified.

"Pirouette is innocent, she was just his apprentice. She didn't know what he was doing; how could she? It was all her father's doing. And he's gone now. She has done nothing wrong! Please, let her go!"

My heart snaps in two, split by a stroke of lightning, hot and searing. Laszlo looks triumphant. The crowd murmurs and rustles, the trees at the edges of the marktplatz reprimand Bran.

"She's clearly not innocent," Laszlo says victoriously. "See how she refuses to speak up, to defend her honor or explain her father. I have no choice but to interpret her silence as guilt. We are fortunate she hasn't taken control of the dark assassin creature, and turned it against more innocents here in retribution. Fear not, good people! I will protect you. I possess the remedy to her dark spells."

With a flick of his wrist and a few more muttered words, the saboteur falls to the ground, lifeless, no magic strings tugging at her. The crowd inflates in awe. Guards come to drag her away, an ungainly rag doll in their arms.

"As long as you serve me and our great territory of Tavia, and shun the dangers that bespelled our forefathers, you will be safe. Take the puppetmaster's apprentice away!"

"No!" Bran yells indignantly. "You said you'd set her free if the truth was told! Let her go!"

Baldrik grips me under the armpits, hauling me toward a waiting wagon. Low in my ear he croons, "We had our suspicions about you, little wench, after your father's deluded tales spilled in the Keep. But I wasn't expecting that double-cross from the tailor's boy!" He laughs savagely.

I can't hear Bran's voice above the fearful tumult of the crowd; I only see his mouth as they pull me away, performing an agonized litany.

"I'm sorry! I'm sorry!"

As if those were magic words that could ease my pain or stop what is to come.

Strangely, all I can think of as I am carried in through the Commoner's entrance at Wolfspire Hall are the new Margrave's hands. Those marble-white hands caressing the saboteur's cheek when I first delivered her, the fine bones fanning protectively across the marionette's face. I'd never seen their like before, pale and smooth, devoid of hair or calluses. Hands that knew no labor, hands that had never seen dirt. Hands that would be like ice to touch. Hands that convicted me and controlled the saboteur with equal power.

I expect to be taken straight to the Keep, but instead I am shuffled along by Baldrik and delivered deep inside the estate. Fear and curiosity wrestle in my chest like a pair of writhing vipers.

Why weren't they shutting me in a cell? How could Bran have betrayed me? Betrayed Papa? His lies were intended to save me, but they only placed me in greater danger.

We reach the landing where the floors bleed from stone to lush carpet; my feet scuffle as I endeavor to keep up with Baldrik's loping gait. We pass the doors of the great stateroom and continue down another ornate hall whose walls drip with ancestral portraits and cloying paintings of fruit in bowls. Every open door I pass reveals more opulence: fat, overstuffed sofas and chaises trimmed in velvet and golden braid, followed by entire rooms tiled in marble just for bathing.

At a turn in the hallway, I'm startled by a row of my father's wooden men lining the hall, the life-sized soldiers propped up against the tapestried walls like fence posts in between mounted suits of armor. These particular soldiers are all clean, looking just as new as when we delivered them. Cold unrolls itself across my scalp at the sight.

They haven't been used yet, not like the ones I saw in the wood.

We stop short at a set of doors painted a deep, glossy black, across which are inscribed two words in gold I don't recognize: LECTORI SALUTEM.

The steward knocks on my behalf and a voice calls from within. "Enter!"

I stiffen at being shoved inside. The door closes soundly behind me. I find myself in a large room paneled by book-shelves that overflow with books. It's dim, lit entirely by daylight streaming from floor-to-ceiling windows overlooking a courtyard.

Avoiding fire, I muse. The slightest drip of hot wax or tip of an oil lamp could cause the whole room to go up in flames. Thousands of books of varying thicknesses and colors are stacked to the ceiling like pieces of scrap wood back at Curio.

I step farther inside, my eyes drawn to an open book illustrating the full phases of the moon, beautiful ring-shaped sketches marking the phases of waxing and waning.

"One never knows what mysteries and treasures one will find in a book," a voice says from a shadowed corner. Laszlo von Eidle, the man who just condemned me, emerges from beneath a ladder with a thick stack of books cradled in his arms. In here, he looks almost benign; far less threatening than he did an hour ago, raking me across the coals from the front steps of the rathaus.

"*Lectori salutem*, Pirouette Leiter."

"What does that mean?" I ask flatly. He's ruined my reputation in front of the whole village; I am in no mood to bow and scrape.

Laszlo drops the heavy stack of books with a thud on the round wooden table at the center of room. It's strewn with papers, writing utensils, measuring instruments, and a hoard of books open and layered one upon the other.

"Greetings to the reader,'" he says matter-of-factly. "The old masters used that term to greet their pupils when they entered training."

"What if they couldn't read?"

"Can't you read?" Laszlo asks incredulously.

"Of course I can read," I say indignantly. "But surely not everyone can. Sounds presumptuous."

"Then I assume you'd hear the master deliver a different greeting. Perhaps *nil volentibus arduum*, in your case."

"What's that supposed to—"

"It means 'nothing is impossible for the willing.'" A pale eyebrow arches sharply over glittering eyes. Their color reminds me of a watery blue paint we keep in stock at Curio.

I stare at him coldly. "Speaking as someone who is here against her will, I wouldn't know what that's like."

Laszlo smiles. "Yes, well. I have high hopes for you. The proclamation you just witnessed was only the first step in my plan. Your complete humiliation was necessary, I'm afraid."

"Necessary! How dare you blame me for how you're using the wooden soldiers. And the saboteur! We made them at your request! And to suggest that I used them to kill the Margrave! And the clockmaker," I rage, dropping my voice low, "is another matter entirely. He didn't even want your bloody position, wouldn't think of it. He wanted nothing from you or the Margrave, though we all know who was more deserving. Yet you destroyed him anyways, using one of my marionettes!"

"One of *my* marionettes. And you may address me as your Margrave now, apprentice," he says icily. "The clockmaker's death was necessary, I'm sure you understand. Though he may not have had any designs on ruling Tavia, I had to be sure. Death is truly the only method of being sure. I've waited long enough for my father to die, I wasn't about to waste any more time wondering about his other filthy progeny."

"Why would you accuse me like that, in front of the whole village?" I continue railing. "I did not animate the saboteur or the soldiers, I did not send them under the cover of night to harm or frighten people."

"Because I am in need of a maker—you, in fact. I had to make an example of you. It's far better for me if you are reviled and feared by the common folk. Your creations will hold much more power in their eyes when I put them to work."

I stare at him aghast. "You need a puppetmaster? At a time like this?"

"I do," he says, dropping to a stuffed chair at the table, ready to conduct business.

"But, you already have so many . . . marionettes." I stumble on the word. "What could you possibly need another for? Especially now? You've raised taxes until the people hardly have anything left to give, let alone eat. You've been buying up most of their food! It's monstrous!"

His lips press together, the pale pink leaching from them. I've disappointed him.

"I've brought you here today, Pirouette, instead of straight to a cell or a burning heap like you deserve, because you are a puppetmaster, quite possibly the best our lands have ever seen. Now, your father *was* excellent." Laszlo moves smoothly past my bristling at the mention of my father in past tense, "But there's something to your work—a realness to your figurines—I've never seen before. That saboteur is outstanding. And I am, as you noted, a connoisseur, a curator, of marionettes and figurines."

The surge of pride his praise evokes burns my throat like solvent. He rises and comes around the table, his fingers grazing the moon book as he walks closer. In his eyes, I read a dangerous mixture: greed and desire.

"Now I need something more; something real."

I edge back toward the door. Even with nary a flame to be seen, the library feels hot and close, void of air.

"I want *someone*, to be precise. And if you'd like to live, you are going to make her for me."

CHAPTER 19

"**Y**OU WILL MAKE ME A BRIDE. A WIFE."

My mouth hangs open. He's completely unhinged. Off his anvil, as Tiffin would say.

"Um . . . " I clear my throat, scrambling for some semblance of sanity. "My lord, you are aware that I am just a puppetmaster's apprentice. Surely I cannot create an actual wife for you—"

"Oh, but I think we both know that you can," he says with a cold smile. "You created the saboteur, and she has far exceeded any of my wishes. Not a bad beginning. Not bad at all." His blinding mouth is all teeth.

"But even if I created such a marionette, you do understand that she would not be . . . real? Alive?" I say, grasping for words to explain reality to him. "Surely you cannot marry a marionette!" My mind spins. The same nausea that overtook me upon discovering the dead soldier in the woods begins to rise in my throat.

His eyes shift to a cloudy gray. "No, surely not." He steps even closer, too close, one hand reaching out to trace my cheek. The marble touch I imagined earlier is not far from the truth. A chill snakes its way across my shoulders as he cups my chin and tilts it, examining my face, this time far more calculating than his performance for the crowd. My whole body goes rigid; I gnaw at the inside of my cheek.

"But then, I don't intend to marry a marionette. You are an excellent example of what I intend, aren't you? You're extraordinary, Pirouette. The craftsmanship . . . it's truly astonishing."

My lungs tighten like corset strings.

"Now, naturally I will want something with more exquisite features, more of an elegant beauty, you understand. And," he looks critically down at my slim chest and narrow hips, "more of a womanly figure to suit my royal personage." He claps his hands together, as if the matter is all settled. "We'll work the details out as we go—I've been preparing sketches."

My tongue seems coated with iron from Tiffin's forge. *How does he know?*

"What do you mean, my lord? That *I* am an example of what you intend?"

"Besides what your friend out there confirmed for me, I had your father here for a little visit to the library recently, while he was staying in the Keep." Blood floods my face. "He wasn't entirely . . . sober, shall we say. Poor man was definitely suffering from some malady, but I brought him up to probe him a bit about his work. To learn from him. It isn't every day you have a great puppetmaster staying in your house.

I intended to take advantage of it."

My anger flares to hear of my father's "stay" in that vile dungeon talked of as it were a cordial visit for tea.

"While he wasn't lucid, he really was very descriptive, you might say, about his techniques and his most special projects. I've always been fascinated with figurines, you see, and the process of making them. I have quite a few books here," he says with a sweep of his hand, "that detail the history and lore of puppetry. It's as old as humankind. But there are some gaps. Some things I didn't know. I needed your father to enlighten me."

"And . . . did he?" I whisper, fearful of the answer.

Laszlo picks up one of my arms, scrutinizing the joints at my elbow and wrist, bending them this way and that, inspecting the delicate skin between my fingers. A memory flashes at me, from when I was newly made: a boy toying with a dead sparrow in the gutter. It petrified me then, seeing the soft, vulnerable under feathers of the tiny wing spread out and contracted over and over again, for sport.

"He told me one very interesting tale in particular, a tale some might consider too fantastical to be true. But I, unlike some, have spent the last twenty years honing my ears." His eyes lock on my own. "When you are a duke who isn't allowed to do much more than sit in the shadows and appear ornamental—a result of my previous constitution, which I assure you is now quite sound—you find ways to pass the time. Me? I've made a habit of listening."

I wrench my arm from his grasp. He still hasn't answered my question.

"What did he tell you?"

"That his prized possession was a child, a daughter made by his own two hands from the very woods surrounding Tavia. That one night, nearly seven years ago, the light of the blue moon brought her to life."

"My father was very ill, my lord. The pressure of keeping up with the Margrave's unreasonable deadlines and the filth he contracted in your Keep destroyed him. You would be foolish to trust whatever he might have rambled in such a state." I lift my chin in defiance.

"Perhaps. But I am not just any fool," he says smugly. "Though, according to the records, you could be, couldn't you, Pirouette Leiter? Look here," he says, reaching for a bound stack of papers from the desk, labeled with the year I came to be with Gephardt. "See," he points with a flourish to a scripted entry that he ruffles in my face, "it's as if you magically appear to exist in the village census. You truly are a girl who came from nothing. One year poor Gephardt is alone and widowed, then suddenly, out of the blue, he has an eleven-year-old daughter and the two of them are thick as thieves. Back at the rathaus, I was only attempting to bring the truth to light. I'm sure most people have wondered about you and Gephardt for ages!"

"I lived—" I begin to spout the lie about my grandmother and stop short.

"With an elderly grandmother, is that right? Yes, I see that recorded here, too. What was her name, Pirouette? Did you have a lovely childhood, growing up in the bucolic village of . . .

what was it called again? This entry just lists the location as 'far away.'"

Anger and fear vibrate through my body. "You know nothing about me!"

"I know more than enough," he says confidently, dropping the stack of census records and picking up the thick book of moon phases. He thrusts it into my hands. "And the tailor's boy confirmed the rest." He grins, pouring salt into the wound of Bran's betrayal. "Now, I need a wife, Pirouette, a duchess built like a royal princess; a Margravina befitting the Margrave I am now." He stands tall, tugging at the lapels of his jacket. "Hopefully, soon I will rule all of Brylov and Tavia, if the stars align. So she must be magnificent.

"I need her built and ready by the blue moon, to take advantage of its power. I'm not waiting another seven years. And it is coming soon, but you're already aware of that, I wager. How lucky for you to get to experience the awakening power of two blue moons in your lifetime. I'm almost jealous," he purrs. "I'm quite sure it will be one of the most exquisite things I'll ever experience."

He talks about the blue moon's power as if it will be a grand spectacle, a show to be put on for his pleasure.

"I can't possibly . . . do you understand what you're asking of me? Surely there's some great lady of Elmslip or Kirkeglenn who would be overjoyed to wed the new Margrave of Tavia?" I stammer, though in the moment I can't name one. "A political or military alliance that would be of great benefit to you? A real noblewoman, someone of proper . . . stature?"

His eyes roll upwards, as if begging the heavens for patience to accommodate my slow mind.

"I will marry a real woman, Pirouette. But I don't want just any woman, born and bred in the common way. You'll find I don't much care for common things," he says darkly.

"I daresay you were born in the common way."

A vein the color of his eyes pulses at his temple. Stepping closer, he wags a pale finger in my face. "Watch your tongue, apprentice. If you refuse, I will resort to whatever measures necessary to render from you what I desire." He turns away from me, pacing with his hands behind his back. "After that display at the proclamation today, it's probable you are already losing the few allies you had left—your precious makers. That tailor's boy especially seems to have turned on you and your father. How tragic." He rolls his eyes, stopping in front of me.

"Who knows, I may decide to burn you alive after all, at our next fall festival. What a show of force that would be! Then you can return to ash and smoke, to the nothing you came from. Or perhaps I'll have my saboteur crush the life from your throat first," he jeers.

Any curiosity about why he called me here has long vanished and is replaced by a feeling I recognize as hatred. It's not a sensation I've had much experience with, but the young Margrave is proving an apt teacher.

"And how am I to make a real bride for you, my lord?" I ask bitingly.

Laszlo whips around with a delighted grin. "Come, my apprentice. Come and see."

"Do you like it?" Laszlo asks, the wobble in his voice betraying a hint of apprehension.

He has dragged me from the library to a room at the end of another lengthy hallway. Wolfspire's main estate is built like a rabbit's warren of tunnels and stairwells and halls; I wonder how anyone finds their way around. Proudly pushing open a set of doors with both hands, he unveiled a gallery unlike any I've ever seen. Light tinted amber and gold streams in through the high windows, painting the room like stained glass. Laszlo enters with a holy air, his posture reminding me of a priest coming to the altar for worship.

Dozens upon dozens of marionettes hang from the walls on custom-built pegs and hooks. Some are tucked into their own small creches. Unlike Curio, these marionettes don't seem meant for play or use, these are for display—a whole museum's worth of characters in arrested motion. The air in this strange chapel is hollow; sterile. Laszlo's fingers skim the dangling bodies, setting them swinging like windchimes. My head spins around. Most are pieces I've never seen before, their craftsmanship more amateurish and crude than I'm used to.

But some—I blink in surprise at faces I've long forgotten. There's a wood nymph the size of a man's arm, wearing a tunic of green leaves and sporting long, forked fingers, who reminds me of the old tree woman. It's surely one of my father's, and the resemblance to the woman, now that I've seen her for myself, is unmistakable.

I reach out to poke the stuffed belly of a dangling circus clown with a rotund, jeering face.

"Ah, ah, ah," Laszlo warns. "Don't touch, unless I say so. Some of these are priceless. Irreplaceable. No one is to touch them unless I give the word. Not even my puppetmaster."

I pull my hand back. In between the ones I recognize are marionettes carved from every color and type of wood, some painted, some plain, with only their natural grain to lend them any features. The marionettes seem voiceless here, afraid to speak. My fingers itch to lift some of them from their hooks, to shake out their strings and set them free.

"Well?" he asks expectantly.

"It's . . . certainly the largest collection I've seen outside Curio," I mumble, desperately trying to say something true.

Laszlo's chest puffs. "Of course it is. The largest in all the territories." He clears his throat in pride, a rough sound that nearly erupts into a cough. "I've been collecting since I was a boy. My father gave them to me, in place of real companions, since he feared contact with lesser-born children might taint or sicken me like it did Mother. And this is only the half of it, my most favorite pieces. Here," he says, plucking a marionette of a small boy from the wall. He thrusts the crossbar control at me, this time forcing me to take it. I lift the puppet up to the light.

The face looks familiar. Too familiar.

"My father had it commissioned in my likeness when I was a child. Gephardt Leiter did it, no doubt."

I brush my fingers against the legs of the wooden figurine, taking in the delicate features, the pale hue my father brushed on the skin, the overlarge and imploring eyes set into the small face that fits in my hands. An unusual series of deep, scarring marks span the legs and back of the puppet. The puppet's face is unmarked, but terrible gouges and scrapes and chipped bits are visible on the back, arms and legs. This puppet seems like it was close to being destroyed—more than once. One leg hangs crookedly from the knee, the foot warped below it. An arm dangles by mere thread.

Laszlo notices me examining the damage and his jaw tightens again. He snatches the puppet back. "Yes, well. When I misbehaved, Father would have the puppet punished in my stead. A whipping boy, of sorts. One can't very well whip the Duke of Tavia." He sniffs. "Apparently I was a very trying child."

Laszlo's puppet-counterpart makes me feel sad. The real Laszlo, though, has an inspired ability to make me remember my anger.

"Why show me all of this?"

He returns the little wooden duke to his hooks, where he stares at me, a pendulous portrait of pain.

"This gallery will be your workshop. I've had a worktable laid out for you with some tools. You'll have space to build here. And you'll have plenty of company, see?" He points to a dark corner on the far side of the room. Tiffin's rack is tucked into the shadows, and from it hangs the saboteur, returned from her spectacle in front of the village. She appears lifeless, but I know what she's capable of under Laszlo's spell.

"I am to build you a marionette . . . here? I can't possibly! I need Curio, my own tools and pigments," I sputter. "And you still haven't answered my question. Even if I build you a beautiful woman of wood, how is she to become real?"

He gestures to a pair of glass doors on the far side of the gallery, unlocks them and flings them open. Warm air rushes in. He nods for me to follow and I do, reluctantly, my sense of unease growing with every step. We emerge in a steamy, elegant courtyard studded with plants greedily drinking in daylight from the foggy, glass-paned roof sitting above us like a domed lid on one of Nan's pots.

"This is the botanical conservatory. Here I will have uninhibited exposure to the light of the blue moon. Perhaps the glass may even magnify its effects—one can only hope. I've done much study on astronomy and the powers of magnification. We will bring her out here for the awakening. I take it there is a set of words, an incantation?" He takes in the raise of my eyebrows. "Yes, well, your father didn't go into specifics on that part. But I gather you know enough of what must be said and what to do so that I will be able to awaken my bride and welcome her to my side."

"This is madness," I dare to breathe out.

Remembering the tree woman's words, I know it's also a chance to release me from my curse. A wild, terrifying chance. *Could it work?*

"One man's madness is another man's magic. *Nil volentibus arduum*," he says in a low voice. "Nothing is impossible for the willing, is it, apprentice? I deserve someone made just for me, a true companion."

I fold my arms across my chest, rocking back and forth uneasily on my feet. My mind cannot wrap itself around the fact that I am in the heart of Wolfspire Hall contemplating such a feat.

"You will begin right away," the duke insists.

I stare at him, balking at the task set before me. The trees in the conservatory cluck like mother hens; I can tell they don't approve.

Fearing I am stuck, I look to strike a bargain. Every good maker knows you haggle before settling on a price.

"Before I can do this, can even *attempt* the task you ask of me, I require a few things."

"Require?" he says testily.

"First, you must tell me how you animated the saboteur and the wooden soldiers."

"First? Is this to be a long list?" he says indignantly.

"Why? How did you do it?" I demand.

He sighs, his patience with me running low. "I needed additional troops in reserve to take on Brylov's men, if that becomes necessary. I also needed a skilled assassin for some special circumstances, as you're now aware. My father has been trying for years to build an alliance with his sister in Brylov, but alas, my dear old Tante Emmaline was never cooperative. She always hated my father.

"So, I needed something to help hasten her end. Something, or *someone*, I should say, who would go undetected by her guards. Poison was always my father's preferred weapon of choice and that at least started the process, gave the saboteur something to administer on her errand across the border. The wooden soldiers were sent to make a show of force, to frighten and confuse the people in her wake. I've just had word the Margravina hangs on by a thread, though not for long."

"But how did you do it?" I ask, as we return to the gallery.

He grins. "For years I have been collecting marionettes, studying their origins. Though I suppose it all really came together when I made a tour to Elinbruk last year. I hadn't been since I was a child. Have you ever been? No? You really should go. It's spectacular in the spring.

"Well," he continues lightly, enjoying watching me squirm, "while my father was busy nosing about for a duchess to woo on my behalf, I found something far more useful in the old royal Bibliothek. I'd heard rumors of it, from my studies, but I honestly wasn't even sure it existed."

"What existed?"

"Hearth tales are never a reliable source of magic legacy; too many tellings and retellings by uneducated fools to be trusted. Full of half-truths and all sorts of moral nonsense, the blathering of old women, best suited for children in breeches. But," he says, absentmindedly straightening the cap of a wizard hanging nearby, "some of the old masters *did* write things down that my great-great-grandfather never got around to burning. Their spells, their poisons, their histories. I've just never had access to them. Father always kept me penned up here, having to rely on what my tutors brought me. It was buried deep in the Bibliothek, hidden inside an old text about trees and the properties of wood. I guarantee you the cleric that brought it to me thought little of it. 'Archaic gibberish,' I believe he called it.

"I wish now that I'd taken the whole book! If I'd only had more time . . . " He sighs. "As it was, I could only take a page with me, but the cleric was never the wiser. Then it was simply a matter of convincing my father to commission the wooden soldiers, speaking the right words over them and then pointing them in the right direction. The directive to kill or maim means nothing to the marionettes; they have no moral objections. With very little effort, they were able to greatly aid my cause.

"I've been waiting for many years for my chance to rule, to not have to sit in a corner and watch a fool give all the orders any longer. He was many things, my father, but a visionary was not one of them. He never appreciated art the way I do," he says, looking fondly at his collection. "He never understood my interest in puppets, never saw their full potential as I do. Now they are proving themselves far more loyal and capable than my human servants."

His eyes glow. I wonder if he envisions a whole estate filled with wooden creatures to do his bidding, serving him without question or reservation. I shudder at the thought.

"But the soldiers, they are not alive. Just . . . set in motion?" I prod, thinking of how the saboteur seemed to listen to me, to respond.

"The only magic I know of to give a wooden figure a fully

human life is the blue moon enchantment your father spoke of. And that I have never found in a book . . . though I've searched. *Believe me.* But until your father told me your whole tale, a puppet turning to living flesh was something I only dreamed possible. I never imagined when I first watched your little show in the square weeks ago that I was watching the work of a creature who represented my grandest notions. I was there just observing the masses, studying them in preparation for my plan to become the Margrave sooner than Father intended. The people were so taken in by it all, eating up your stories like they were starved.

"I must thank you for that, for it was your dramatics that inspired me to request the saboteur in the first place. I was planning to poison my aunt and Father the old-fashioned way, you know, by hand. But after seeing your theatricality, suddenly using a puppet seemed far more elegant."

I blanch, feeling sick. *He used the saboteur not only to poison the Margravina of Brylov and mortally wound Emmitt and the soldier in the wood, but to kill his own father. The count keeps rising.*

"What will happen to the masses, to the people of Tavia if I am to make this bride for you? Surely there is a better way to force a union between us and Brylov than a battle."

I think of the Maker's Guild and all the village people who will suffer if we are forced into a war.

"I am loathe to discuss politics, especially with a maker. It's so dreary."

"Concerned the terms are too difficult for a commoner such as myself, *my lord?*" I ask in a huff. My attitude is well beyond the bounds of propriety, but I have ceased caring. It's this or the Keep, and all his efforts tell me the new Margrave needs my skills here.

He glares at me. "You are making my point. But, if you must know, with Tante Emmaline nearly sleeping on death's pillow, I've already sent a dispensation to Elinbruk to petition the king to allow me to rule both territories. I'm sure he will agree; Tante Emmaline has no children, and I am my father's only heir. A von Eidle has held the territories in the southern seat for generations. It seems only right that I join both of our lands together. Together, the south will be even stronger."

And your own pockets far fuller, I think.

"And if Brylov resists?" I ask. "Or the king disagrees?"

"He won't. My father was one of his favorites. But, in that rare case," he says, "I not only have my own regiments whose ranks are bolstered by my new wooden soldiers, but I also have a whole village of common men to call up at my command. If we must go to war to unite the territories, we will."

He brightens. "And won't the citizens of Brylov and Tavia be delighted to attend the wedding of their new Margrave? People will be so tired of death and squabbling by then. Think of it, the feasting and dancing! Such a celebration will surely unite us all!"

I nod grimly, letting him think I am in agreement with his preposterous plan. If we actually make it to a wedding, I'll be the first to dance a jig at the feast—if I'm not strung up by my neck.

"Is there anything else, apprentice, to add to your odious list of requirements? You should know that ordinarily I would not brook such demands from a maker. I am the one who gives the orders here."

"If I am to build for you anything remotely resembling a princess," I quickly begin thinking out loud, "then I shall need the best materials."

"Naturally."

"I must return to the woods to secure the right pieces. And to Curio to select the tools I will need. What you have here is . . . adequate," I gesture to the tools that have been laid out for me in the gallery, "but they are not my own. A maker can't be expected to work with tools they are not comfortable with."

Laszlo grimaces. "Fine. But you will be shackled and accompanied by my steward and return here later tonight. You will sleep here and stay here, so that I may keep an eye on your progress. We haven't much time. The blue moon is less than a month away, and I want her to be perfect. Can you really do it, Pirouette Leiter?" he asks, clasping his hands. The marbled knuckles turn purple where he presses his fingertips in between their ridges. His eyes remind me of the puppet in his own likeness hanging behind him: far too earnest. "Can you make me a princess? A Margravina to put all others to shame?"

If I don't answer honestly, I'll be explaining splinters to him. I'm not eager to give the new Margrave anything else to hold over my head.

"Yes. I can." I sigh.

Cursed if I do, cursed if I don't. I don't wish to, but I will make him a princess marionette unlike any he's ever dreamed of.

"Though if she is to live—that, my lord, I have no control

over. I've never attempted what you speak of . . . an awakening."

"Leave it to me to arrange the perfect conditions," he says confidently. "If you know the spell, it can't be that difficult, no more than a few magic words spoken in moonlight. After all, your father, a mere maker, did it. And look at you now!"

Yes, I think, my stomach turning sour, as I am ushered out and turned over to a waiting guard. *Look at me now.*

CHAPTER 20

J UST OUTSIDE THE ENTRANCE TO CURIO, THE STEWARD WAITS impatiently, having sent another guard round back to make sure I don't escape. I hurry inside to find most of my makers cloistered in the workshop, looking miserable—Bran, especially. I cannot bring myself to meet his eyes.

"Piro!" Nan throws her arms around me. "Where did they take you? What have you been sentenced with? Are you free to go? Surely this is all a terrible mistake!"

"Don't believe a word of it, Piro," groused Fonso. "He's a barmy liar! None of this is your doing. He's just using you!"

"A fool always looks for an easy mark," Tiffin growls, clapping me on the shoulder. "I'm so sorry he chose you."

Bran stares at me helplessly.

"I'll be all right. But I must make a special order for the duke—er, the new Margrave. I'm just here to get my things and am ordered to return to Wolfspire Hall. I'll be staying there now," I say stiffly, motioning to the broad back of Baldrik keeping watch at the door.

"Staying there?" Bran repeats dismally.

"What was it like, Piro?" Tiffin asks. "Did you see the weapons Mort and I have been making? Is everything in the living quarters covered in gold? Have you seen the kitchens? I've heard they're storing all the bread a hundred loaves deep in straw, piled to the ceiling!"

Fonso knocks him in the chest with a thump of his hand. "Is food the only thing on your mind at a time like this, you lanky duffer? Piro's just been given a terrible sentence by the new Margrave, folks are scared witless about a possible skirmish with Brylov, and you're thinking about bread."

"I'm blasted hungry," Tiff mutters, "and I've never been inside Wolfspire Hall. If I'm going to die in service of the Margrave, I'd like to know how the other side lives before I go."

"None of you are going to die in service to our Margrave or his offal," Nan growls. "Not if I have anything to say about it."

"It seems like nothing we say makes any difference at this point," Fonso offers glumly.

Nan utters a blaze of furious oaths in the direction of his despondency.

"Well done, lover boy," Tiffin rolls his eyes.

"What can we do, Piro? What do you need?" Nan says. "Can Fonso hide you in the theater wagon and spirit you away from here? Anything to keep you from the Keep?"

"There's nothing you can do for me. What's done is done. Help me pack. *Just you*," I say shoving wordlessly past Bran.

Nan follows close behind.

In the workshop, I fill an old trunk with necessary tools and paint to take back to Wolfspire Hall. I can't help but think of my father as I layer in our best chisels and calipers and spokeshaves.

What would he say if he were here now? What would he do?

My stomach sinks, imagining he might quietly go along with Laszlo's orders, making whatever the man desired simply because we could use the money. Francs have no allure for me now. I don't even know if I will be paid for what I am about to do. We never even discussed it. Right now, I don't have the luxury of considering anything but saving my own neck.

Wedged like a shim between Laszlo's orders and fear of losing the life I have left, I recall my father's words, uttered when a board broke or a marionette's delicate joint vexed him: "A maker will always prevail."

That's the only way to make it out of this alive. I tighten my fingers around the comforting weight of a hammer, the handle silky from years of use. *Find a way through.* The hammer falls into the trunk, ringing like a bell against its fellows.

Next, I will head to the wood to claim the right trees for Laszlo's princess. I don't know when I'll return to Curio again, if ever. After I pack, Nan leaves me to walk briskly from room to room in our tiny home upstairs, hesitating at the doorway of my father's bedroom where he took his final breaths. I run my fingers over the cracked and fading wallpaper, look through each window to savor the view of the village and the wood in the distance. I miss my father very much. I'd love nothing more than to tiptoe out and see him waiting in his chair by the kitchen fire, glad to see me. He was always glad to see me.

Bran finds me upstairs in the kitchen, after everyone else has said their goodbyes. Baldrik lurks below, stomping about grumpily. I turn my back to Bran, to get one last glimpse of the world outside this window.

"I did it save you, Piro! He said he would let you go if he had the truth. I thought pointing him toward your father would distract him, give him enough to keep him satisfied. I hoped it would set you free. Gep would have wanted it, would have been willing to do anything to save you. I had to! You didn't say a word. We all know you're innocent!"

"I *couldn't* say anything!"

"I know. And I was a fool. I'm sorry." His voice breaks. "I'm so sorry."

I shake my head, still unable to meet his gaze.

"I asked for one thing when I told you about my past, Bran. One thing, in exchange for revealing the truth. And you couldn't give me that one thing?" I let loose a sob. "I thought I meant more to you than that. I thought you *understood*. You knew what could happen! And you threw all the blame on my father, cast his reputation and good name out like it was slop for swine! I was protecting him!"

"You do, Piro," he pleads, taking a few steps closer. "You mean everything to me! I went mad, couldn't stand to see you bound like that, paraded in front of everyone. I said the only thing I could think of to spare you!"

My heart is a battleground, wanting him to come all the

way over here, to hold me and slay the dread overtaking me.

"Please, forgive me." Bran puts a tentative hand on my shoulder.

I stiffen and shrug it off. For now, I must draw the circle tighter around myself. Bran can't be fully trusted.

I experience a sudden pang of shame, remembering Laszlo's chilling examination of my hands and limbs, as if I was something he'd love to tear apart and understand, something to be studied for his own purposes. My scalp crawls. No one else understands what it's like to be in my skin, and they never will.

"He only knows what he wants to know, Piro," Bran insists, practically reading my mind. "Men like him only see what they want to see and shut their eyes to the rest." He falls quiet a moment. "You must protect yourself. Let him think he knows who and what you are. Let him underestimate you."

"And what am I?" I whisper sharply, needing to hear his answer.

"You, Pirouette Leiter, are *beyond*. Beyond brave, beyond good, beyond real. Your hands make magic with wood that mine can only hope to make with gears and winding wheels. You exist far beyond anything he can see. So let that ill-bred weakling see what he wants, but do what you must to save yourself."

"He wants me to make someone like me," I hiss. "He thinks I can bring another marionette to life by the light of the blue moon. How can I? I don't have any magic of my own, despite what you might think."

"You'll have the blue moon, won't you?" he offers

hopefully. "Perhaps that will be magic enough. A girl like you and the blue moon. What can't you do?"

Whirling around, I march past him, pocketing the extra key to Curio hidden on the kitchen mantel.

"Thanks to you, I'm about to find out."

Chapter 21

WHERE TO BEGIN? I WONDER, LEANING BACK AGAINST THE long worktable in the gallery room adjoining the botanical conservatory. I was escorted back to this same room with my supplies as soon as I returned to Wolfspire Hall, and this time I was locked in. I've been given a closet at the far end of the gallery for myself, a tiny walk-in outfitted with a single bed, rickety old chair, and cracked washbasin.

I am informed by the disgruntled steward that he is leaving to go to Brylov with a regiment of men for surveillance, but that a guard will be posted outside at all hours. Laszlo himself will inspect my work daily until he is satisfied. "See to it that you obey the Margrave, little drudge. We can exchange your living quarters for something more simple in the Keep without any skin off our back. Your father's cell is still empty and waiting." He leers.

Until the blue moon's rising, I will remain here, breathing

the dust of a dream Laszlo has been long waiting to animate.

Morning light stretches itself through the windows facing the conservatory courtyard.

Though I just barely convinced the Margrave and his guards a moment ago that I would only be able to begin my work on his princess marionette *alone*, in here I feel anything but. Laszlo's prized marionettes hover all around me. In the quiet I can't help but study their faces and forms, taking in the many eyes that center on me or longingly search the air, dreaming of a handler to materialize and save them from their hooks. Rebelling against Laszlo's orders, I walk around and touch each one, feeling the weight of a leg here, the length of a creature's tail there. Who knew what Laszlo saw in each to prize it among his favorites?

I stop before the saboteur.

Whatever magic he summoned to send her on her deadly missions is snuffed out. She rests limply in the cage, though I swear when I graze her arm, admiring my own handiwork, I feel a pulse flutter, a quickening within her wooden frame.

"Will we ever be free from here?" I whisper.

A hollow sound threads up my fingers, the barest strand of a voice. "Find courage, and you will find your freedom."

Courage. Freedom. Let's hope I live long enough to once again be in possession of both.

Laszlo reviewed all of his sketches with me first thing this morning; there are detailed descriptions of what he envisions his bride looking like, complete with measurements. From the stack of them, he's been working on them for quite some time. I envision him in his library, sketching away at his conception of a perfect woman. The drawings are a boy's fancy, what callow youth imagines a perfect bride to be: a sort of hollow, obedient, too-obvious beauty. I take them politely, tucking them away among my tools and nodding agreeably the whole time he animatedly describes how he desires her chin to curve and how daintily her waist should tuck in. And how she should be free from strings. He doesn't want her mobility facing any impediments. It requires all my fortitude to keep my true thoughts to myself.

At the worktable, I spread out the pieces of raw wood I harvested specifically to build Laszlo's princess. The Margrave's guards hauled them up for me, after following me home from the forest. I am pleased to see the clear flesh shining from beneath the bark I've stripped for her head and torso is so fine it nearly glows. I focus on it a long time, the way I always do when I begin a piece, asking the wood to tell me how to shape it, how much to keep, how much to take away. I must sit with it for a while, become acquainted.

When the lines of a woman's face emerge along the creamy grain of the halsa, I pick up my chisel. It is time. The blue moon waits for no one.

The days meld one into the other from the moment I make the first notch into the wood. Within five days, I have a rough body laid out on the table, and piece by piece I set about shaping

228

her legs and feet, her neck and torso. I begin calling her Prima, naming her after the first puppet my father made for me. There's something about the pattern of this wood that reminds me of her; I hope I can do my father's miniature justice in full scale.

Missing Bran despite everything that's happened, and worried for my makers, I throw myself into the labor of construction. The work reaches a feverish pitch I've never attained before, my hands moving of their own accord in rhythm with my carving knife, hammer, and saw. I try as much as possible to ignore Laszlo when he appears at odd hours to cast an eye to my progress.

I hate being watched while I work. Some days it's as if I have a gnat, an insufferable royal gnat, constantly buzzing about my face, making insidious comments. When he makes a suggestion or offers an observation, I make an admirable effort to hold my tongue, or so I think. At night, when I lie down to rest for a few bleak hours, I worry that I may not make it to the blue moon with my sanity, or my bitten tongue, intact.

The more time I spend in his presence, the more Laszlo reminds me of an overgrown child, not unlike his small puppet. He is a man overseeing an entire territory with a Margrave's part to play, yet he seems to know very little about how the world outside his stone walls works. Having long outgrown his tutors, he seems starved for company beyond his library of books and his collector's gallery. He would never admit this ineptitude and loneliness to me, but I suspect it explains why he hangs about incessantly, inspecting my tools and questioning my process.

That and his need to converse with his marionettes. I've

woken more than once to the sounds of his hushed conversations in the gallery. In lieu of real companions, he seems to have built his own small guild of wooden friends to confide in. I cannot judge him too harshly for this, however, since I too talk to the marionettes more than most.

On the morning of the sixth day, as I'm carving the princess's face, carefully sculpting a high brow with long, subtle strokes, Laszlo drones on beside me about the unique appearance of the light of a gibbous moon. A thought strikes me hard, like the felling of a tree.

"My lord?" I interrupt his prattle.

"What?" he snaps, annoyed I've dared intrude upon his line of thought.

"Isn't it so that I should use only the best materials as I build your princess?"

"Yes, yes, we've already gone over that." He waves his hand, once again appearing to find me inordinately slow-witted.

"Well, as I am about to begin her eyes, I believe no *common* carved eyes will do, not the sort I might create for any other marionette. We should requisition glass eyes for her. They will be exceedingly lifelike and the most exquisite shade of green."

The Margrave did request green eyes; I figure I can concede that small detail to his whims. I love green.

Laszlo straightens up, weighing my words. "Glass? Well, of course," he says, as if I have suggested the most obvious thing in the world. "Much more refined and elegant. Where do you propose we get them?"

"Well, that's the unfortunate part," I say with sigh. "I

fear we shan't have any way to get them, though the finest glassblower in all of Tavia happens to be a friend. With the threat of impending skirmish in Brylov and you raising taxes, I imagine his shop must be closed now and his furnace left to grow cold. It takes a day or so to even get it firing hot enough to blow the glass. I suppose I shall just have to carve her eyes by hand and paint them green. I'm sure it will make no difference when she awakens—"

"No! She must see perfectly. I want only the best for her!" he says emphatically. "Give me the name of that glassblower. I will have him brought in."

"Of course, my lord. Let me write up the requisition for you, so that he might have proper measurements to make for a perfect fit. He will need to be paid, of course, to secure the best materials."

After I dictate Fonso's information to Laszlo and hastily write an order, he rushes from the room to send a messenger after my redheaded giant of a glass smith. A small part of my heart untangles itself, finally able to breathe. I feel triumphant. Even if I only spared Fonso from a week's worth of hunger or lessened his chances of being sent to Brylov to fight, it's worth it.

While I sit smoothing the forehead of Tavia's presumed future Margravina, a plan unfolds itself quietly in front of the two of us.

Why didn't I think of it sooner? Can I help them all and still manage to build a marionette beyond the Margrave's wildest dreams?

I cast a glance at the saboteur. Remembering when she pressed her own hand to mine in the wood, that moment I felt her strength push back against my own, a smile lifts the corners of my mouth.

The old tree woman foretold that the heart of the maker would determine the course of the marionette. I pick up my small planer with renewed vigor and shave more curls from the princess's rough scalp. If I can build into the very fiber of this princess the various strengths of the Maker's Guild—and if she really does wake under the blue moon—she will be a force to be reckoned with. A force the new Margrave will never expect.

I didn't realize what I was doing back then, building the saboteur. I couldn't have fathomed then what kind of powerful being might be wrought from wood, couldn't have imagined how someone might use her for their own desires. And she isn't even alive!

Though I come from the same place as these two grand figures I've labored over, I never considered that I might possess powers of my own. Yet here I stand, an assassin created by my own hand within arm's length and a princess in bloom on my worktable. The saboteur was built with fevered glee, using the wildest stretches of my imagination. To build this marionette, I must tame that wildness and turn it inward—into cunning.

Laszlo may intend to provoke our neighbors to war and force me to do his bidding, but I will wage war in this gallery of my own accord. I come to this battleground armed with the weapons I know best: a rebellious piece of wood and the tools of my trade. I cannot say yet if I believe Prima can be awakened, but if she can, she should be the best of all of us. Exactly the match this Margrave deserves.

CHAPTER 22

ONSO ARRIVES AT WOLFSPIRE HALL FIVE DAYS LATER, just as I am carving Prima's ears. I sense his presence in the hallway before I even hear him enter the locked gallery. With a rush of happiness, I run to him despite the guard hovering at his back. He is wearing a wide smile, clutching a velvet pouch I desperately hope contains the princess's new eyes. Either that, or a slow-acting poison I might slip undetected into the Margrave's tea. After enduring a two-hour soliloquy today from Laszlo on the superiority of navigating sea journeys using constellations—from one who has never stepped a single well-shod foot on a ship—I would be grateful to receive either.

It's all I can do to keep from flinging myself into Fonso's massive arms. Seeing his dear, coppery head again makes me feel connected to home, to all the makers. But with the guard watching, I know it won't do to seem over-familiar with the glassblower. For Laszlo and his guards, Fonso's presence here must be all about the work. They mustn't suspect my plan.

"Fonso Donati, glassblower, here to deliver and set a pair of glass eyes. Have I arrived at the right place?" he says, trying to keep a laugh from his voice, though I see his eyes are pinched at the corners.

"Indeed," I say, pointing with a flourish to where the princess lies in bits and bobs all over the worktable at the center of the gallery. "I am ready to place the eyes, if you'll be so kind as to follow me."

I am bold with the guard, wanting him gone. "We will need complete silence and no distractions to make sure these are installed properly. Please wait in the hall."

"The Margrave ordered me to—"

I summon up an icy stare; my best impression of Laszlo. "Well the Margrave ordered *me* to build him a perfect marionette. If I don't set her eyes properly and she turns out to be a cross-eyed hag, I will know *exactly* who to point him to for that, now won't I?"

The guard rolls his eyes at me and shuts the door all but a crack, positioning his back on the other side of it.

I whirl around to see Fonso caught in the middle of the room, staring wide-eyed at the young Margrave's marionettes. He whistles low and slow.

"I'll be honest, Piro. It's worse than I imagined." He reaches out to touch the boot of an old witch whose black robes dangle nearly to the floor.

"Tell me about it. I love marionettes, but this place is

not Curio." I grip his forearm tightly and pull him to the worktable. "Don't touch anything. Come, sit. While I set the eyes you must tell me what's been happening. I need to know everything, how you and Tiffin are faring, how the Sorens are, what Nan's—"

"Easy Piro, slow down, there. Take a breath. Surely we've got a little time." He drops on a stool that groans beneath his weight, and lays the velvet bag gently on the table.

"Who knows how little, Fonso, if the Margrave has his way. I can scarcely scrape together five minutes of quiet 'round here."

Eagerly, I inch the drawstring of the bag apart and slip a hand inside. Swaddled in cloth, the glass eyes feel as heavy as jewels. I unwrap one and watch as it rolls onto the palm of my hand. The glass is cool and smooth to the touch. The iris is a deep, quenching green, the color of the woods after a hard spring rain.

"Oh, they're spectacular, Fonso! Just what I needed!"

"How are you faring, Piro? It's barbaric that the little duke won't let you go outside."

"Don't let him hear you call him that!" I mutter, drawing my pot of glue and a pipette closer. "At least I can go out in the conservatory. I can see the sun."

"Nanette is fairly raging to see you. She worries over you being cooped up in here."

"You know she worries just as much over you, even if she won't admit it. How are the others?"

It's only been days since I left Bran behind, but already

it feels like another lifetime. His false accusation against my father still plagues me like a thorn, but my heart—that most traitorous of creatures—longs to know how he is.

Using a paintbrush, I gingerly coat the backs of the fragile eyes with a special resin, and use the pipette to create a well of the resin in each of Prima's eye sockets. While Fonso tells me all the latest news, I slowly and meticulously position each eye.

" . . . there were pieces of your wooden soldiers littered about in the streets, Piro. I don't even know enough to say what happened there, but it wasn't pretty, I'll tell you that. Men have been stalkin' about with torches, threatening to burn any wooden soldier that crosses their property, but the wooden ones keep coming just when we think we've gotten them taken care of! They keep peering in folks' windows and threatening them with their swords, which are quite real, even if the buggers are wooden beasts themselves. I think they're meant to keep everyone afraid, to round us up and force us to march on Brylov as soon as the Margrave gives word. But they're frightening the children! I don't know how he's doing it!"

A miserable sigh escapes me. If only my father had known these wooden men were destined to harass and intimidate the village . . . that the Margrave is making a travesty of his life's work. *Of our work.*

"Now he's taken to having his men parse out rations instead of letting folks sell at the market. So people are mostly keeping to the village limits, shut up inside their homes to avoid the soldiers, trying to share food when they have some to spare.

The smart ones are hiding what they get, storing up for the worst if winter comes early. Most are mighty nervous to go about at night, fearing *that thing*"—he points to the saboteur with a leery eye—"will be after them if they do anything the Margrave doesn't approve of. It's bad out there, Piro."

I swallow.

"How *is* he doing it? It's magic, isn't it?" Fonso growls, his voice low. "Spells and such?'

"I don't know exactly," I say truthfully. "I believe he's practicing some spells of his own, and blaming me to cover up his misdeeds."

"You're not to be blamed for anything, Piro," Fonso says solemnly, putting his massive hand gently on my shoulder. "We all know that. There's talk of finding allies in Brylov, of overthrowing the young Margrave and appointing someone of our own choosing, should the King agree."

"Overthrowing?" I whisper. "Is that even possible?" I adjust the position of the right eye just a nudge. Despite what I said to keep the guards away, I won't allow my princess to start life cross-eyed.

"It's possible," Fonso says, eyes gleaming. "The young Margrave is weak, though he's doing his bloody best to hide it. He may have the threat of magic and your saboteur on his side, but he doesn't have the support he needs beyond that. And surely the King would be upset to learn our young master poisoned the royally appointed Margravina of Brylov. The old lady just turned the bucket, heard it myself at The Louse and Flea."

"And will the King learn of that?" I murmur.

"He will if the Maker's Guild proves our worth. The tailor and Anke have some connections in Elinbruk and hope to spread the word. And also, if we have our way, your stay here will not be long."

As his hand drops casually from my shoulder, he deftly slides a small, folded note into the front pocket of my work apron. He does it so subtly, I doubt I would have noticed had it not been right under my nose.

"Truly?" I say in one breath, and then in the other, "It's too dangerous. Don't waste your energy on me. Laszlo would think nothing of pulling you all away from your homes and tossing you into the Keep, or worse, if you're caught plotting against him. I fear he aims to make an example of me."

"We'll see," Fonso says mysteriously.

The note begins to burn where it lies, unopened against my chest.

"What of the others?" I ask.

"All well, mostly just hungry and bone-tired. Tiffin is more of a grouchy lummox than ever—being cooped up in the smithy day and night hasn't improved his mood—but all send you their good wishes. 'Specially Bran."

"Well, if I have *my* way, there will be more work for each of you, hopefully sooner rather than later," I say, giving Fonso a knowing glance at the body of the princess marionette. I can tell from the light in his eyes he understands that I, too, am up to something.

"Fonso, you still have a cousin who works in the kitchens?

A serving lad?"

"Marco Donati, the kitchen porter. The Margrave kept all his personal servants and inherited a few of his father's. Got to keep those noble bellies full and their backs scratched."

"Good. I need you to ask him something for me on your way out, if you can manage it. I would do it myself if Laszlo ever let me out of his sight, but so far I have a guard with me at all times and can't roam."

From a crate on my worktable, I lift out a pouch of thirty gold francs. Hastily, I scoop them up and drop them into the pouch Fonso used to deliver the glass eyes to me and pull the strings tight.

"If anyone asks on your way out, consider this your payment for your services, for our most generous Margrave did leave it for you. I know it's not much. But I have an idea, if you can convince Marco to work with us and think he can be trusted."

Fonso strokes his red-bristled chin. "Does this idea involve breaking into the hoard of food being stored in Wolfspire Hall's rathskeller?"

"It might," I whisper back, "if you are willing. Help yourself to whatever is left in the coffers at Curio. The shop is locked, but Bran knows a way to get in without being seen. Papa would want you to have it.

"Then, on your way out, give this to Marco. It should be more than enough to allay the risk of Marco smuggling out several loaves of bread and vegetables each day from the cellars for you all, and some oats for Burl. The Soren girls are seeing to him.

"Arrange for Nan to stop by the Commoner's entrance each day and have Marco slip the supplies to her with the normal rations, perhaps hidden in one of her large pots—you know, the kind she likes to show off around town by balancing on her head. Tell Marco that, after today, I will leave any additional francs that can be spared for extra food for the makers under a teacup on the tray the guards bring me."

Fonso nods slowly, but whistles again. "Piro, that will buy a goodly amount of bread. Aren't sure you shouldn't hold a little something back for yourself?"

I shake my head. "They feed me, and Laszlo hasn't killed me yet, so that's enough for me for now. But I can't stand to think of Gita and the children or Nan going hungry when I'm sitting several stories above a mountain of food that is surely going to waste. If there's enough to share with the neighbors, they'll know who needs it—"

The door is thrown open suddenly, and Laszlo drops in on us like a hawk circling his prey.

"Well? Can she see?"

Fonso stands, trying to look courtly by sucking in his belly and puffing out his chest.

"See for yourself, my lord," I say, gesturing to the eyes of the princess, set like green gems in her face.

Laszlo leans in close, putting a slender hand on either of her cheeks, which are still rough.

"Yes, those are just as I proposed. Excellent work, erm—"

"Donati," Fonso pipes up. "Alfonso Donati, glass smith."

"You are to be commended for your fine work. I'll have one

of the guards show you out. I'm sure you're eager to get back to your little shop, so we shan't keep you here any longer." He sniffs impatiently. I can tell he doesn't trust Fonso, doesn't like having outsiders in his private sanctuary. He's proud of his collection of marionettes, but smart enough to know most people consider his obsession with them a bit . . . odd.

"I love what you've done with the place, my lord," Fonso says, straight-faced, with a nod to all the marionettes gathering on the walls. "So many toys in here. It's all very *enchanting*."

I bite my lip at Fonso's little dig. Laszlo glowers, his cheeks staining. "Isn't it? I find it very restorative to spend time among my collection. I assume you find it scintillating to be among your fires and furnaces? How quaint. You must prefer the heat."

"Surely don't mind it," Fonso says unflinchingly, and he bows. Just out of the Margrave's view, the glass smith flashes me one last wicked grin. The coins in his purse chink together quietly as he leaves. The sound makes me happy.

If I have my way, we'll be using von Eidle gold to pay for food to feed the very people they stole it from. I pick up a chisel and return to work, ignoring Laszlo, who lingers like a bad smell in the gallery. I can scarcely wipe the smile from my face for the rest of the day.

Later that night, I finally dare to light a candle. Though Laszlo has a deathly fear of fire for the damage it might do to his marionettes, he does allow me a few slow-burning candles behind glass with which to work at night. If I was only able to labor by daylight, I'd have no chance of completing the princess on time.

With a precious candle flickering, I slip the back of my chair under the door handle, barricading myself in my closet. I curl up on the bed to read the note. Unfolding the paper, I instantly recognize the handwriting scrawled in black ink.

Dear P—

When a gift arrives for the Margrave, so will your means of escape. If you can, send word through Fonso's cousin that day. After dark, make your way to the rathskeller so I can meet you. I'll be waiting. Always.

   —B

An escape? A gift? And I have to get past my guards? They are all much larger than me and seem possessed of very little humor or goodwill. Years of working in the old Margrave's employ has long beat that out of any I've encountered. I don't even know their names.

I suck in the first breath of hope I've had in days. *Can I really leave?* I hate to think what might happen if I fail.

I burn the note in the candle's flame and bury the ashes at the feet of one of the gingko trees planted in the conservatory. I huddle against its trunk, watching the stars blink their eyes at me in never-ending astonishment through the glass-domed roof.

I am torn at the prospect of rescue. The thought of leaving

Prima unfinished and abandoning the saboteur carves painful grooves of worry in my soul. I can't leave them behind, pawns for the Margrave to play against Tavia. I'm grateful for the gesture, but my Makers don't understand the real danger I'm in. If I don't stay and complete the spell, I'll miss my best chance to realize the removal of my curse, like the old tree woman said.

Not to mention that leaving before the blue moon's spell is uttered will surely awaken the sleeping dragon of Laszlo's rage. If escaping Wolfspire Hall doesn't kill me, he will gladly finish the job.

CHAPTER 23

"**W**HY ISN'T SHE FINISHED YET?" LASZLO SNAPS, KNEADING the back of his neck with one hand while pacing erratically alongside my worktable.

It is only the fifteenth day of my work in the gallery, and yet it feels like my fifteenth year. The Margrave grows noticeably impatient, and ever more anxious. His appearance is normally impeccable, every stitch perfectly tailored and pressed. But today he wears a jacket deeply lined with furrows and the same vest he had on yesterday, flecked with crumbs. Very unlike him. I wonder if he's been sleeping, noting the deepening bluish shadows under his eyes, the pale skin stretched more tightly across his high cheekbones.

"I ordered the saboteur from you and she was completed in fifteen days' time." A cough escapes him at the end of this angry observation, a rasping growl. Sometimes I wonder at the return of his insipid cough, despite his insistence that he is hale and stronger than ever. What if the spells he's been using to animate the saboteur and soldiers are exacting a price from him already, just as the blue moon will?

Putting those thoughts aside, I steel myself for another tirade. "My lord," I remind him wearily, looking up from where I am fitting Prima's forearm and connecting the joints together with pins, "this marionette is not the saboteur."

I gesture to the assassin's cage, where she's hung for days, and balk; she's gone. I didn't even hear her leave. She must have gone in the night. *That doesn't bode well.*

"If your bride is to be as regal as a princess," I continue, trying not to think about the absent saboteur, "and if you wish her to be perfect, perfection takes time. We still have another ten days before the blue moon shows its face."

He paces like a hungry bear emerging from its den. "Precisely. Only ten days, and she is nowhere near complete!"

He is right about that. Prima is shaping up beautifully, but her face still needs to be refined and painted, her hair needs to be stitched on and she is missing her hands. There is still much to be done to turn the raw materials into something truly royal and noble-looking. I spend each day working on her and now, thanks to Bran's note, anticipating the arrival of the gift that is supposed to bring me a chance at freedom. Freedom I'm not sure I'm ready for. In the meantime, I'm still plotting ways to give Prima what she needs to be complete.

"Is she to have a name, the princess?" I ask.

"Of course she is to have a name. She cannot be a Margravina without a name, a *proper* name."

"Have you named her then? Because, if you haven't, I have a suggestion."

"You have a *suggestion?*" he says, the word dripping sarcastically off his lips. "Let's hear it, by all means."

"I noticed in one of your books, one from the library you left on the worktable, that the word 'first' was listed in the language of the old masters as *prima.*"

It's true; I saw it just yesterday, in black ink on paper. The meaning of her name caused a glow at my very core, making me feel certain I was born to sculpt her, that she was destined to be made. That she isn't just a creature conceived in Laszlo von Eidle's reclusive mind.

"I thought it might be a fitting name for her, for she will be the first of her kind. The first *Margravina* of her kind," I clarify.

Laszlo gives me a dirty look. "Prima sounds like something one would name a cat. The princess shall be named Ulrika Desdemonia, after my great-grandmother."

I cringe, thinking his choice sounds more like the name of a deadly pox than a princess. The noble families do have their own strange way about names.

"Perhaps," I suggest lightly, "once she awakens, she might choose her own name?"

The Margrave rolls his eyes.

"Then, in keeping with your desire to have only the best for her, I was wondering if . . . no, I don't suppose we could," I murmur, holding the stumps of her arms, which end in rounded joints at the wrist.

"Spit it out, Pirouette, we've no time to waste on your inane wonderings!"

"I've thought of a new way to build very delicate and life-like body parts, like the hands, but it requires skills beyond my abilities."

"What way?" he demands.

"A metal armature, a skeleton if you will, is forged and shaped, each bone and joint soldered together. Then, a sculptor lays clay on top to create skin, fingernails, and everything to match. It would be very realistic and refined, far more elegant than what I can carve with the wood alone."

The Margrave looks thoughtful, but I can tell he remains highly irritated. I wonder if he's received a reply from the king about his proposition to rule Tavia and Brylov, and the news wasn't to his liking.

"And I suppose you just happen to know an artisan or two who could produce such work in the time we have left?"

"Of course. I am part of a collective of makers and have many craftsmen and women whose work I rely on when a task is outside the scope of my skill."

"And I also *suppose* that these artisans must be summoned here to help you," he says drily.

"If you wish, yes! The makers I have in mind are Tiffin Hale, the blacksmith, and Nanette Li, the potter. If it's perfect hands you want for your bride, they are the ones to make them for you. If a messenger could be sent—" I watch Laszlo's face carefully. I am treading on unsteady ground today.

He looks out the windows to the conservatory. There must

be a good chill in the outside air today, for the windows of the botanical conservatory are clouded with vapor.

"Fine! If it will give her the best sort of hands, and you know I only want the best, then fine," he says petulantly. "Write up the order and I'll have it sent. But take care, apprentice, who you are so quick to invite into my private gallery."

My neck prickles.

"My lord?"

He turns to face me again, drumming his fingers slowly on the table. "Ask whoever you wish to aid you in making my bride, as long as they are the finest artisans in Tavia. But you may want to be a little more choosy. I've just been told your glassblower had an unfortunate accident with his furnace after his visit here."

"What?"

"You heard me."

Prima's unfinished arm drops from my hand to the table with a thud.

He's hurt Fonso! His ill-advised jibe in Laszlo's inner sanctum must have been too much for the Margrave. *Another maker hurt and the saboteur missing again, and it's all my fault. When will this end?*

I can't bear to press Laszlo for further details, for I know he will only delight in giving them, so I bite down my bitterness and pin my eyes back on my work. I was counting on his vanity and pride to save us, to allow me to bring in each of my makers to give Prima something special and take home a little extra food and protection. My thoughts fly to the wicked, selfish fairy in the tinker's tale, cruelly turning the maiden's bread to stones.

One by one, he will harm them, if he feels threatened by their presence. We must be so cautious.

"Tell me, apprentice, have you given any thought to what she might wear?" the Margrave asks, toying with one of Prima's legs. I am still seething over the news of Fonso's injury. *What did the Margrave do to him?*

"Wear, my lord?"

"Well, surely I can't have her looking like this," he says, pointing to the marionette splayed on the table. At this stage, she looks like the ghost of a woman who jumped off a bridge, arms and legs all afloat.

"Is she to be awakened in a royal ball gown or a wedding dress? Something that looks quite regal? Or should she appear in something more demure, as is befitting a bride? We really should have a tailor round to take measurements," he says, his eyes narrowing. "Don't you agree?"

"A tailor," I breathe, my mouth dry as sawdust.

"Of course, a tailor! You must write up an order for him as well. Do it quick. But *not* the younger tailor," he says, chewing on his lips. "No, I want the older tailor. The younger can stay put," he says, his face cracking into a smile, the first I've seen in a few days. "For I may have special need of him."

I force myself to continue joining the princess's elbow. He's trying to goad me.

"Very wise, my lord. Benito Soren will create a gown for her that will be both spectacular and uncommon. He's the best," I say, slowly and evenly.

"I should like to oversee the design. Otherwise it may not be grand enough. Tell the tailor he must consult with me as soon as he arrives."

"Of course," I manage to choke out. "I'll send the orders with a guard right away." I move the princess's forearm back and forth, inspecting how smoothly the joints rotate on their pins, blinking back the tears that threaten to spill from the corners of my eyes.

"See that you do," the Margrave says, "you know we're pressed for time. Some of us more than others."

Later that night, after sending for Nan and Tiffin and the tailor, I fall into the narrow bed in the closet, winding my aching hands beneath my head for a pillow. My doubts are as numerous as the scratches and bruises on my weary body.

When my chance at escape comes, do I take it? Do I choose freedom from the Margrave over liberation from my splinters?

Everything in me revolts at the idea of abandoning Prima and the saboteur to Laszlo. I feel a bond with them, a kinship. If I leave before the blue moon, before taking the chance to awaken Prima, who knows what the Margrave will do with her?

I'm garnering every tool at my disposal to ensure she comes together as a woman of strength, valiance, and beauty, hoping she can hold her own against the Margrave and do Tavia some real good. Making her is my act of rebellion; I'm hoping to give Laszlo more than he's bargained for. But maybe my efforts and intentions won't be enough. Maybe she'll wind up just another tool of the Margrave, another blade to be wielded as he wishes.

With the saboteur loose among the people again, I consider that it might be best if Prima is not awakened after all. Alive, this princess may be even more powerful than I anticipate . . . or more deadly.

Still, selfishly, I have to consider that waking Prima is also my best chance at being freed from my curse, at leaving that last vestige of my past behind. Yet what good is it to be set free from the splinters only to be trapped here the rest of my days? I have no guarantee Laszlo will release me when I'm finished. For all I know he intends to keep me installed in the gallery permanently, a lifetime sentence as his own personal puppetmaster. The thought curdles the remains of my supper.

Or if I stay and the spell works, I fret, what if the grief and rebellion in my own heart causes her to be cursed, to suffer as I do or with a malady far worse? What if by repeating the blue moon's magic, I am cursing another to suffer in turn? It's not fair!

Oh, Papa. What do I do now?

Thinking of my father only causes more doubt. I know the moon's magic will exact a price, just as it did for him. *What if the price the blue moon demands is one I am not willing to pay?*

Flocks of questions haunt me unceasingly, a swarm of ravens returning to pick at my carcass, tearing me apart piece by piece. The weightiest fears land on my chest after the clock strikes twelve.

What if, instead of building a masterpiece . . . I am making a monster?

Knowing what's become of the saboteur, the most formidable question of all claws its way into my heart.

And if I am capable of making a monster, what does that make me?

CHAPTER 24

THE NEXT DAY, THE DOOR TO THE GALLERY BURSTS OPEN LIKE the advent of a winter gale and Laszlo strides noisily forth, shutting out the guards in the hall.

"Look what's just arrived," he crows, placing a small wooden chest on the worktable.

Wiping my hands on a rag, I come over to inspect the object. A stab pierces my heart. I recognize it. *It's from Curio.*

"Open it," he gloats.

"But, don't you wish to open it?" I stammer.

"Already have. I want you to see it. Something new for my collection."

The Margrave is positively giddy, which I take as a bad sign. Tentatively, I drop my rag and use my thumbs to shift the outer locks on the wooden chest. I lift the lid carefully.

"Oh!" I gasp, unable to keep the memories from rushing in.

Gently, I lift a marionette I had long forgotten from the

crinkled paper wrapping. A queen, an exquisite puppet my father made years ago—far older than me. She has jet black hair and a delicate face, smooth as glass. She's clad in a gown the color of milk, studded with pearls and lace, and remains untouched by the years that have passed, looking just as fresh as when I last saw her. This was a marionette Gephardt created to please his late wife, a portrait of her in puppet form.

"The Lady Cosima," I whisper.

"Is that what she's called?" Laszlo asks, swooping in with greedy hands to snatch her away. "Funny! Leave it to the puppetmaster to have a piece like this stashed away in the muck and damp somewhere. No doubt she was rescued from Gephardt Leiter's stores where she would surely gather dust and rot. This one should most certainly be on display in my collection, where she can be truly appreciated!"

He walks to an empty rack on the gallery wall, one right next to the small puppet version of himself, and drapes the Lady Cosima triumphantly over a waiting hook.

My father only ever showed her to me once, when I was asking questions about his wife and what she was like. Papa unswaddled her with great ceremony from her wrappings high in the large wardrobe in his room, opening the rustling onionskin paper as delicately as if he were handling gold leaf.

"How did you—" I falter.

"A gift! Delivered by hand from the Maker's Guild. In honor of my newly acquired position as Margrave, or so the note read. And, I suspect," he says with a dark smile, "a peace offering, an attempt to get back into my good graces after the glassblower's accident. Perhaps you are not all as thick-witted as you seem. At any rate, I am never one to refuse a new marionette, especially one so fine as this. She deserves to be with me, rather than locked away in a box. Look at those hands! Those eyes! That dress!"

His eyes light up. "*That dress!* We must send the tailor revised instructions immediately. The dress my own bride will wear should match this one exactly!" He stops to laugh a second, looking from the Lady Cosima to Prima and back.

"Why, it's uncanny! The resemblance! Have you noticed it? How perfect," he says, stroking Prima's smooth cheeks. "If you ever misbehave for me, darling," he croons, pointing to Lady Cosima's small hanging form, "we shall have your own whipping girl at the ready. How splendid!"

I stare at Lady Cosima, appalled.

"Now, I have some important matters to attend to. Pick up the pace, Pirouette. The days are waning. Send them in!" Laszlo yells to the guards out in the hall.

Nan and Tiffin are brought in by the guards, laden with materials and tools. They must have been waiting in the hall all this time, after handing over the marionette. Laszlo looks them over with a shrewd eye while they quietly ready their things to begin constructing the princess's hands just as he ordered.

Earlier this morning he was berating me for the princess's own cheekbones being, in his opinion, too wide. I managed to stop that rant by plying his vanity with compliments and explaining they brought balance and strength to the rest of her features. It's requiring all my wits, but I shall say whatever

I must, short of lying, to not have him ruin her face with his own peculiar tastes.

"Send word about her new dress immediately. The tailor must return in a few days' time with her gown. She must be ready!"

Ten days left 'til the blue moon. The days are slipping away from us like sawdust.

"I will, my lord." I say. "*We* will." Tiffin bows his head and Nan does a little bob and curtsy that nearly makes me choke at the sauciness of it.

When the door shuts behind Laszlo with the guard safely on the other side, I launch myself into Nan's arms, hopping up and down with happiness. Tiffin stands awkwardly to the side until I reach out and grab him too, pulling him into our embrace. Together, they smell like iron and sparks, glaze and paint—everything good and real about the world outside these doors.

"How I have missed you! What news of poor Fonso? Did the food reach you, Nan? Has it been enough? What about the Sorens? How is Bran?"

Nan laughs and squeezes me back. "Hold tight to your questions, Piro. First, I must get my bearings or I'm not going to be able to see straight. Too many eyes on me. Far too many eyes." She pulls back and I let her go because I understand her need to gape at the cloister of marionettes.

Tiffin takes the opportunity as well, murmuring, "Bloody brimstones, Piro! How in the blazes did you end up in here? Is this his private chapel where he worships them or something?"

I shake my head. "This is the gallery, the best of his private collection. Apparently this is only half of it."

"We're out there with barely enough food to fill our bellies, being terrorized by wooden soldiers, with the threat of a fight against Brylov hanging over our heads all so he can win some seat at a bigger table than the one he has here, and he's playing at puppets . . . " He rubs his eyes in disbelief.

"He's not exactly *playing*," I say quietly. Bran is the only one who knows the true nature of the project the Margrave has commissioned me for. The rest of the makers know I am here, building a special marionette at his request, but that is all.

"What do you mean?" asks Nan.

"He has hopes to bring her to life," I point to Prima, finding myself unwilling and unable to lie. "He is the one reviving the old magic, all while hiding behind me, blaming me for it."

Tiff's eyes grow wide, the whites looking sharp against his dark skin. "Preposterous," he scoffs. "And just how does he think he's going to do that, eh? A few magic whispers and that thing will be up walking around on her own, living and breathing? That deranged wastrel!"

Nan walks around the gallery, chewing a fingernail, looking angry and repelled all at once.

"No offense, Piro, I know you and your father love mario-nettes, but this is beyond anything I've ever seen. They are just so . . . so gruesome." She motions to the body of a man who bears a wolf's head. "How on earth are you working here, let alone sleeping here?"

"Well, I can't say it's been restful, but I don't have much

of a choice, now do I? You must ignore all of that," I say, taking her by the hand and directing her eyes back to me, to the wooden princess lying in state in the center of it all. "You must tell me, how is Fonso? What's happened?

Her eyes grow pained. "Someone—or some*thing*—attacked him in the early hours, when he was up stoking the furnace. Nearly shoved him in, but you know Fonso, he has the strength of a bull and is just as stubborn. Still, he's suffering—great burns all up his arms. 'Twill be some time before he can work again. We're all taking turns, seeing to him, but Anke's been especially good. Makes her feel useful, with Emmitt being gone." Nan's voice drops low.

I pull her to me, hugging her tight again, feeling devastated at the torment visited upon my small clan. Feeling, as always, that I am to blame.

"You and Tiffin must be alert," I whisper in her ear. "I fear the Margrave may try the same with you, if he senses anything not to his liking. Close your studio, run to the Sorens or to the woods, whatever you need to do if you feel unsafe. I'm worried for you all. We must act quickly now, I don't know how long we'll have alone."

"Don't worry about us," she whispers back. "Worry about yourself and take the *gift* of freedom when it's offered to you," she says with a knowing wiggle of her eyebrows. "Leave every-thing behind and go as soon as you have the chance."

Tiffin reaches out to awkwardly pat my shoulder. Nan throws him a glare, her voice still low. "It's not as if we're sending her to the gallows, you clodding oaf. She'll be fine."

I look at her skeptically. "I don't know how . . . how am I to get past the guards?"

"You'll think of something! Charm them with your feminine wiles!"

"What? What wiles?" I ask, alarmed.

"Can't we get started now?" Tiffin interrupts, looking around nervously. "I don't want to spend a minute longer in here than I have to. No offence, Piro."

"Right," I say, my mind still baffled at the idea of escape. "Tell me, have you all been getting enough to eat?"

Nan's eyes light up again, and I can immediately tell the intrigue of smuggling food from the Margrave's stores is a delight.

"Yes! Remarkably, there's been more than enough to go around. Now," she says, suddenly very business-like, tossing her braid over her shoulder. "Tiffin, these hands aren't going to build themselves. Let's get to it."

"That's what I'm saying," Tiffin slumps onto a stool at the worktable.

Despite the forced strangeness of being together in the gallery, I am eager to see what he's brought and how a pair of iron-forged hands might look on one of my creations. I've never tried this method before with a marionette and I know my father would have been proud to see it attempted.

Tiffin pries open the lid of a wooden crate he brought along and lifts out a set of well-matched metal armature. The wrists are delicate, the finger-bone rods splayed out from iron bands that form the palms, the five slender fingers attached with knuckles of hardened metal. Though they are just the skeleton of a woman's hands, they look strong and aristocratic; bones that might brandish a cup of tea and a knife with the same grace.

He looks up at me, his eyes filled with one question. "Good?"

I nod. "Just right."

"At least something in here will be."

While Tiffin attaches the wrists to Prima's forearms, drilling with his awl and securing them with screws, Nan begins kneading a huge batch of white-gray clay I know is usually reserved for her finest pieces, for fragile platters and vases and such.

Once Tiffin has the hands properly attached, Nan begins her half of the work. The hours pass quickly with them here, watching them work. Laszlo flutters in and out to watch our progress.

Under Nan's deft fingers, the princess's bones begin to bloom with skin and structure. Rounded fingernails emerge from the fingertips as if they grew there. Nan pads the light muscle of Prima's palms, gently creasing her knuckles at the joints, drawing each wrinkle across the skin with precision. When she finally looks up at me, the daylight has vanished from the gallery windows and her face is flushed from concentration.

"What do you think?"

"Brilliant," I say, sad to break the happy reverence of the afternoon. "I could never have achieved that same effect with wood."

She wipes her forehead with a dusty sleeve. "Well, to each

element its own strength; wood has qualities that clay can never match. But, if I do say so myself," she says, standing to stretch and clutch at cramping muscles in her neck, "that's a pair of beautiful hands, fit for any noble lady."

"They're amazing, Nan," I say, reaching out to run a finger across the palms. The ridges in my fingertips drag across the smooth, still-wet clay, leaving a tiny smudge.

"Don't touch, Piro! You know we can't fire them, it would ruin the whole thing. You must allow them to air-dry without disturbance."

As Nan and Tiff are returning their tools and materials to their carrying cases, the Margrave billows in again to see what's taking so long. The makers keep quiet while he bends over the wooden princess, examining her new hands. I can tell from the way Tiffin throws the tools into his kit and the fury in his eyes that he's considering yanking one of the Margrave's marionettes off the wall and beating him over the head with it. Nan reaches out, steadying the smithy with a firm touch of her hand.

Laszlo makes an inane series of speculative sounds, little grunts and murmurs, the sounds of an expert surveying a new treasure. He finally pops his head up, looking extraordinarily pleased.

"Exceedingly lifelike. I would never have thought clay and iron together could make something of such elegance."

Nan takes his back-handed compliment in stride, throwing her satchel over her shoulder. "It's amazing what a maker can do with such simple elements, isn't it, my lord?"

"Indeed. I will keep note of your names for future projects," Laszlo says, trying to sound magnanimous.

"Delighted, my lord," Nan replies. "Might Pirouette see us out? I want to make sure she understands my instructions for proper drying and ventilation of the clay."

Laszlo's pale brow wrinkles. He hasn't let me off this floor since I arrived. I've taken all of my meals here, used a chamber pot in the conservatory that's emptied for me daily, and have generally only been keeping company with him, the guards, and the marionettes in the gallery.

"No," he replies, though I can tell he struggles to resist the allure of Nan. "She must stay here and keep working. My guards will see you out. Back to work," he bids me, gliding out after them.

When the moon rises that night, I allow myself one candle for light and creep from my closet, praying Laszlo isn't underfoot in the gallery, consorting with his marionettes. Bran wrote that when a gift came for the Margrave, so would my means of escape. Nan also intimated as much, though she didn't tell me specifics.

What would it be? A door left unwatched? Help from the kitchen porter? I've had no interruptions from anyone for hours and the saboteur still hasn't returned to her cage.

"Keep watch!" the trees call from the conservatory.

Drawn to her like a moth to the flame, I pull the Lady

Cosima down from her hooks. *Perhaps she's my means of escape. She was the gift, after all.*

Heart thundering, I pilfer her dress, feeling along the seams and under her voluminous skirts for where a key or weapon might have been sewn in along the ribbing. Nothing. Feverishly, I turn her upside down, sliding my fingers along her joints and body, tapping my fingernails against her skull. I shake her. Nothing comes loose. She's not hollow; her body is solid linden. When I've gone over every inch of her, turning out every possible place to hide something sharp, I nearly throw the puppet to the floor; I barely stop myself from destroying a piece that was so important to my father.

Nan clearly said, "Take the gift of freedom when it's offered to you," didn't she?

That's when my eyes fall on the chest Lady Cosima arrived in, still open on the worktable. Cautiously, I run my hands over the lid and pull out all the paper stuffing, shaking it out. The small chest is empty. *Except, if this was my father's . . .*

"Remember," the trees jabber from outside.

I trace a fingertip on the floor of the little wooden chest, examining the grain for any hint of inconsistency, for something unusual but inconspicuous. Suddenly, a small pit in the wood, a tiny blond knothole, just barely catches against my skin. Breathlessly, I tug along one of the walls of the chest and feel the whole inner wall give ever so slightly.

My fingers follow the steps of an old dance from childhood; they know exactly what to do. Pulling the left interior wall up and out of place, where it shimmies free like a sliding tile, I flip it around and press it back down in position. With a soft *plink* a hidden tray pops out from the base of the chest, gliding open like a shallow drawer. There, in the tray, lies a small blackened key.

How on earth did they manage it?

I know that even with a key I'll have to get past the Margrave's guards. I never sent word through the kitchen porter to Bran, so he won't be waiting for me below. I'm on my own. I console myself that it might be safest to go now, when no one, not even Bran or the makers suspect it. That way, if I fail, I fail alone and put no one else at risk. Even the kitchen porter would be in danger for aiding me. Shakily, I palm the key, sweating through my dress, still wavering.

Do I go now? Or do I wait? Should I take my chance at freedom from the Margrave and run, or wait and hope to gain freedom from my splinters?

I know without question who snuck into Curio through my bedroom cupboard and discovered the chest and the Lady Cosima and knew how to use them to help me. I hate to leave my marionettes, but like a stick honed to a point, my resolve to take the chance to be out from under the Margrave's thumb and free to be with the boy I love grows sharper. Bran and all my makers have sacrificed so much to help me escape. Do I dare scorn their hard-won gift by staying here?

Seeing Prima, her hands still wet and drying, tears fill my eyes and I know what I must do. Regardless of her final end, I know I've done something good by building her, something worthwhile. *She may never be finished, but perhaps that's for the best.* The Margrave will be forced to find a bride elsewhere, and she'll never be awakened to suffer his presence. As much as it hurts to leave her behind, I convince myself I am doing her a kindness. Giving Prima a final kiss on her bare scalp, I grab my cloak and walk around the gallery, saying my goodbyes.

In just a few short days, the Margrave will be expecting just as much from me as he will from the blue moon. I still haven't given him the words of the spell that awakened me; I avoid the subject whenever he brings it up. I fear that both of us, the moon and I, shall prove to be a grave disappointment.

CHAPTER 25

PLACING MY HAND ON THE THICK WOODEN DOOR OF THE GALlery, I put my ear to the crack. At this hour, the halls are silent. Hopefully the man stationed at my door is drowsy. Do I create a disturbance, bringing him in so the door is unlocked for me, or do I attempt to use the key? I'm unsure of how to talk my way past the guard once the door is unlocked, so I opt for a diversion. Unlike Nan, I have no faith in my feminine wiles.

Thinking quickly, I grab the Margrave's little whipping boy and wrench the nearly broken arm completely from his body. Using my candle, I pass the torn arm through the fire, charring the wood and rapidly setting it aflame. I toss it through the open glass doors onto the stone floor of the conservatory and throw the rest of the body after it, hearing it crash to the floor in a pathetic tangle.

Good riddance. I despise that ugly, sad little puppet.

Then, I scream. In seconds, the door opens and a guard rushes in.

"Quickly!" I implore him. "There's a fire in the conservatory; it's one of the Margrave's favorite marionettes!"

At the mention of fire, the guard turns ashen and runs into the domed greenhouse. Like a wraith I slide through the open door and into the hall, free for the first time in weeks. I decide not to go the way I remember being brought in, figuring that will take me past the Margrave's main living quarters and library, and instead look for a back hall or passage, one the servants might use.

Drawing my hood up and clutching my key, I trail my fingers on the stone walls, watery torchlight my only guide. I make a left, and then a right, trying to scurry but not outright run, keeping my feet light, as I imagine my saboteur would.

Where is she now?

Up ahead, I see a glowing doorway, overflowing with men's voices droning over ale and cards. I press myself against the wall and slide along, flattening around a far corner, attempting to move without making a sound. I breathe a sigh of relief when I succeed in remaining out of sight.

Ducking around the next corner, I inhale a scream as I come face to face with new obstacles. Wooden ones. The Margrave's animated wooden soldiers stand sentry in the narrow hallway, three abreast, each with a fresh sword from the blacksmith in their grasp.

Seeing me, they tilt their heads and square their legs for a fight. Their eyes remain wide and unblinking, seeming to see everything and nothing all at once. I cannot go back the way I came, knowing the guard at my door will have put the fire out and realized I escaped. He will be on me in a moment. I spot a far door past the wooden soldiers and decide that's where I need to go.

The wooden soldiers tower over me. *How did we construct such massive pieces?*

I remember each of their grim faces, which appear sullen in the dim torchlight. They are still under whatever spell Laszlo is using to keep them at his beck and call. If only I had some way to break the hold he maintains over them, some way to get them to listen to me instead—but other than my blue moon lullaby, I possess no magic words.

Quickly, I take a step forward, to see what they'll do. They hold their position steady, waiting. I take another. They stare, weapons held at the ready. The closer I get, the more they seem unsure of themselves, possibly recognizing me as one of their makers, yet fighting an internal directive not to let an intruder pass. The confusion within them rattles their joints, their arms trembling. I shuffle closer. They waver on their feet, but don't advance on me.

If I can just get close enough to touch one of them, to hear their voices . . .

Cautiously, I reach out and grasp the middle one's wrist, at the base of the carved fist where a sword handle has been tucked. The other two draw their swords on me in an instant and I am breathing hard, trapped in the middle of their blades. The soldier's voice comes to me through the wood, vague and shallow, "*Schützen consurgé!* Guard and protect . . . rise up and protect . . . *sister* . . . "

Despite their spell, they recognize something in me that is like them, wood calling to wood.

"Let me pass," I whisper. "Please, let your sister pass. I don't wish to fight you."

Slowly the shaking soldiers lower their swords, and I keep my hold on the middle one until I am sure they aren't going to run me through.

"Thank you! Keep watch," I tell them, willing my voice to bleed through their wooden ears into their hearts, into whatever part of them might still understand me. "Don't let the others come after me."

Then I drop the soldier's hand and dart between them, running as fast as I dare now down to the end of the hall they were guarding. A stairwell!

I tear down the steps two at a time, clutching my key. I pass the first floor and continue down, down, until the twisted stairway runs out and I am forced to another door. Pressing my hand against it, I wait a moment, listening. I hear a faint clatter and scraping sounds from above.

I must go through.

I try the handle unsuccessfully.

Time to use the key. I probe the latch, the seconds passing like eons, waiting for the moment when it gives. The key slides around, but eventually, after some fearful wrangling, I feel it catch. Quietly as I can, I nudge the door open.

Large barrels tower in pillars on the other side, stacked

three high. *The weinkellar. I've got to be close.*

I lock the door, hoping to slow down anyone coming behind, and quickly dash among the oaken barrels storing Wolfspire Hall's supplies of ale and mead. I have to unlock the next door as well; it opens into another cave-like room lit by a single lantern, this one filled floor to ceiling with brimming baskets and crates. I discern tipsy piles of vegetables and overflowing heaps of fruit and sacks of grain from the lumpy shadows.

This is where he's storing all the hoarded food, that greedy swine.

My instincts note that the cellars seem empty of what I imagine is the usual swarm of servants. *This seems too easy,* my gut warns. *It's far too quiet.*

My eyes seek among the teeming shelves and baskets, searching for any sign of a guard or the kitchen porter. I see no one, though I can hear voices nearby. I move quickly, to keep the voices from catching up. Weaving my way through the maze of the rathskeller, I finally open a door that turns me out into a room with no light. It's as dark as a tomb in here, but the smell of fresh cut wood is bracing. I breathe deep, comforted by the familiarity.

This supply of kindling and firewood must feed the great stoves and hearths. Once I shut the door behind me, the lantern light from the previous cellar fades and I am left to wander by touch through the stacks, looking for a door on the other side.

A hand strikes like an adder from the blackness, grabbing me.

I shriek, but my voice is muffled when I am pressed into a warm body and hugged tight.

"Piro, it's me!" Bran whispers.

I melt into him, my heart a thunderstorm.

"How did you—"

"Shhh . . . I hoped you would try tonight. I've been waiting in here for hours. Marco let me in. Quickly, we have to keep moving," he murmurs in my ear.

He takes my hand and I follow him into a low side passage that requires crouching.

"I take it you found the key?" he whispers.

"How'd you steal it?"

"Didn't. Tiffin made it, from a mold of Nan's clay," he murmurs proudly. "It's the steward's skeleton key. Supposedly opens everything from the Margrave's parlors to the cells in the Keep. She snuck a tile of wet clay to the kitchen porter, who managed to bump into the steward on his return from Brylov, carrying a tray full of food, knocking that vulture flat on his back and heaping him in hot parsnips. He keeps the key at his belt, on a long chain. Marco was nearly flawless, landing right atop him! The fall left an impression in the clay and the steward was never the wiser."

He stops me short. "Here, this is where they bring in the kindling. When I open the door, be prepared to run."

I squeeze his hand to show I understand.

"Piro, there's so much I want to say to you, but there's not time. It will have to wait. You ready?"

I nod, my stomach seething, knowing freedom is so close at hand. If I can just make a stop at Curio under the cover of darkness I can flee to the woods, or perhaps, to Brylov. I will have to hide anywhere I can, to escape Laszlo's grip.

Bran puts his hand to the door and gives it a shove. Together we peer into the night, finding ourselves looking up from the dug-out cellar door into Wolfspire Hall's kitchen farmyard. The way is clear. Bran mounts the steps and starts to run. I am right on his heels.

We make it to edge of the sheep pens before a shadow drops like a poacher's net from a steeply pitched barn roof. The shadow tackles Bran to the ground, pinning him soundly. The silhouette binds him with ease and then looks to me, seeming to judge whether I am going to run or join in the struggle.

It's the saboteur, of course. I move toward her, hoping to employ the same trick I did with the wooden soldiers, to see if I can read the spell ensnaring her, but I am stopped by heavy boot-falls. A hand clamps roughly around my neck.

"Only you would try something as foolhardy as this." The gravelly voice of the steward rakes across my ears. "It's getting tiresome, having to fetch you puppetmasters back over and over again. If I have my way, you'll be going straight to your own cell."

"Please," I plead, "if you let us go, we'll leave and go far from here. The Margrave never has to know you helped us. We can't let him continue to do this, to practice the old spells and harm his own people. It's all against the old laws! You know it's not right. It may cost me my life!"

"That's the price you pay for being a maker," Baldrik growls, turning me around to march me back into Wolfspire

Hall. "You must do what you're told. Your services to the Margrave have yet to be rendered, and you'll not fail to meet them on my watch."

The saboteur keeps in step with us and carries Bran handily over her shoulder, unconscious and limp as a sack of grain.

"He'll be heading to the Keep. As for you, you're going straight back to your room and I don't envy you the consequences of the Margrave learning of this indiscretion. The young lord doesn't take kindly to treason."

He stops suddenly and pats me down, feeling in all my pockets. He quickly comes up with the key and utters several choice curses while sticking it deep into his vest pocket.

I failed. I failed everyone who risked themselves to save me.

"You'll be watched now, closer than you've ever been watched before. And you'll not rest until you've made that *thing* you're building exactly as he wants it."

"But don't you see what he's doing?" I cry in protest. "He's using the very magic he claims is unlawful. And he's using it against us all! Surely you're in as much danger as I, if he were to turn on you!"

"I have served him and his father since he was a spindly lad, knee-high. I know my place and am well compensated for it," he snarls, shoving me ahead. "And if you'd like to keep your head attached to your neck, little puppet-wench, you'd best learn yours."

CHAPTER 26

HE MARGRAVE RAGES AND BELLOWS AT ME FOR HOURS THE next morning, after learning of my near escape. He's irate about the damage done to his little whipping boy, and slices me across the knuckles with the remains of a broken, charred arm while the steward holds me firm.

"I hoped you could see the benefit of what you were doing, Pirouette Leiter. Hoped you understood the great gift I've offered you, to see another life given by the power of the blue moon. I would gladly do worse to you and your hands right now, if I didn't need you to finish my bride.

"You obviously cannot be trusted. So, in addition to the guard at the door, I've set the saboteur to keep watch on you, so that her keen eyes may keep you at your task when my own cannot. And now," he sneers, "you must be chained. I was hoping it wouldn't come to this."

A shackle is brought in and I am cuffed at the ankle,

tethered by a long chain to one of the beams holding up the roof in the corner of the gallery. I can reach my small room to lie down and hobble over to the worktable, but I cannot go out into the observatory any longer to talk to the trees.

As for the saboteur, Laszlo seems satisfied that I am being watched by an assassin. He doesn't realize I don't fear her, so I cower when she draws near and he's in the room, playing into his misconception. While she is under his spell I don't seem to be able to affect her at all, to command her as I did the wooden soldiers, but I still talk to her when we are left alone, appreciating the company. She mostly stalks around or hovers like a black fly over Prima and me. Sometimes she returns to her cage, where she seems to be resting.

With my heart heavy and my hands smarting, I return to work on Prima. With each stroke of my chisel and blade, my despair grows. My father and Emmitt are gone, Fonso has been hurt. Bran's been tossed in the Keep. Laszlo von Eidle will not stop until he has every last thing of mine he wants in his collection.

When the tailor is brought in the next day, I can barely look Benito in the eyes, knowing his son was sent to a cell because of me. But he seems glad to see me, ever kind and gracious despite the deepening wrinkles around his eyes and new strands of white dusting his black hair. He shies away from the saboteur crouching in the corner, trying to keep his focus only on the marionette on the table.

"In all my years working with your father," the tailor remarks, his sharp eyes taking in the proud arch of the princess's head, the dip at her throat, the sturdy limbs and capable hands, "I've never seen a piece like this, Pirouette. Magnificent!"

I flush. This is high praise from another master, from a man I respect as much as I did my own father.

"You truly are a puppetmaster in your own right, Piro."

"Thank you, tailor."

"Yes," quips Laszlo, a little too brightly. "Isn't our little Pirouette a marvel?"

Ignoring the sickly-sweet way Laszlo jabbers about me to the tailor, as though I were a coin plucked from the gutter, I change the subject. I hope he soon tires of maker talk and will scuttle back to his own rooms.

When the Margrave isn't in here, I think he's sifting through the vast tomes in his library like a fiend, trying to uncover anything else he can about the blue moon and its power. I suspect he is eating and sleeping even less, for he has grown increasingly pallid.

Tailor Soren lays the box with the gown on the table, gently pulling back the tissue. I am astonished. In the few days that have passed since he received his commission, I can't comprehend how he constructed such a dress. The bodice is a pure, creamy white, edged with gold piping, and is a near match to the Lady Cosima's. It's sleeveless, just as I requested, knowing it would be too dangerous to pull narrow sleeves over newly sculpted hands. The waist gathers high, just below the bust where the gown descends in a riotous waterfall of ivory and gold, each layer of the skirt interlaid with intricate swirls of flowers and leaves stitched in gold threads. It is perfection.

Just the dress for a bride of nobility.

The tailor and I lift her torso from the table and carefully fit the top over her head and maneuver each limb into place, ever so slowly. Tailor Soren talks me through the process of dressing her quietly and calmly, with a needle and thread pursed in his lips, whipping out his small scissors to snip an errant thread here or tuck a seam in line there.

It takes us quite a while, with Laszlo looking on anxiously, interjecting such helpful advice as: "Watch her arm there, Pirouette, you're going to break it clean off!" and "Do be cautious, tailor, she mustn't be *so* sewn into that thing!" He's nearly out of breath during the whole process, though the tailor and I are doing all the work.

The tailor remains unfazed by Laszlo's blather and somehow, together, we manage to get Prima fully dressed, elegant hose, pretty shoes, and all. I suspect that working with six children constantly on hand at The Golden Needle has sharpened his ability to focus on his work in the face of constant distraction.

I step back, looking the princess over from head to toe. The Margrave is too excited now; I see no chance of him leaving me alone with Benito, not even for a moment. With less than four days remaining, I still must refine and polish Prima's face, add some color to her skin and lips, and attach her hair. Right now, her scalp is smooth as an egg, and I have plans to create a special cap to which I'll sew swathes of horsehair to create a wig of dark locks. But even now, without her hair or any warmth to her skin, she is still lovely in a simple, unadorned way.

Laszlo stands with arms crossed. "It is the very dress for a princess," he says gravely. "Well done, Tailor Soren." As he swoops about, fingering the fabric and straightening her skirt within an inch of its life, he continues. "Such a shame you had to build this without the help of your son. I assume he is enjoying his time in the Keep?"

The tailor holds his tongue, quietly packing up his things.

"Thankfully, your little stitching shop doesn't depend on your apprentice's assistance. *You* are the finest tailor around. I've checked."

Just as the tailor is about to join the guards who will escort him out, Tailor Soren stops, as though remembering something. Quickly he comes back into the gallery and tucks a small fabric envelope into my hands.

"A sewing kit, Piro. Just in case you need to do any last-minute alterations to the gown. I trust your fingers have enough skill with needle and thread to do them." His dark eyes spark, reminding me of Bran's.

I nod, and take it, watching helplessly as the tailor is hustled from the room, nearly like he is a prisoner himself. Laszlo follows, pausing for a long look back at me.

"Don't get any ideas about visiting the tailor's son in the Keep, Pirouette Leiter. You have a task to finish and until it's complete you shall remain here. Now, seeing as my bride is still hairless . . . " He raises his pale eyebrows to indicate I should get on with it before slamming the door shut behind him.

My anger at him burns hot and slow. At the princess's side, observing her frozen loveliness, I realize I know exactly what gift she should have from Bran, the final addition to make her complete. I must act quickly, so Laszlo won't see.

Picking up a carving knife, I pull back the bodice of Prima's new gown and expose the pale swell of wood where her heart will be. With a steadying breath, I plunge the knife in deep.

During the final days leading up to the blue moon, I work at a frenzied pace, stitching segments of long, silky strands of hair to the spiderweb-style cap I wrought together. The horse hair I receive from Wolfspire Hall's stable hand is black as midnight. Though Laszlo initially wanted golden, I managed to convince him that dark hair, like his mother's, would best match the princess's coloring and regal features. It helped that there's a serious shortage of golden horse hair in the village.

Once I secure the hair to her scalp and glue the cap in place, I play coiffeur and trim the ends, winding it high on her head and using the tailor's handy little sewing kit to stitch tiny pearls into the coils.

I spend hours with my sanding tools, smoothing and refining the features of her face and preparing the surface for paint all while thinking of Bran in the belly of the Keep far below, and my friends struggling in the village.

When I'm left alone for a few hours each night and should be sleeping, I continue work on the secret compartment I've built in place of Prima's heart. I carve it just deep enough and round enough, to fit the watch Bran made for me, the one thing from him that I brought to Wolfspire Hall. Tucking the blue velvet ribbon around the edges, I rub my thumb over the "P" embellishing the case. My breath catches at the scrolling pattern of leaves and flowers engraved on the case. The tailor wove the same pattern into Prima's dress, in golden threads.

I smile at the match, knowing it's fate at work. Nestling the watch in its new refuge, I carefully replace the wooden panel I made to conceal it. It isn't quite as clever as my father's puzzle boxes and their false layers, but it will do. When I finish gluing the panel into place I sand the surface yet again, until the faint echoes of my handiwork disappear seamlessly into the wood's grain.

I feel satisfied, placing my ear to her chest, content that the faint ticking will continue until the blue moon or some other force bids it to stop. Thanks to Bran, she will have a steadfast heart. And from Tiffin and Nan, hands with the strength of iron. From Fonso, eyes that will see things as they truly are. From the tailor, a gown to set off her beauty and conceal whatever she might wish to keep hidden.

And from me?

"Well," I whisper, as I pick up a brush to add some final touches of color to her lips and cheeks, "I give you the gift of being just as you are meant to be. Yours is not the face that Laszlo sketched, nor is it one that I merely dreamed up. Yours is the face I saw in the wood. You are what was already there, growing at its core, unfolding in its heart. You and I, I've learned, can't be anything other than what we are. It's both a blessing and a curse, this ancestry of wood."

Prima's subtle voice coming from the wood is always eager. "Soon," she hums under my fingers. "My time is soon."

The nearly full moon strides high above the dome of the conservatory, casting a pewter luster through the windows. Tomorrow it will undergo a transformation of its own, becoming blue and brazen. Laszlo's marionettes light up in its beams, even the saboteur resting in her corner. The air fills with many voices, a series of desperate cries; I cannot normally hear a marionette's voice unless it's one I've made, but for a moment I hear them all.

"*Wake me!*"

"*No, me!*"

"*I am more deserving than she!*"

"*I am the oldest of us all—I should be the next to live!*"

I close my eyes against the onslaught, knowing they watch us, me and Prima and the saboteur, with greedy gazes and longing stares. The Margrave has already chosen among them who will live and who shall remain forever asleep, dreaming in wood. I don't even want to think about what some of them would be like, coming to life instead of Prima. The black witch, the gruesome clown. It would be a nightmare.

"Will you really awaken?" I whisper to the princess. "Or is this all just a hearth tale? One where the exhausted puppetmaster finally meets her untimely end?"

"Soon."

Spent, I lay my head down at the worktable. My father's words resound in my mind, in tandem with the muffled ticking of the princess's new heart: *A maker will always prevail. A maker will always prevail. A maker will always prevail. . . .*

I fear its truth and my failure in equal measure.

CHAPTER 27

T HE DAWN OF THE BLUE MOON IS A STRANGE ONE. I WAKE TO
one of Laszlo's heavy stares. He has joined me in the
gallery, dressed in what I assume is his wedding finery: a
jacket of cream, layered over a white shirt and fitted trousers,
everything awash in reams of gold braid. He perfectly matches
his princess, except for the dark slash of crimson across his
chest. It doesn't escape my notice that he's added many of his
father's own adornments and medals to the sash.

"Today is the day," he says brightly, while I rub the sleep
from my eyes. "*Nil volentibus arduum*, apprentice," he reminds
me. "Nothing is impossible and the moon is almost ready, I
can feel it!"

"She is ready, at least," I say tiredly, motioning to where the
princess lies complete on the table.

For I've done it.

No—*we* have done it. The makers and I, combining our

skills and strength, have constructed the most beautiful, life-like figurine our part of the world has ever known. I am sure of it. Her eyes glow green and her skin is smooth and soft to the touch. Her hands wait, open, ready to be grasped. Her lean, muscled arms and legs rest now, but they can, I imagine, wield a sword or ride a horse with ease.

"She is everything I imagined," Laszlo says softly. "Everything a Margrave should have."

I clear my throat to disguise the sarcastic laugh that threatens. She's *nothing* like the creature he imagined and sketched for me, and yet somehow he is too blind to see it, too blind to remember. Perhaps it's because I conveniently lost those sketches. Or maybe the power within the wood convinced him all on its own, I don't know.

"The wedding banns have already been called. My marriage to Ulrika Desdemonia will take place immediately upon her arrival."

"But, my lord," I say, startled, "that will be in the middle of the night. Shouldn't we allow her some time to adjust? To see that she's safely through from one form to the next? It might be a difficult transition—"

"By the dawn of tomorrow, I want to be married and to show her off to the rest of the territory as my bride."

"But you said the people will want a wedding, something to look forward to? After all they've been through?"

"The commoners can go hang! The clodding lot of them are rebellious, vile, and can't be trusted. They're always plotting! They've tried to turn the king against me! So we will marry tonight, after she awakens. What better thing to come to life for, than to become an instant bride, an immediate Margravina? She'll never want for anything!"

Except a few moments' peace.

"You are to go and bathe yourself; make yourself present-able for her," Laszlo says, looking me over with distaste. I know I have glue in my hair and paint on my cheeks. My dress is rumpled, my apron dirty, and my hands are in a ghastly state. "Rest a bit, if you must, for you will be unshackled only to perform the blue moon ceremony tonight," he says begrudg-ingly. "I will stay here and keep my bride company."

I look to the saboteur's cage; it's empty. She's been sent away again. So I shuffle off to my closet of a room, where someone has already hauled up a tub of water and left a meager sliver of soap. I scrub myself from head to toe, using up every bit of the soap trying get off as much paint, glue, and resin as possible while in my chains. Then, I put on the only other clean dress I have from home. I brush my short hair, knowing it will dry quickly, and lie down on the bed.

If Laszlo will be spending all day at Prima's side, I don't think I can stomach joining him. I'll stay in here. I need time to think.

I don't know what the blue moon will bring for Prima and me; we may be trapped here at Wolfspire Hall the rest of our days. But I cannot allow Bran to rot. The thought of Bran never recovering from the Keep, like Papa, breaks my heart. *Can I at least help him escape, even if I can't help myself?*

When the guard knocks and leaves my luncheon tray, I am

forced to rise and eat. After drinking some tea, my thoughts clear. Tea will do that for you. To my knowledge, neither Laszlo nor anyone else is wise to our scheme and Marco has kept mum about the whole thing. I reach for the remaining few precious francs I siphoned off from paying the tailor to place some below the teacup's downturned shell so that Marco will have money to bribe the guards managing the food stores.

A new thought arrives, like a chisel driving through the soft wood of my brain: the tailor's sewing kit. I still have it in my dirty apron. I dip into the cloth envelope and pull out two needles pinned in some wool, a wee pair of scissors, some white buttons, and a tool I haven't yet needed: a miniature seam ripper, the size of my little finger. Just the tool you could use to pick a lock, with its sharp end curved like a fish hook.

With my heart in my throat, knowing the Margrave is on the other side of my door, now always slightly ajar from the intrusion of my long chain, I snip a piece of thread from a tiny spool in the kit. Quickly I bind the seam ripper to the small hidden stack of coins. On a scrap of paper, I scratch out a quick note to Marco, hoping my few words will make sense, and that he might be willing to risk using these francs to bribe a guard at the Keep. Or to take the risk and deliver the seam ripper to Bran himself. I realize I am putting a lot of faith in a man I have never met, but he has come through for me thus far.

Let's hope your cousin is still up for it, Fonso.

I fold my note into a discrete square, placing it just below the coins and seam ripper. I set my empty teacup upside down on top of the whole lot, praying it remains undisturbed until

Marco's hands reach for the dishes. Bran's fate rests in the hands of the kitchen porter and the shelter of a teacup.

When the guard comes for the tray, I hold my breath as he carries it away, the empty dishes rattling past both me and Laszlo out into the depths of Wolfspire Hall.

When the dinner tray comes, I find I have no appetite. The worry of waiting for the moon to rise is more than enough to fill my belly. I check under the fresh teacup on the tray to see if there is any sign from the kitchen porter that my message has been received, but there's nothing.

Laszlo spends the day pacing around the worktable, talking to himself, the princess, and the other marionettes. I try to stay quiet and well out of his way. I tidy and pack up my most prized tools brought over from Curio, hoping against hope that one way or another my time in the gallery is nearly at an end.

As night draws close, Laszlo has my shackle unlocked and insists I help him carry the princess out to the conservatory. He has a special table prepared, and while I think it looks like a funeral pyre, I keep quiet; he is so proud of it. He had thin hazel switches cut and woven into a bed, interlaced with willows and greenery. Among the greenery he placed flowers, late-blooming white lobelias and fall lilies. Together we lay Prima upon the springy bed, and we wait. The trees growing up through the conservatory floor hum anxiously. They know the blue moon is on the rise, and what a special occasion it is.

"Be warned, young one, be wary," they trill.

Looking up through the glass-domed ceiling, Laszlo's

anxious eyes watch the sky. So far, the moon is just a pale, light-blue glass eye in the heavens. We must wait until it is directly overhead and shines with the bold silver-blue of the rarest of all moons.

"Shouldn't be long now," he says, pacing around the conservatory, tugging at a branch here, pulling a dead leaf from a plant there.

He's forbade anyone but me to join him in the inner sanctum of the glass enclosure, but I know plenty of guards are posted just outside the gallery doors. I caught their curious glances earlier as they peered in. I wonder what they think of their Margrave and his strange obsession. He doesn't want anyone else to see us use the blue moon's spell; besides his fear of giving anyone else magical knowledge, if things go wrong, I understand I alone am to be blamed.

"Are you ready? Do you know the words to say? You'd better. You still haven't told them to me," he sulks.

"I do know the words, my lord, I have them in my memory from childhood. But I must warn you that it isn't as simple as saying a spell. The person making the cut and spilling their own blood will lose some of their life in exchange."

Laszlo nods, taking that in stride. "It seems a fair trade, exchanging some life for another."

"Perhaps, but it is unknown how much life you might lose. Take my father, for instance. He was still a young man; he could have lived many years yet had he not made me. It could be that awakening your bride takes from you days, even years. Or it may take something else from you, something like your sight or your hearing. It's impossible to know."

He tightens his jaw, scoffing. "Don't lecture me on how I might spend my own life, apprentice. I am the Margrave of Tavia, and if I think it worthwhile to create a mate, a bride, made just so, even if it takes years from me, I consider that time well-spent. Surely it won't require much blood as noble as mine to awaken her."

"Perhaps I could be the one to make the cut, on myself, to spare you the sacrifice, my lord?" I offer, remembering the old tree woman's words: "The heart of the maker will determine the course of the marionette."

Even though I constructed her, if Laszlo's blood gives her that last bit of power needed to take her from wooden to human, I can't say what will happen. I cannot account for the state of his heart. Especially when the state of my own frightens me.

But this is my one chance to be rid of my splinters forever. I've come this far. I cannot let the Margrave get in the way. I must think of something.

"Certainly not," Laszlo spits. "I will be the one to make the cut and use my own blood. We can't have your non-noble blood tainting hers. Now, shouldn't the rest of them watch?"

"Who, my lord?" I ask. I thought he didn't want an audience.

"The rest of my marionettes, the best ones. It's only fitting!" he says, leaping up to rush back into the gallery. "Surely they will be jealous, won't they?"

I watch, feeling mildly ill as he brings out about twenty

marionettes of all shapes, sizes, and characters to hang on the plants and from the nearby branches of the conservatory's grove of trees. The newly scorched whipping boy is placed in a prominent position near the princess's pyre. Laszlo forced me to reattach his broken arm with wire as part of my penance.

"Well? Aren't you going to go get her?"

"Who, my lord?"

"The saboteur," he says with a knowing grin. "She should be able to see, too."

Licking dry lips, I proceed into the gallery, where the saboteur's been returned to her rack. She is lifeless.

"I don't think I'm ready for this," I mutter under my breath, tugging the cage, feeling it creak and roll beneath my hands.

I wheel the saboteur into the courtyard of the conservatory and place her at the edge of the viewing circle, among the others the Margrave has strung up in the trees.

And so we wait, the Margrave, the puppets, and I, for the moon to reach the crest of its travels. At its pinnacle, I sense it immediately, a crackle in the air, the shock of stocking feet against a rug, the flare of a knife against flint. The air is full of ripeness, laden with the sense that the mere spark of a single word might set everything around us ablaze.

The first blue moon I've seen with human eyes hangs heavy and burdensome in the sky, straining to stay put. The ring of color reminds me of a blade thrust into Tiffin's forge, a white-hot molten blue. A strange aura bathes the waiting audience in the conservatory in a silvery wash, suspending us all beneath a cresting wave of moonlight.

It is time.

Laszlo knows it, too. Before his audience of many painted eyes, he retrieves a small, pearl-handled knife from the pocket of his wedding clothes.

"Say the words, Pirouette."

"You must make the cut and paint your blood over where her heart will be," I instruct, my own heart racing, knowing his fingers will land right where I planted Bran's watch.

He nods, readying the knife to draw across his palm.

"Bitter moon—" I begin.

"My lord!" a voice interrupts.

"I told you I wasn't to be disrupted!" Laszlo shrieks.

"The new prisoner, the tailor's son, has escaped the Keep. Word just came from the Keep's watch. We thought you should know." The guard waits anxiously at the door to the conservatory. "You'd said to keep an eye on that one."

Laszlo's icy eyes narrow. He immediately turns to me.

"Do you have anything to do with this?" he erupts. "Now is not the time! We don't have *time*! I can't wait another seven years for a blue moon. Did you help him escape to distract me from waking my bride?" He jabs his knife at my face, eyes glazed in fury, his jaw twitching.

"You don't want me to awaken her, do you? You all want me to be alone forever! You're just like my father, never letting me have anyone for my very own. I've had no one, do you understand? For years he kept me shut up here. Like a caged beast. *Alone*. So tell me," he spits, pressing the blade tip against my throat to punctuate each word. "Did you do this?"

A familiar storm rises within me, the thundercloud of truth and lies rumbling in my chest. I don't even think twice. The lie passes hot and easy off my lips.

"*No.*"

He examines me warily. I say it again.

"No, my lord, I don't know what you're talking about. If the tailor's son escaped, it was thanks to his own wits and a sad lack of security in your prison."

I wait on pins and needles for the familiar pricking, the thrust of a splinter breaking ground through my skin. It doesn't come, at least not until Laszlo has cursed me soundly and dismissed the anxious guard. Then, just as my pulse begins to slow, a sliver of wood the size of his knife blade rips its way out through my neck, and neither my cry of pain nor the splinter escape Laszlo's notice.

"I knew it!" he says, both furious and triumphant, pointing at the splinter. "You are *exactly* what I thought you were. Wooden to the core. This proves it! Was it your lying lips that prompted that? Ha!" He begins to laugh, gleefully. "It's better than I imagined! Inside you are just the same as they are!" he says, gesturing to our wooden audience. "You truly are a girl made of nothing, and you are a liar of the worst sort!"

"And what sort is that?" I ask, yanking the splinter from my neck. The pain is stifling, a burn that takes my breath away. I grip the splinter between my fingers, registering the feel of the sharpest end against my thumb. For the first time in my human life, I'm grateful for my strange curse. Of all my splinters, this one may prove worthy of a greater purpose.

"The sort whose own lies destroy them. This will be your end, apprentice. Now that I have proof of what you truly are, we must find a place to keep you on display. Perhaps in the gallery, hanging with the others? After this, I can't have you running about, creating more like yourself. My bride must be the only one."

Blood pulses from my neck, hot and angry.

"Now," he says, dragging me by the collar to where the princess waits under the blue moon, "I don't care where that worthless tailor's son is, or what grand plan you've constructed to thwart me, you will speak those words and awaken my bride, or something much sharper than a splinter shall pierce your throat. *Begin*," he growls.

With a voice that scarcely sounds like my own, I slowly speak aloud the words my father taught me, the words of the old tree woman from many blue moons before my time.

"Bitter moon and solemn blue,
blood of earth and sap and dew,
wake a second life anew."

While I say the words, Laszlo makes a great show of slicing the skin of his hand, reaching out with two fingers to sloppily paint a bright smudge across the princess's heart.

But with blood already on my hands, I get there quicker.

I smear crimson across her bust before he can reach her. I cringe at the stain spreading on her exquisite gown, but it can't be helped. Laszlo shrieks, horrified. I wait, pressing those same fingers back against my neck to stop the bleeding. I wait for the magic to unravel. For him to try and take my head off with his knife. For something, *anything* to happen.

The Margrave yowls at me in panic and we both look frantically to the sky. The moon is still blue as ever, waiting expectantly among the stars. Nothing stirs.

"It didn't work because it's your disgusting blood!" he sneers, furiously smearing his own on top of mine. "Say the words again!" Laszlo commands. Once again, I repeat the precious words, though each one tastes more bitter on my tongue.

Still, nothing. The princess lies on her bed of boughs, appearing the same: lovely and wooden.

The Margrave glares at me with a vehemence I've not yet seen. No longer am I just a tool for his use. I am clearly his enemy.

"This is all your fault! You've destroyed everything, you wooden wench, and you did it on purpose! I will take every pitiful tool you own and have you tortured with them in the Keep. We'll see if you can outlast your father down there! Will a puppet girl fare better than a puppetmaster? Maybe that will be too slow. I should have a burn pile made ready for you!"

He grabs me, shaking me by the shoulders so hard that my teeth catch on my tongue. His knife nicks my arm as I strain and struggle to maneuver the hand clutching my deadly splinter closer to his throat. Entangled in a mad, twisted embrace, we hear a new voice, strong and musical, interject into the fray.

"Do you dare to dishonor the blue moon?"

CHAPTER 28

WE STOP, INSTINCTIVELY OBEYING THE VOICE. LIKE A warrior queen raised from the dead, the princess's bloodied dress and high-coiled hair quickly betray her identity. Prima's back is ramrod-straight, her curving chin proud, her skin the same creamy color of raw halsa. Her eyes flash green in the moon's light, like moss aflame. Something about her makes me feel the way I did around the old tree woman—not fearful, but not exactly at ease, either. This is an untamed, wild creature. Still unstained by her own humanity. Unless you count her dress.

Laszlo's mouth drops open and for once, words fail him. The three of us are locked in a triangle of wonderment, staring until it becomes apparent that one of us should say something. That one of us, of course, is the Margrave.

"My darling! You're finally here," he croons, hastily dropping the pearl-handled knife with which he had been threatening me. He approaches the princess as if she'd just arrived for tea, taking her hand. She stiffens, unused to human touch.

"I've been waiting for you. Waiting so long."

He kneels at her feet and proceeds to kiss her hand. She regards him with the same disdain one might show an unwelcome stray dog off the street; she looks to me, bewildered. I feel an instant kinship with her.

I remember what it was like in those first few moments, the strangeness of the sounds, the feel of skin stretching across my bones, the endless beating of my own heart. The sheer overwhelming sensations of a human body are a lot to comprehend.

But if I've built her well, with her many secret strengths, and if some of my blood courses through her veins, she will soon find her words and speak them.

"Why are you fighting?" she asks him simply. Her words come out slow, even. "Why do you hurt her and dishonor the moon?"

Laszlo gets to his feet, waving me off. "Nothing for you to be concerned about, Ulrika dear—that is to be your name, you know, and what a grand one it is! Named after my great-grandmother, on my mother's side. She was a legendary beauty, though already no one in all of Tavia can hold a candle to you." He turns around and sneers at me for good measure.

"Now, let's come in to the gallery so we can have the church cleric summoned. We are to be wed at once!" As Laszlo prattles on, he blocks my view of her, trying to drag her toward the gallery door, intending for me to give them some privacy. Now that he has what he wants, he wants me out of the way.

But I can't stop staring at her, nor does she stop trying to peer around him to see me.

I sense that she recognizes me, recognizes that I am somehow a part of her, just like the saboteur. But if Laszlo takes her away, I might never get the chance to speak to her. She will need someone to explain everything; I long to tell her things Papa was never able to tell me.

She is having none of this manhandling by a stranger, however. She pulls back from Laszlo's greedy grip, and I hear the Margrave's breath intake sharply as she wraps a hand like a vise around his forearm, digging her patrician fingers deep into the cuff of his wedding jacket. With pride, I note how he immediately crumples in pain. Nan and Tiffin's gifts at work.

"I don't know you, yet you speak to me as if I *belong* to you," she says, dragging out the word "belong," further entrenching her fingers in the flesh of his arm. "I am new to this world, to this way of being, but I find that very strange. I *belong* only to the wood, to earth and dew and moonlight. To the wind singing through the trees. If you ever earn my favor, perhaps, someday, I could belong *with* you. But *to* you—no, I do not belong to you."

With that, she releases him, and I exhale a long breath of relief. She is everything I hoped for. Prima begins to traipse around the conservatory, examining the plants and talking to the trees like they are old friends.

I want to go to her, but Laszlo has wedged himself between us, whining and pacing like a rat in a trap.

"You did this!" He turns on me. "You did this *on purpose*! You've made her hate me! How dare you spoil the one beautiful, good thing I would have for myself! The one thing I needed to be *real*! You've ruined everything!" He's sweating and runs his fingers through his fair hair, which becomes streaked pink from the blood still seeping from the cut on his hand. "My father always said, 'If you want something done well, do it yourself.' Well, that old fool never let me do anything and look how it's turned out!"

Laszlo rails against his father and my treasonous hide, all while yelling for the guards to send in the cleric posthaste. The blue moon remains, though it's slowly fading. The magic will soon be lost.

But it worked. Prima is alive and real in a way she has never been before.

I take advantage of the Margrave's preoccupation with my vulgar origins and shuffle over to step on his forgotten knife. The princess's eyes flash from across the courtyard, lighting up with awareness. I bend down, ostensibly to adjust my shoe and neatly pocket the blade. Now armed with both my splinter and the knife, I know I must find a way to end this.

I will not doom Prima and the saboteur to a life here, tangled up in the strings of the Margrave. If I can somehow convince Prima to help me carry the saboteur and make a run for it, maybe we can find Bran.

Vincenzo the cleric, who I remember from Papa's funeral, arrives looking like he spent the day taste-testing Wolfspire Chapel's communal wines. His face registers surprise at the sight of the new Margrave's intended, leaning against and fondly talking to a gnarled tree growing through the conservatory floor. I inch closer, hoping I won't scare her into climbing its branches. I'm not sure we'd get her down without a fight.

"Come, my darling," Laszlo says to the princess, his voice like tightly strung wire. "It is time for you to assume your rightful place at my side," he coaxes. "Come and stand with me, and I will make you a Margravina, a lady of the dew and the moonlight, whatever breed of lady you wish. As my bride, you will be free to do as you please."

"You are already free to do as you please," I pipe up.

Anger pulses on Laszlo's face. Prima regards him warily and doesn't move from the tree.

"She's just jealous of you, of your beauty and your position, my Margravina. Disregard her. She's nothing but a common apprentice. You are royalty. Come and stand here with me, and let us talk awhile. Or, if you prefer, you needn't speak at all. You must be tired from your . . . journey. We can let the cleric here do all the talking for us, isn't that right, man?"

Vincenzo nods, holding up the lantern he brought with him, looking utterly mystified by the beautiful woman in the bloody dress who won't let go of the tree.

Prima looks from Laszlo to me, and finally speaks after a long silence. "I will stand near you, but only if *she* is at my side," she says, pointing to me.

Laszlo smiles through gritted teeth, "Of course, my darling, whatever you wish. The puppetmaster can be a witness to our joy." He hurls another warning glare my way. If Laszlo's looks could kill, I'd have been dead days ago. Too bad for him I'm still breathing.

And so is Prima. She walks deliberately toward me, and reaches forward to clasp one of my hands in her own. I feel the reassuring pressure of her fingers, gripping mine like our lives depend on it. She is even more astonishing up close. Her skin is warm and clear, her eyes bright. Her face is a sea of expressions, shifting from wonder to confusion to revulsion and back again. I don't know how to explain the awe I feel, seeing someone who is like me, in the flesh, but someone already so much more magnificent than I will ever be. Someone I helped bring into being.

Laszlo is just pleased to have his bride in the vicinity of the cleric. He approaches cautiously; I don't doubt that his arm is deeply bruised where she seized it. Before the cleric starts to intone the standard wedding fare, the princess's hand quickly releases mine and plunders my apron pocket, quick as an accomplished thief.

I panic. The Margrave's knife will be all too visible in her hand, for she has no sleeves. But my fears are allayed when from the corner of my eye, I watch as her hand is swallowed up by the deep folds of Tailor Soren's exquisite dress. The skirts are so voluminous; it seems she's discovered a secret sewn-in pocket that I missed.

My face cracks a smile at the tailor's provision and Laszlo, who has just turned to face us to begin his vows, notices. His eyes darken. The air around us is still tinged blue from the moonlight, though it's quickly losing its deep luster.

"Cleric, you may commence with the ceremony and do what you came here to do."

"I object," I say staunchly, letting my splinter drop from my sleeve, keeping it hidden in my palm.

Laszlo rolls his eyes. "You get no say in the matter. I am the Margrave of Tavia, and this woman is to be my Margravina."

"I object," Prima calmly repeats after me.

"The lady objects," I concur.

"I do," she agrees.

"Oh my, there are objections already," Vincenzo stammers. "We've not even begun!"

"Shut up! All of you!" Laszlo screeches. "You," he says, pointing to Prima, "you were *made* for me. Made to my exact specifications. If you have any semblance of a brain in your head, it's only because I told the puppetmaster's *apprentice* to put it there. I've half a mind to string you both back up inside with the others. Like it or not, Ulrika, I own you." He grabs her roughly by the shoulder and pulls her to him. "Now, cleric, begin," he growls impatiently.

The cleric licks his lips nervously and begins to shuffle through the pages of his leather-bound book of prayers. I wait for just the right moment, intending to surprise Laszlo with my splinter—but the princess beats me to it.

CHAPTER 29

As soon as Vincenzo begins mumbling the homily, Prima throws off Laszlo's grip and uses a well-heeled wedding slipper to kick the book from the cleric's hands and shove the bewildered old man out of the way. Quicker than he can blink, Laszlo is her prisoner. Her arm wraps unflinchingly around his neck, pressing his own knife against his throat. She is nearly as tall as he, and, it appears, outranks him in strength.

"My name, you gutless man-creature," she says evenly into his ear, not even breathing hard, "is not for you to choose. I already have a name."

"Let me guess," he says, his windpipe bobbing under the blade. "Is it Prim or Prissy or Pretentious? It's clearly not *Prudence*," he spits, followed by a hollow cough that seizes his chest in its own spell.

"My name," she says, twisting his collar tighter like a

noose, "is Prima. I am the first of my kind, the firstborn of my maker's blood."

She heard me. She knows her name.

"And you, one born the common way, couldn't possibly understand." Every time she speaks aloud, her voice grows in strength and eloquence. Pride breaks open in my chest.

I am somewhat useless now, brandishing my splinter in Laszlo's face, but I don't let that stop me. "You're going to let us go now, *my lord*," I say, dripping with sarcasm. "Neither of us belongs to you and we never will. One cannot buy or collect the things you need most: love and companionship, for starters. But don't worry, you shan't be left alone. You can be grateful we let you keep your head intact, and your precious collection for company. I would say you have the cleric as well, except he seems to have fled and left you in the capable hands of your bride," I say, noting the empty place remaining where Vincenzo scrabbled off in fear, his lantern left behind, upset on its side.

Laszlo remains frozen beneath the princess's knife, hating us both with a vicious smile.

"No. It's you who don't understand, my wooden darlings. What can you possibly know, one of you an ignorant maker, and the other only alive for five minutes? I have given my life to the study of puppets, of dark animation—mostly the conjurer's kind. If I can't have the bride I wish, then at the very least I will have a show."

He chants an incantation in a language that sounds like it's from another time. I don't have to understand it to know it means something ruinous.

"*Exsurgencia, exitarneum. Exsurgencia, exitarneum . . . leben-surge.*" His eyes gleam with expectation as his voice builds. Prima instinctively tightens her hold on him.

A flash of movement among the trees catches my eye. The marionettes. The ones the Margrave brought out to watch . . . every marionette in the courtyard and in the gallery begins to quiver. The moonlight hangs over the slow ballet beginning in the conservatory like a curtain. Laszlo continues to spew his spell and though Prima hurriedly clasps a hand over his mouth, it's too late. His words have taken hold.

The magic unfolds as a series of sharp twitches, bolts of lightning to the puppets' strings. The moon only knows what secrets Laszlo uncovered in his late nights of research in the library; all I know is that in the last few weeks, when he wasn't in the gallery with me he was there, *studying.* My blood turns to ice.

The marionettes gain vitality with every passing second. Soon they rip free from their strings, tearing away with hands and paws at branches and wire, away from the pegs that brace them, away from anything holding them back. One by one, they drop to the ground or gambol down the limbs of the trees to encircle us.

They are all here: the wolf-faced man, the clown and witches and wood nymph, even those crafted by my father, Lady Cosima included, all under Laszlo's spell. Among their number are masked and jeering faces, knights and soldiers, wizards and plain stick men whose ancient, bare faces have only their arms and legs to commend them to a human form. The emptiness of their faces fills me with fear.

They perch on the princess's wooden pyre, crouch among the trees and roost on the edge of the fountain at the center of the conservatory. There are dragons and birds, beasts and monsters. None of them breathe, none of them speak or question. They just wait. Wait for the next tweak of their strings.

Laszlo is ecstatic at his accomplishment; his laughter bubbles out high-pitched and delighted. Prima hasn't abandoned the knife at his throat, but the fear in her eyes matches my own. Together we are strong, but there are only two of us against dozens of mindless marionettes, each ready to spring into action at Laszlo's words. More trickle in from the gallery walls every second. When the saboteur steps from the shadows to join them and cocks her head, listening for her next command, my heart sinks. I saw how she captured Bran and handled him as if he weighed no more than a feather.

The cleric chooses this moment to return with two guards, and the three men rush into the conservatory, only to quickly realize the Margrave's call for help has been answered in the most absurd and astonishing way.

"My lord?" Vincenzo squeaks, clinging to the arm of the nearest guard for fortitude. "I have brought . . . help."

The Margrave bites down hard on Prima's fingers, triggering release of his mouth.

"*Captismarenach! Captismarenach!*" he shouts.

The puppets act without question. They surround Prima and me, pulling her from Laszlo. I begin kicking them as fast as I can, but they swarm me like ants. No sooner is one flung aside than another takes its place. Prima heaves them into the trees. The unmistakable smash of broken glass abounds as the conservatory windows are severely battered from her efforts. I cannot hear the voices of any of the marionettes or trees in the thrall of the battle; the sounds of struggle are too chaotic.

While I slash wildly at the oncoming horde with my splinter-dagger, Prima rips the head off a large dragon puppet, swinging the broad tail-end around to knock others away. But the Margrave's marionettes are just too numerous; they climb her elegantly moving body and soon, Prima is restrained under their weight. Before I can blink, the saboteur, who was lingering at the edges, has seized me, swiftly bolting my arms to my sides. She lifts me easily off the ground and holds me in front of her, never flinching while I kick and twist.

"You're a little late, cleric," says Laszlo, rubbing his throat and glowering at the man. "I clearly don't need your help to subdue my rebellious bride. Now get over here and perform your duty."

The Margrave's own disfigured boy-puppet has capered up into his arms like a puppy, where it stares balefully at Prima. Vincenzo slinks closer to Laszlo, stepping delicately over and around the marionettes covering the ground like a swarm of locusts. He and the guards can't quite believe their eyes; the full depths of the new Margrave's eccentricities are illuminated like never before. This is magic like no one living has seen. Wooden soldiers walking among us was just a foretaste. The guards back away, slinking off to wait in the hall.

My arms ache where the saboteur's claw-like hands clench

with steadfast pressure. It hurts worse, though, to have looked into her empty eyes and realize that my own creation has betrayed me, that I have unleashed upon the world a figurine that can destroy and kill. I strain to hear her voice, to gain some reassurance in our shared connection, but I sense nothing; she is an empty vault. She must be completely consumed by Laszlo's spell.

In the ghostly glow of the blue moon, we appear to be the cast of a deranged theatrical, with the bride pinned to the ground like a furious butterfly and the groom giddy, holding a miniature likeness of himself in his arms. The cleric clears his throat and begins to address the wedding party.

"*Leben sorgere, leben consurge,*" Laszlo commands. Slowly, the puppets begin to lift the princess, forcing her to stand. Her eyes blaze and she struggles, but the strength of many hands and wooden paws on her body is resolute. Under their insistence, she stands and stays put.

"Don't do this!" I protest. "Just let us go! Please! You could have any bride in all of Elinbruk or Tavia or Brylov that you wish! What you truly want cannot be bought, or made, or forced."

"Proceed," he says to the cleric, ignoring me. Though he seems calmer now, he keeps himself a safe distance from Prima and her wooden sentries.

Vincenzo wipes his graying brow and licks his thumb, trying ungracefully to locate the place in his book at which he might be given some words to address the unseemly crowd before him.

At last, he finds them. "Let us celebrate today, the union of these two souls, who wish to be joined together in accordance with the laws of the territory of Tavia, and the greater laws of Elinbruk, which guide us all, in the most sacred of—"

"I. Do. Not. Wish. It." Prima says through clenched teeth.

Still rattled, Vincenzo looks to Laszlo. "She objects, my lord."

"Proceed," the Margrave says nonchalantly. Because of the spellbound puppets, he now has everything he wants: the princess and the upper hand.

The cleric swallows and continues his ramble.

My thoughts are racing as I try to work out how to maneuver Prima away from here. I've given up hope of connecting to the saboteur. She's lost to me.

When it comes time for the princess to say her vows, she refuses, of course, and Laszlo commands the puppets to move her mouth for her. All that comes out is a garbled snarl, but that is apparently good enough for the Margrave and the cleric and the sovereign territory of Tavia. A jeweled ring, beset with emeralds, is jammed roughly onto her finger by a small monkey marionette; his tiny paws make quick work of prying open her resistant fist.

"And now, by the power vested in me," Vincenzo hurries, only too glad to be at the end of his part in this whole debacle, "I pronounce you man and wife, Margrave and Margravina." He bites his lip. "You may, should you wish to, er, kiss your bride?"

Laszlo takes one look at Prima's incensed face and turns

even paler. "Later, perhaps," he says, handing the boy-marionette to the cleric with an air of loftiness. "We'll save such things for *later*. When we can be alone."

Swiveling away from his bride, he saunters up to me, admiring the immoveable strength of the saboteur holding me in place.

"As for you—I'm finished with you now, puppetmaster." He grins, his face thrust far too close to my own. "We," he says, spreading his arms wide to include the entire bastion of marionettes and Prima, "have no need of you or your craftsmanship any longer. The moon is nearly drained, and your father's precious spell, which I have now memorized for the future, has done its work. And while I would find it vastly amusing for one of your own kind to do the honors," he says, picking his knife off the floor from where it had been tossed free of Prima's grasp, "as you know, I have a bad habit of saving the best things for myself."

CHAPTER 30

FEAR NESTS IN MY BELLY LIKE A BIRD DIGGING ITS TALONS. I look to Prima; her eyes are wide and ferocious. Were it not for the many puppets holding her back, I have no doubts Laszlo would be flattened on the ground, crushed beneath her fury. I squirm in the saboteur's hands, but no matter how I thrash, I cannot free myself. I cannot help myself at all.

Sudden laughter bubbles out of me, sad and surreal. *This is how it must feel. For all of them.* To not be able to move of their own accord. Your body cannot obey your will when it is restrained by stronger forces, even one as simple as a string.

Laszlo looks at me as if I've gone mad, shaking his head in mock sorrow. "Better for this to happen now. I'm doing you a kindness, Pirouette. Better to die here, a puppetmaster in the company of a Margrave, than a wretched corpse in the bowels of the Keep, eh? What else could someone like you wish for, than a better death than your father's?"

"You forget that this will be my second death, my lord. I have lived two lives, and one of those began long before you were ever born or thought of," I spit. "If I die under the light of a blue moon, the same light to which I was born, who knows what will happen? It's never been done. Perhaps I'll become everlasting, like an evergreen. Or perhaps my body will be buried, biding its time like a seed, and at the first drop of rain I'll return to haunt your every sleepless night. Either way, if you kill me now, neither of us knows what will happen next." I sound far more brash than I feel.

With one final, angry roar he thrusts the knife toward my chest. Prima screams and my eyes squeeze shut. My last breath inflates my lungs like a bellows heaved full of air. I wait for it, for the piercing finality of the blade, but it never comes. Instead, the knife strikes something hard. Something more solid than flesh and blood.

I open my eyes. It's the saboteur. She's lifted an arm on my behalf to ward off Laszlo's blow. Enraged, Laszlo rears back and tries again, this time attempting to slash across my throat. He's blocked again by a nimble swipe of the saboteur's gloved hand.

"No!" he shouts at her. "*Arrestivan!*" he commands, parrying and thrusting with his short blade like it's a rapier. "*Arrestivan! Mertenhalten!*"

But his commands don't work on the saboteur. Somehow, she is fully animated, but able to ignore his desires. The rest of the puppets, however, cannot. One by one, the marionettes holding Prima loosen their grip at their master's command to halt. Like ropes falling away, the spell's hold is shed and she begins to shake them off.

"No!" Laszlo shrieks at his tiny army. "No, no! Not you! Don't you stop! *Leben consurge!*"

But Prima is already fully unleashed from her prison of clawing hands. She tears a long, thin switch from her awakening bed and thrashes it about like a whip, knocking puppets from the trees and the fountain's rim, scattering them away. The old cleric himself is knocked to the floor by the soaring marionette of a shepherdess who smacks him soundly across the face with her staff.

Laszlo seethes. "You will obey me, saboteur. You've killed for me before and you'll do it again. *Valder mortifikanto.*" He repeats the directive to kill over and over again while trying uselessly to butcher me with his blade.

The saboteur doesn't seem to hear him. She shoves me behind her, her whole body now a shield between me and the Margrave. When she fights, she is a thing to behold; Laszlo has studied the art of fencing and fighting, to be sure, but only ever with an opponent who wished to keep his head at the end of a lesson. The saboteur is a creature who cares not for her own welfare. She is focused solely on winning the fight.

Her arms and legs fly so fast, Laszlo can't see them coming; the saboteur interrupts every strike. He begins screaming for the guards, but they have retreated in fear, leaving the cleric, Prima, and I to fend for ourselves against the Margrave's horde.

The call to kill *was* heard by the other marionettes. They skitter toward Prima and me and Vincenzo, who has scrambled to our side, hoping to find sanctuary behind the saboteur. Puppets who can still crawl or march come at us in waves. They've broken off branches of the trees, snatched up the gardeners' tools, grabbed whatever they can find to use as weapons. The wounded ones twitch on the ground, some with limbs missing or still dangling like forsaken fruit from the trees. A few heads roll haphazardly on the ground, searching in vain for their wayward bodies.

In the distance, through the domed roof, above the uproar, bells begin to chime. It's the unmistakable song of the glockenspiel, fully resurrected, bells and all. The eerie melody rouses Laszlo to a new level of fury, no doubt reminding him of the victory he thought he had claimed over the clockmaker.

My heart surges with the bells, knowing who climbed up there and set them in motion, completing what Emmitt was never able to. Though I normally detest the glockenspiel's song, right now it renews the fight in every swing of my arms.

The saboteur delivers a powerful blow to Laszlo's jaw, sending him flying back into the fountain. Blood pools in the water. Eventually, he lifts his head and comes up sputtering. The saboteur turns toward Prima and me, who are still battling with the other puppets, I with my splinter and she with her whip of wood.

The saboteur seizes the cleric's lantern from where it fell and holds it high, turning to face us while Laszlo struggles to emerge from the fountain. Her gaze is still the same as when I'd painted it, intense and sure. Her mechanical chin drops like an open door, and the only word I'll ever get to hear her speak aloud is released from its depths.

"*Run.*" The command is a sharp bark, the sound of heavy boards clattering together.

I falter. It feels wrong to leave her, especially now. There's something in her, some spark of me or my father, some ele-ment of goodness itself ingrained in her wood. Something the blue moon brought to light tonight. Something impenetrable to Laszlo's misery and destructive spells.

"Run!" she bellows again, pointing intently to the shadows among the trees. Her mouth snaps shut like a sprung trap. She turns her back on us.

Laszlo limps bitterly toward her, looking like one of the maimed marionettes coming back for more. For a second, I think she's going to wallop him with the lantern, but instead, the saboteur smashes it broadly against her own chest. The globe shatters across the stone floor and oil douses her body. The flame follows.

"No!" I scream in tandem with Laszlo.

Prima uproots me where I stand. She drags me behind her, toward a slew of broken windows. I cannot take my eyes from the saboteur.

My *saboteur.*

Like a wooden torch, her whole body is marvelously alight, glowing with leaping licks of flame. Tears stream down my cheeks. She lifts her arms, darting and whirling among the trees, touching every branch and marionette she can reach, with hands that singe and burn. Laszlo howls like a wolf in pain; his worst fears are come to life. When she reaches out to enfold him in her embrace, his wails cut through the crackling flames like ice.

The last thing I see as Prima hauls me through the smoking grove is my saboteur, destroying everything she touches, danc-ing beneath the blue moon like a scorching star fallen to earth.

CHAPTER 31

OWITH EVERY FREE HAND OF WOLFSPIRE HALL RUSHING TO put out the fire and save whatever's left of the Margrave and his collection, Prima and Vincenzo and I are hardly noticed as we dart through the back stairwells and halls. We don't have a key this time, but I hope with Prima on our side we can barrel our way through any guarded doors.

Suddenly a very large redheaded man runs up the stairs toward us. He flattens himself against the wall, wheezing at the sight of us.

"Fonso?" I ask, squinting in the stair's weak torchlight.

"Marco," he pants, trying to catch his breath. "Piro?"

"Marco!" He looks so like his cousin, I want to hug him on the spot.

"I was just on my way to see if I could help, but you've made it without me, I see. Heard all the commotion of the guards."

"Oh, thank you! Can you lead us out of here?"

Marco nods, his copper beard bobbing reassuringly. "Come!"

The four of us start to descend, but then a sudden thought trips me and nearly sends us all plunging down the spiral steps in a heap.

"Wait! What about the others?"

Prima looks to me. "Others?"

"Those in the Keep," I say, thinking of the poor souls who still remain.

Marco turns around with a grin. "The only reason the tailor's Golden Boy isn't here right now is that he had a bit of an errand to run first. As far as the Keep goes, we already got things started." He pulls the tailor's seam ripper from his pocket. "Your friend Nan and I picked all the locks we could. She had a second copy of that skeleton key made, stashed for safekeeping. It's just as well we got there when we did. By the time Bran was out, the other prisoners were already near to tearing the doors off their hinges."

"Thank the stars. How did you get past the guards with the seam ripper in the first place?"

"Those blokes are a dirty lot. Your extra francs were enough to grease a few palms. A few less mouths to feed in the Keep is of no consequence to them."

Energized by this news, I run faster, dragging the cleric behind me by one of his vestments while Prima brings up the rear as lookout. Outside, we all gulp huge mouthfuls of fresh air, eager to have done with the smoke and flames. I try desperately not to think about what's been left behind, my saboteur lost to the flames.

Outside the gates, Nan sits atop the driver's seat of a familiar wood-hauling wagon.

"You made it," she says with whoop. "Looks like we're just in time! Who's your new friend? Another captive of the Margrave's?"

"We've really no time for introductions, but you already know the cleric of Wolfspire Hall," I begin.

"Regretfully true, lass. The puppetmaster and the Margravina, they saved me from the fire," Vincenzo says humbly. "Our Margrave is a very disturbed young man. Dark magic . . . dark indeed," he mutters to himself. "Never thought I'd live to see the day . . . "

"Margravina?" Nan asks, confused.

"Nan, this is Prima. She's only just been . . . she's only just," I say hesitantly, trying to delicately explain her existence.

"Begun," Prima speaks up. "I've only just begun."

The bells in the high tower of Wolfspire Hall peal frantically, the same pattern rung the night the old Margrave died, the same ones that sang while my father slipped away. Those bells can only mean one thing . . . Laszlo is gone.

"They're sounding the full alarm," Marco says. "The fire must be sweeping through the whole castle." He begins to run back toward the Commoner's entrance.

"Come with us, Marco! There's room in the back of the wagon!"

"No, not yet," he calls. "The guards will all be fleeing their posts—and they'll forget."

"Forget about what?"

"The Keep! I need to make sure everyone got out! Otherwise, any poor sots left behind who can't walk'll roast alive. I'll check, you go!" The big man bolts, determined to make sure every inhabitant of the Keep is set free.

"Prima, let's go," I start to say, turning to find her lifting the cleric like a sack of meal onto Burl's back.

"Oh, I can't possibly, my lady," he says, fumbling apologetically and awkwardly trying to dismount. "You should be the one to ride. You are our Margravina now."

"Margravina?" the newly made girl asks. "What is that? Everyone keeps saying it."

"Yes, milady, if the duke, er, Margrave, had survived the fire, they wouldn't be ringing the high bells as they are. Therefore, you are not just a new bride; you are the new ruler of Tavia. I myself conducted the ceremony. Your marriage to him was legal and binding. The puppetmaster witnessed it with her own eyes."

"I did," I say, in shock. "If Laszlo is truly gone, and they were married before he . . . then that would make Prima the new Margravina."

Prima looks to me. I can't speak for a minute. There are so many questions we'll have to answer. How can we invent a story for her, a believable history, without betraying both of our origins? She doesn't even know yet about the splinters that plague our kind. And a girl cannot be a Margravina from nowhere. She needs a family, a noble bloodline.

"What do I do?" she asks, her green eyes unsure.

I look to the smoking castle behind us and the village below. The blue moon has bled out all its power. It's back to being that pale, milk-glass eye once more; pretty, but impotent.

"What if the fire spreads to the village—to the farms or the wood?" I ask in alarm.

"We got almost everyone out of the village already, Piro," Nan says. "For days now the women and children have been quietly fleeing to the woods, hiding from the constant patrols of wooden soldiers. We can stay there until it's safe to return. The others are waiting for us."

I breathe a deep breath of relief. "Then let's go. We'll retreat from the fire. And hope that there's something left for us all to return to."

"I will see to it that your reign is uncontested, milady," Vincenzo says, bowing as best he can from Burl's back. "After the horrors I've seen today, it's the least I can do. We've been too long under the rule of the old von Eidles, if I do say so myself. A new Margravina shall be a breath of fresh air indeed!"

"I need you," Prima says to me, taking my hand, her eyes locked intently on mine. "You will help me?"

"We'll help you," I say, pulling her up to sit on the wagon seat beside Nan and me. "My friends and I."

Burl takes off at a clip through the darkened streets. Just as Wolfspire Hall begins to shrink behind us, the deafening sound of an explosion engulfs the ringing bells and rocks the cobblestones beneath us. Clinging to each other, we look back to see the glass-domed conservatory roof completely collapsing. The roof pops like a glass bubble, leaving nothing behind but air and smoke. The acrid smell of burning wood and charred brick rides the wind ahead of us. Nan tries to calm Burl, who is pulling hard at the reins, following his instincts to flee the noise. She stops the wagon, looking back at the carnage and then to me and Prima.

"Let's keep going," I command.

"Good, I was just going to suggest that," she says.

But a few moments later, in front of the rathaus, I spy a light on in the clock tower and beg her to slow the horse. Though the glockenspiel has finished its refrain, the great clock above is keeping accurate time again.

"Wait for me," I say, leaping from the wagon before the wheels even grind to a halt. "There's something I need in the tower."

CHAPTER 32

I FIND BRAN JUST WHERE I THOUGHT I MIGHT; HIGH UP ON the scaffolding, boxing up Emmitt's tools and watching the smoke spew from Wolfspire Hall. As soon as he hears my footsteps, he quickly drops down the ladder, his eyes hungrily searching my face. I try to ignore the carousel behind him, and the memories that will forever haunt this clock tower.

"Are you all right, Piro?" I can tell he wants to pull me to him, but he hesitates, unsure if I'll allow it. "Were you hurt? Did he do anything to hurt you?"

"No. I mean, yes, I'm all right. You?"

He's filthy, and that peculiar smell that followed my father home from the Keep lingers on him. But he is Bran, and he is here, safe and real.

"I'm so sorry, Piro. My carelessness could have cost you everything!" he says, looking over his shoulder to the fire and smoke on the hill. "I could have lost you in there! I feel like a fool, taken away to the Keep and unable to help you. I had no idea, Piro—what it was like in there . . . " His voice breaks. "I would have come straight to get you myself, but Nan overruled me. She didn't trust my strength after being in that horrible place. So I came here, to fit the last piece in, for Emmitt."

I take a small step toward him, drawn as ever to his warmth, which even Wolfspire Keep could not extinguish.

"I'm glad. I think he would be proud to hear the old bells roar to life again. The Margrave, however, was *not*."

Bran smiles a wry, sad smile.

"But then," I continue, "you and I well know something the Margrave never learned; a maker will always prevail."

"Always," Bran agrees, reaching tentatively for my hand. I happily give it to him.

When Bran touches me, there is none of that probing measurement there once was with Laszlo. A sameness flows between us now, a current I could get lost in. In his eyes, I'm not a thing made of parts and pieces, an apparatus cobbled together to fit his purposes; I'm much more than that. *I am loved.* Perhaps that's one of the ways we each find ourselves becoming more human, by that strange magic of being seen all at once for the whole marvelous and terrible creatures we are and not just the odd scraps of our faults and frailties.

The Maker's Guild and the Tavians who fled to escape the spreading fire sleep in the thick of the wood that night, among the old giants. There are released prisoners from the Keep who are much rejoiced over, mingling with housewives and butchers and shopkeepers. Whatever food was liberated from Wolfspire's cellars is gladly shared among them all. Fires dot the forest floor, keeping everyone warm against the cutting night air. Though most were afraid of the wood's nooks and dark hollows, they find safety and shelter in its shadows now.

But sleep refuses me. I leave our dwindling fire, around which the others dream soundly—Nan and the Sorens and Fonso and Anke on one side, Tiffin and Mort on the other, with Bran keeping an eye on the cleric and Prima in the wagon. Quietly, I wrap my cloak around my shoulders and venture into the black curtain of trees.

The others took to Prima without too many questions; I even caught Tiffin staring at her like a royal dunce more than once. She moved among us serenely, not saying much, but her every movement was deliberate, every flash of feeling across her face aristocratic and bold.

When it came time to introduce her, I completely froze, only to be saved by Bran, who made her acquaintance on the drive to the wood. Like any good tailor, he spun a story for us all.

"Makers, meet Prima von Eidle, daughter of a distant noble of Elinbruk. Milady was wed to the Margrave just after midnight tonight, so she's had a bit of a shock, you could say, what with being very suddenly a widow and finding herself our new Margravina to boot. Tiffin, get her a blanket. Mort, make room by the fire. Mother, would you heat her a bowl of stew? No doubt our lady is quite hungry after her trials."

Vincenzo confirmed Bran's story by spouting a long and very sensationalized tale of Prima's bravery in the midst of the fantastical events that occurred in the conservatory. The little ones listened in awe from their sleeping pallets, but the elders were rightfully skeptical of the account of the duke's marionettes come to life, especially as the cleric's yarn grew ever more outlandish each time he brought his cup of ale to his lips. I didn't mind. His tales would spread Prima's story far and wide, saving us the trouble.

Restless, prowling among the trees away from the camp, I startle at every noise and blink at every moving shadow. The cover of night makes me imagine the saboteur might step from among their number at any moment. *I almost sense her here.*

It's hard to comprehend that one of the greatest works of my life is reduced to ash drifting on the wind, her strange beauty settling like black snow on the stones of Wolfspire Hall. *I couldn't save her. But she saved me. She saved us all, really.*

Leaning against a linden for support, I slide down to my haunches, my chest racked by sobs. The weight of all I've lost is crushing. After the saboteur, and now Prima . . . can I ever create again? Would it even be right? How can I continue as a puppetmaster, knowing what wreckage and ruin can stem from my hands? I shudder, remembering Laszlo dancing to his death in the saboteur's arms.

In the process of wiping the wet from my eyes, I feel a hand on my shoulder. My lungs tighten. *It can't possibly be . . .*

No, the hand is not gloved and wooden like I hoped, but

gnarled and work-worn, its hold strong as roots of oak. The unflinching face of the old tree woman bends over me like a branch offering shade.

"It's the maker's pain, isn't it? I feel the same torment each time one of my seedlings is chopped down, or a great giant is felled by lightning and the flames take hold."

"How do you bear it?" I ask, my eyes welling up again.

The old woman smiles a twisted smile, the wrinkles in her face rippling like ridges in bark. "Because each end, each small death, gives life to the new. In every tree that falls, creatures will find shelter and birds will drop seeds to sprout from its rotting depths. A tree only grows by rising from the layers of many deaths that came before."

She gently tugs my arm, pulling me to my feet. I am taller than she, but even so, I do not feel like I am looking down on her. Quite the opposite.

"So must you, Pirouette Leiter; find a way to grow, to squeeze life from the ashes left behind." She grips my hand roughly, trying to imbue some life into me.

"But what if it happens again?" I ask her, clinging to her branch-like fingers. "What if more lives are ruined by one of my creatures? I feel as if I should never touch a chisel or blade again. If I never see another blue moon, it will be too soon."

She shakes her head. "You should know by now that magic, just like the truth, can't be hidden. The blue moon will always rise and men will always hunt for ways to make the things they most desire. But you will know the moon's power and your own strength next time as a master, not just as an apprentice."

"*Next time?*" I don't think I'll ever be ready to face another blue moon. But before I can say as much, the old tree woman releases me and turns away. Soon, she is nothing but a mist fading into the night. Though it won't be night much longer. A rim of early morning ruptures the sky above me.

I press my cheek to the tree's knotted side and close my eyes.

"How?" I ask the linden. "How can I begin again after all this?"

The wind ruffles the tree's remaining leaves above. It lifts the dried remnants of fall off the forest floor and whips them into the air, only to set them down again. But the tree does not answer.

It dawns on me slowly, like a leaf dropping from the canopy, that I cannot hear the linden's voice. I press my hand to her side, shoving my ear up against the bark.

Silence.

I feel my way to the next linden, and the next. To the oak, and the halsa nearby. All quiet. The only sounds that reach me are the wind and her sighs. I slam my hands angrily against the tree trunks, one after another. I've been shut out, locked away from a world that used to belong to me. *The trees' voices are lost to me, too.*

"Lost," I whimper, a great silence rising up around me like a barricade.

When did it happen? How had I not noticed?

And then I realize: Prima. When I awakened Prima. I couldn't hear the saboteur's voice either, when she held me fast. The demanding blue moon had taken its tithe already; it could be nothing else.

In the next heartbeat, I wonder, *What of my curse? Was it taken too?*

"Piro." Bran's familiar voice pulls me back from the deep silence. "What are you doing out this far?"

I whirl around to search the dark for his face.

"I don't know. I don't know what I'm doing any more."

He finds me, lacing his fingers with my own. "It's so dark out here, so far from the fire. Even with the moonlight." He shivers, looking around. "This is what I was talking about. These woods make me uneasy. I know it's different for you, but aren't you ever afraid out here?" he asks, looking up at the towering trees.

Am I afraid?

There's only one way to test it.

"No," I say shakily, taking a deep breath. "I am not afraid." Then I hold my breath a long moment, waiting.

I *am* afraid. Of everything.

Of what comes next. Of not knowing how to live without my father. Afraid for Prima, with a whole territory-worth of burdens suddenly resting on her shoulders. Afraid of what I might build that could take on a life of its own. Afraid of what it means to no longer have the guidance of the trees.

But I stand with Bran, breathing long and deep, as many breaths as I dare, feeling my fears wash over me, one by one, like wet strokes of paint. No splinters besiege me. No slivers surface to wound me. I can hardly believe it.

"Come on," Bran says, wrapping a blanket around us both. "Let's go back. You're freezing." He pulls me closer, sliding his hands beneath my cloak to curl me tightly against the wall of his chest, another barrier against the night. "Or if you're not quite ready yet, we can stay a little longer, as long as we stay together?"

My eyes seek the moon and find it over his shoulder, that enigmatic, silver-blue face full of shadows.

"You did it, Piro," Bran whispers into my ear. "You and the blue moon. Remember? You never know what might happen with a beautiful girl under the moonlight. You might get—"

"Moonstruck," I finish, thinking it the best possible word to describe my quiet awe. The moon's magic has taken its tithe, but in its place, I find the gift I've always longed for.

A few days later, when the turrets of Wolfspire Hall no longer burn like coals, the Maker's Guild and the people of Tavia return from the woods to reclaim their shops and farms. Some of the Margrave's wooden soldiers were lost in the great fire; the rest, when their lifeless husks are discovered, are chopped up and used as kindling.

The accusations flung at me by Laszlo are dismissed by the villagers and my fellow makers as further proof of his foolishness; they saw the marching men and the creeping black soldier with their own eyes. They understand it was he who used illicit magic to keep power tightly in his grasp.

Thanks to the Maker's Guild, word reached the King about the untimely demise of the Margravina in Brylov, though Laszlo will never receive his due punishment for that crime. The steward has disappeared too, vanishing like smoke. We're still awaiting the cleric's return from Elinbruk, to confirm that the King has granted Prima the right to rule us in her husband's stead. Everyone is happy to leave Brylov well alone, glad to not be forced into a battle none of us wanted to fight.

Now that the streets are safe again, the Margravina of Tavia joins me, her newly appointed advisor and puppetmaster, on the walk back to Curio. I have hopes that with Prima as our new ruler we can start to change things, begin to loosen the grip of the old laws and fears that would have us accusing our neighbors and looking with suspicion on magic that we don't understand.

Prima and I stand solemnly on Curio's doorstep.

I thrust something small and much older than me into her capable hands. "I know you have many questions. But first, a gift. I have a story to tell you, and this is the only place where I know how to tell it."

Prima takes the heavy, brass fob and tries Papa's key in the lock. When it turns and the latch drops, her face lights up. She steps inside and I follow.

"I know I've never been here before," she says, breathless at the overflowing shelves of treasures, "yet I feel as if I know this place. I feel as if I *remember* . . . "

The perfume of wood shavings and paint still lingers strong, though everything is coated in a thick layer of dust. For a second, I nearly call out to my father to let him know we have a guest. I can almost hear the echoing rasp of his sander and the chink of his chisel. *What would he make of Prima? Of me?*

"I will remember for both of us," I say, drawing back the curtain, opening up the heart of Curio to us both. "Always."

ACKNOWLEDGMENTS

HIS BOOK IS BROUGHT YOU BY NUMEROUS CUPS OF TEA, the musical stylings of Danny Elfman, and the merciful grace of God.

Nathan: If I were to carve a marionette of you, it would be that of a nimble jester, with a hero's cape and dagger. Thank you for being my best friend, first reader, and action-scene sounding board. (Also, first-rate child-wrangler and take-out food purveyor.)

Alicia: Thank you for being an ever-trusted critic and bosom friend. Your magical red pen has saved me from many a grievous error and brought me a good laugh when I needed it most.

Mom & Dad: Thank you for putting books in my hands and giving me a childhood full of magical adventures. I love you!

Chad & Leslie: Thanks for reading my stories with such